TOUCHPAPER

By David Dodds

Copyright © David Dodds 2025

The right of David Dodds to be identified as the author
of this work has been asserted in accordance with the
Copyright, Designs and Patents Act 1988.

All rights reserved. No part of this publication may be
reproduced, stored in a retrieval system or transmitted in any
form or by any means, without the prior permission in writing
of the publisher, nor to be otherwise circulated in any form of
binding or cover other than that in which it is published without
a similar condition, including this condition, being imposed on
the subsequent purchaser.

No part of this book may be used or reproduced in any manner
for the purpose of training artificial intelligence technologies or
systems. In accordance with Article 4(3) of the DSM Directive
2019/790, David Dodds expressly reserves this work from the
text and data mining exception.

All the characters in this book are fictitious,
and any resemblance to actual persons, living
or dead, is purely coincidental.

A CIP catalogue record for this book
is available from the British Library.

ISBN: 978-1-0685669-0-5

Cover design and typeset by Raspberry Creative Type, Edinburgh

*For Rona,
who puts up with me.*

PROLOGUE

On the rocky outcrop which forms the summit of Arthur's Seat, a tall, languid figure reclined on a convenient rock, his gaze drifting over the street-lit city below him. He ignored the piercing chill wind and, under a shock of dark hair, his brows occasionally moved together, as his mind worked through a problem. His substantial nose and full mouth twitched from time to time, as if in sympathy with his indecision. A large, dark garment, a sort of cross between a cloak and a greatcoat, was half-open, revealing a pair of knee-length tan-coloured boots, with the patina of extensive use. He sat with his legs crossed, the heels resting on a smaller rock, the left one tapping irregularly.

A bat flew past, diving to catch an insect. He glanced sideways, scowled at it, and returned to his thoughts.

Before him the lights threw shadows onto Edinburgh's buildings: Victorian tenements, the Georgian majesty of the New Town and the late medieval jumble of the Old Town. The castle loomed over it all on its vast volcanic plug, but the watcher appeared oblivious to it all, until something changed and caught his attention.

In the distance, a brief glow of intense pale-yellow light suddenly illuminated a tall Victorian tenement before rapidly fading away. The foot-tapping ceased instantly, and his face cleared as he leaned forward, gazing into the semi-darkness.

His stare lengthened, and he made a sound that crossed the boundary between a snort and a spit before muttering one word, 'Arseholes.'

The figure stood up rapidly, inclined his head, slid through a gap in the air and was gone. There was no dramatic moment, simply a sudden and inexplicable absence. The bat flew by again, corkscrewed in flight around where he had been, and jinked away as an echo of his voice said, 'And you can get stuffed too.'

1. SCEADHU

Losing my parents six years ago, and in quick succession, gave me the excuse to leave Edinburgh, travel, and squander my inheritance. But now, with the excessive self-confidence of someone who has learned hard lessons along the way, I had returned to pick up my degree course. My resentment at the world had finally run out of steam, and it seemed the obvious thing to do. But now I was meandering home on a damp October afternoon, musing that the obvious thing is rarely the right thing. I stuffed my hands in my pockets as I slouched along, when a car horn made me jump. I turned to see a gleaming BMW speeding away. Something white lay in the road and I realised it was a small dog. I stepped onto the road and knelt by it. He was a grubby, thin-looking, nondescript sort of terrier with white, wiry hair. His ears sat unevenly on a whiskery face and his deep brown eyes stared up at me. His breath came in shallow pants and his flank was red with a liberal coating of blood.

I looked around, but seeing nobody, I picked the dog up and walked as quickly as I could towards the local veterinary surgery. The dog whined occasionally as I walked, his breaths coming quicker, making me wonder briefly what I'd do with a dead dog if he expired before I got there.

The vet took one look and lifted the terrier from my arms. A few minutes later, the door burst open, and she stormed back out, followed closely by the dog, clean and trotting along jauntily. She stopped in front of me and jabbed my chest with her forefinger. 'Do you think this is funny? Do you think I've nothing better to do than waste my time? And where do you get off using an innocent animal for your stupid games?'

'What do you mean?' I gaped at her and then at the dog, who was now sitting, licking his genitals energetically.

'There's nothing wrong with this animal! The blood isn't his. He hasn't been in an accident. He's absolutely fine.' She stood with her hands on her hips, glaring at me.

'I know nothing about that,' I protested. 'He's not even my dog. It looked like a car hit him, so I brought him here. What else would I do?'

She stared at me for a long moment, sighed and then said, more calmly, 'Well, he's got no collar and no microchip, so we'll never know, will we?'

The dog sat up and looked at me. He raised one paw off the ground, cocked his head, and whined.

Sometimes in life we do inexplicable things without really knowing why and I heard myself say, 'I'll take him.' I stooped to pick the dog up. He licked my face, and I turned to leave, wondering what the hell I was doing.

'He should go to the cat and dog home,' the vet called after me, but I just kept walking.

Arriving at the dingy front door of my flat, I put the dog down whilst I searched for my key. As soon as I opened the front door, he trotted in as though he owned the place. 'You cheeky little sod! Just make yourself at home, why don't you?'

The flat was small and just as scruffy inside. I'd tried to make it comfortable, but there was no hiding the low-budget nature of the place: shabby-chic, with the chic missing. The small living room housed little more than a sagging sofa and a cheap coffee table on which sat my lap-top and a scattered heap of books. A battered door led into the small kitchenette. The dog strolled in and sat down. He scratched his ear, then faced me and wagged his tail, looking at me expectantly.

Two hours later, it seemed as if the dog had lived with me all his life. He shared my meagre dinner (not entirely with my agreement), crapped in the little muddy garden and curled up on the sofa beside me, alternately snoring and emitting little 'pfft' noises from his rear end.

I scratched the dog's ear. 'I think I'll call you Crockett,' I said. He opened both eyes wide, then with a movement remarkably like a shrug, he curled up again and resumed his slumbers.

The next day, I discovered Crockett didn't seem to need a lead, trotting alongside me wherever I went. After being refused entry to the university lecture theatre, he simply curled up by the door and waited for me to return. The unexpected faithfulness was quite touching.

With the lecture over, I took him to Princes Street Gardens, stopping off to buy a tennis ball on the way. 'Fetch,' I called, throwing the ball for him. Crockett looked at the ball, looked at me, and sat down. Two passing teenagers laughed as I retrieved the ball and tried again. Crockett looked around and then lay down, his nose between his front paws. After a couple more failed attempts, I gave up and sat on a wooden bench. He crawled over and lay down beside me.

'You're not the average dog, are you?' I asked, and his tail flicked lazily twice in acknowledgement.

Just then, a slight movement caught my attention. I watched as an ant emerged from a crack between the paving slabs, followed by another and a moment later by a third. 'Must be a nest of them,' I told Crockett, fascinated by the purposeful movements of the tiny insects. Two more emerged, then five, then even more, building into a minor flood of tiny dark red creatures, pouring out of the crack. Crockett got to his feet, thrusting his snout towards them. He took a rapid step backwards, swiping his nose with a paw and whining. I laughed at him. 'You berk – you got stung on the nose, didn't you?'

I looked back at the ants and, to my astonishment, they were forming into a shape on the ground. A right-angled arrow was clearly visible, the ants forming it, writhing and moving, making the shape seem alive. Crockett barked and jumped at me, pushing me back from the shape. 'Geroff, dog,' I snapped. I took out my phone to grab a picture, but when I looked again, there was nothing to see, just some ants running here and there, carrying crumbs and bits of detritus back to their nest. 'Did I imagine that?' I asked, but Crockett just sat, looking mutely back at me.

*

'There's something weird about him,' I said, nodding at the dog, who was curled up under the pub table. Across from me, my only friend, Jamie, was using his fingernail to draw a face in the condensation on the side of his pint glass.

Towering over most people, Jamie's shock of ginger hair, shaggy eyebrows, stubbled chin and burly figure made him look as though his preferred activity was single-handedly charging a line of terrified red-coats, brandishing a claymore and screaming blood-curdling Gaelic oaths. In fact, he was laidback to the point of horizontality. Dropping out of university soon after I did, he had lurched, bemused and chaotic, from girlfriend to girlfriend, making ends meet with a string of low-paid, undemanding jobs.

'How so?' He slowly added strands of hair to the condensation face.

'I found him covered in blood, but it wasn't his. What was that about?'

'Maybe he killed a pigeon or something,' Jamie added eyebrows and ears.

'The vet said it wasn't his own blood.'

We were sitting in our usual pub, The Reekie Lum. The pub was narrow and old-fashioned, a line of small tables facing a long teak bar with its polished brass foot-rail and gleaming pumps. We drank there regularly, partly because of its well-managed beers and uncomplicated atmosphere, but mostly because we both worked shifts behind the bar, qualifying us for a staff discount.

'What about his behaviour?' I asked. 'You couldn't ask for a more faithful or well-behaved dog. He goes everywhere with me.'

'Isn't that a good thing?'

'Of course. But it's like he's always been my dog. I don't seem to have to train him: he's always a step ahead of me. The only time I've fallen out with him was when I tried to put a collar and lead on him – he was having none of that.'

Jamie moved his attention to a beer-mat, systematically separating it into thin layers of paper. 'From what I can see, you've got a hassle-free pet. He doesn't need a lead because he strolls along beside you. He doesn't act like a pillock much; he's good company – what's not to like? Besides, women like a cute dog – he could help you end your emotional famine, monk-boy.'

'Just because I don't leap into bed with anyone who has a pulse doesn't mean I'm deprived,' I replied. Jamie frequently found amusement in the contrast between his highly active love life and my own rather limited one, but

I refused to engage. 'Anyway, I still think there's something weird about him.'

Jamie changed the subject to the only consistent thing in his life. 'I've found a second-hand spoiler for the Carpy!' The Carpy was a heap of junk, which Jamie liked to think of as a "classic car". It was an old Ford Capri in a startling shade of orange, mottled with rust. When he bought it, the receipt was mis-typed as "Carpi" and the name "Carpy" was born. To fix it, I had bought him a rubber fish, which hung from the rear-view mirror.

'Well, I'm sure that will make it go much faster,' I said.

He narrowed his eyes. 'That car's an investment.'

I picked up my jacket. 'It certainly seems to eat up cash, but I doubt you'll ever see a return on your money. I'd better be going. See you soon.'

'Yeah. Good luck with super-dog!'

I gave him a wry smile and left to have a think.

A sea-haar had rolled in from the Forth, shrouding the Edinburgh street in a clammy, swirling greyness and making me shiver as I emerged from The Reekie Lum. Crockett followed me out, stretched, and trotted to my side.

Spiked iron railings topped a wall next to the pub, and I tapped each railing with my finger-tips as I passed. A jackdaw sat on the last spike of the railing, glaring at me. As I approached, instead of flying off, it continued to stare, its pale silver eyes gleaming. Surprised, I stopped. 'Hello,' I said – well, what else should you say to a big black bird? It tilted its head and responded, 'Tchak.' Enchanted, I moved closer. 'You're quite something, aren't you?' The jackdaw responded, 'Tchak-tchak,' and continued to stare, the pale eyes seeming to grow. Suddenly it stretched towards me, opening its beak wide. 'TCHAK!' it shrieked, flapping its wings wildly. 'TCHAK! TCHAK!' It gaped and clicked its beak and I stepped back and clapped my hands to scare it, but it continued to shriek and flap its wings at me. I hurried past. The bird didn't follow, but its cries followed me until I turned the corner. Crockett seemed unsettled too, looking about him as we walked, and raising his nose to sniff the air.

I turned into Greyfriars Kirkyard, my sidekick still trotting alongside me. I liked Greyfriars. Outside the tourist season, it was quiet, especially in the late evening gloom. Despite its historic fame for grave-robbing and for the story of Greyfriars Bobby, the dog who guarded his master's grave, it was a peaceful, reflective place, and I liked to wander amongst the lichen-covered grave-stones and think. Hemmed in by grimy sandstone tenements and by the kirk itself the kirkyard was an essay in the Victorian fascination with death, mausoleums and monuments of every shape and size, with skulls featuring widely.

Crockett cocked his leg against a large, pollution-blackened monument with carved stone urns on the corners, and started sniffing intently around its base. Suddenly, he gave a start and stared across the kirkyard, his hackles slowly rising as he gave a low growl. He crept forward, hugging the ground.

This was a new behaviour and quite alarming. 'What is it, Crockett?' I asked him. 'It's not that bloody bird again, is it?' Ignoring me, Crockett continued to slink forwards, growling. Then he turned and ran, hurtling away as fast as his little body could move and in a moment was out of sight. 'Crockett!' I made to chase after the dog, but a peculiar sound behind me caught my attention and I half-turned towards it.

In a dark corner of the graveyard, partly hidden by the monument, I glimpsed a movement in the shadows. It grew in depth and shape, and a pair of crimson eyes formed from the depths and glared fixedly at me. I took several steps back, while a deep susurration combined with a rough, arrhythmic vibration seemed to rattle and vibrate my inside. I shook my head, trying to rid my head of the all-pervading sound, and a wave of nausea swept through me, making me retch. A chilling sensation filled me as I realised it wasn't something *in* the shadows: it was the shadows themselves that were moving. The shadow, now towering over me threateningly, moved steadily closer. Tendrils of dense shadow reached towards me, smoke-like and yet with structure and solidity. I kept stepping back, gasping and gagging, but the massive, terrifying form kept enveloping me.

Suddenly a golden-yellow light washed over the kirkyard. At its centre stood a tall, statuesque figure, whose straight blond hair fell to his shoulders. Blue eyes surmounted a slim, straight nose and full-lipped mouth, and there was a determination in his square, clean-shaven jawline. A white robe extended to the ground and his skin seemed to glow with amber light. His right arm slowly extended towards the dark shape, fingers outstretched.

In a confident, precise tone, he intoned, 'Vile denizen of the lowest pits, I command you to be gone from this place.' The shadow turned its attention to him and seemed to recoil slightly as he continued undiminished, 'Beelzebub's spawn, you belongeth not on this clean earth. Go now, withdraw, and be gone forever. I command you to–'

A thick tendril of shadow shot out from the creature and batted him sideways. The figure hit the graveyard wall and fell into a crumpled heap, the golden glow dimming and flickering.

The massive, dark shape turned its burning eyes back towards me and I gasped and scrabbled backwards as another burst of nausea hit me. The horrible sensations grew in intensity. Panicking, I staggered further back, losing my footing as I collided with a small gravestone. I scrabbled sideways around the stone as those dark tendrils of shadow stretched and flicked towards me. I had no time to understand what was happening: the sound and nausea had me in its grip and I couldn't think.

A sharp thrust thumped into the small of my back, driving the air from my lungs and propelling me face down onto the damp grass. The turf filled my mouth and, as I choked and gasped for breath, a boot pressed roughly on my back, holding me down. A harsh voice said, 'Stay down, you fool.'

As I fought for breath and struggled to free myself, I felt my body weakening. Consciousness slipped away, though I heard the same voice say authoritatively, 'I don't think so. Not this time. Unless you want to start a war, you won't win.'

2. TRAGGHEIM

I became aware of a peculiar, moist, sensation moving vigorously across my face. Gradually, memories appeared: the crimson eyes, the golden man, the overwhelming nausea, the horrid susurrating sound. I slowly opened my eyes and found myself slumped against the kirkyard wall. Crockett stood in front of me, with his front paws on my chest, thoroughly licking my face. Pushing him aside, I spat out a mouthful of grass and earth and rubbed at my face.

As understanding returned, I tried to get up and fell back. A hand roughly pushed my shoulder down and shoved the dog to one side. A face stared into my eyes. It was angular and unshaven, with dense black hair and dark eyes that bored into me. The man betrayed no emotions, just said, 'Why you? Who are you? What do you have?'

I shook my head, unable to process what was happening. 'I... I don't. I'm not really...' I shook my head again. 'Who are you? And what was–'

'What was that? A sceadhu – a shadow. The thing that occupies your nightmares. Or would do if you had a sufficiently twisted imagination. It's gone now.' He stepped back. 'I am Archer.' He rubbed his chin and looked directly into my eyes. 'And if you're of interest to a sceadhu, you've just become my problem.'

I suddenly remembered the golden figure. I grabbed a projecting stone on the kirkyard wall and hauled myself up. 'There was an angel. It tried to stop that thing.' I looked at where the golden figure had fallen, but there was nothing to see, the figure was gone.

'Angel? Yes, he was one of the angelii. Did anything strike you about him?'

'It... *he* glowed and seemed... well, somehow perfect.' I got my breath and suddenly it made sense. 'This is a wind-up, isn't it? It's good though.' I looked around. 'So what's going on? Are you with one of the ghost tours?'

'No. This is not a pretence. This day a sceadhu has attacked you and I need to know why. The angelii won't help you.' Archer snorted. 'Yes, he looked golden and shiny. But think! What did he actually do?'

'He... tried to stop the scead-thing.'

Archer looked down at the ground for a moment. 'But did he succeed?' He answered his own question. 'No. Of course he bloody didn't. You're oh-so-excited about the shiny pretty boy, but fail to notice he was as much use as a paper condom! I never cease to be amazed at how easily your race falls for a bit of glitzy marketing. These things are shiny and glowing and try hard. But when the situation gets serious, all they actually do is get in the way and make things worse.' He paused. 'And if you're being hunted, you may as well get the name of what hunts you correct. It's sceadhu – shay-ahd-hoo.'

I stared at him. There was far too much realism here for comfort. 'Hunted? Look, what the hell is all this?'

Archer leaned forward, effortlessly pulling me up by my collar so our faces almost touched. 'Listen, boy. Your life and your soul are at grave risk. It wasn't smoke and mirrors, it wasn't pyrotechnics and it wasn't an audio-visual effect. It was real, and it wants you. Neither of us has the faintest idea why, so let's stop passing the time of day and get you away from here.'

'Wait! Who... What are you? Why is this happening? How–'

'Later,' snapped Archer, giving me a shove.

I looked around for Crockett.

'Come on. The fleabag will follow when he's finished.'

Finished what? I thought. But what else could I do? I followed.

Archer's long legs carried him quickly and sure-footedly over the wet cobbles, his weather-worn boots clicking and thudding as he hurried along. The folds of his long black coat billowed round him, revealing dark leggings, a deep purple waistcoat and a grubby blood-red neckerchief. Behind him, I struggled to keep up, tripping and slipping in my efforts.

It was curious that Archer never seemed to break step, despite the many people on the Royal Mile. They didn't appear to notice him at all, yet seeming to flow naturally around him, like river water around a prominent rock. Behind him, though, I constantly had to sidestep people and change direction.

Archer turned, swiftly disappearing into a narrow close, before turning into an even narrower one branching from it. At the end, facing us, was an impossibly narrow shop door, below a weathered pale blue sign that read, "Traggheim & Associate – Chronometrists & Labe-Smiths", in ornate gilt lettering. Archer wrenched the door open and stepped inside. I considered making a run for it, but curiosity made me follow him.

Inside, there was barely enough room for us both to stand. Surrounding us were floor-to-ceiling shelves, piled to overflowing with clocks, parts of clocks and every kind of mechanical item imaginable. Astrolabes were crammed beside boxes of gears and cogs. A heap of watch springs leaned against a teak-boxed barograph in which an ink pen slowly scribed onto a paper cylinder. A rack of fine watch-making tools jostled for space with a small lathe. Brass swarf crunched beneath my feet and the scents of warm oil and etching acid mingled in the air. I turned around, fascinated, thinking there was nobody in the shop and no space for a shopkeeper, until a deep, rumbling voice behind me said, 'Who have you brought me, Archer?'

I birled round to see the clutter had somehow parted to create a space occupied by a short, balding man. Oil stains and burns on his worn leather apron betrayed his work. His thin, pointed nose and yellowish-white goatee beard surrounded a thin-lipped mouth. He fixed me with piercing pale blue eyes, topped by incredibly hairy white eyebrows, and spoke courteously, with a faint North European accent. 'And more importantly,' he continued, 'why?'

'Good evening, Traggers,' said Archer, jovially. 'This is Drew Macleod.'

The old man frowned at the irreverent greeting. 'Of course he is.' He stiffened slightly. 'Grosscott von Traggheim, at your service.' He paused. 'Metaphorically speaking.'

'What do you mean, "of course he is"? How did you know I was coming?' I looked at Archer and back at Traggheim, trying to make sense of what was happening. 'What the hell is all this? And how do you know my name?' I glared at Archer.

Traggheim glanced at Archer. 'You're right, Mr Macleod. You have a right to some answers.' He pulled at his beard and looked pensive for a moment. 'Tea. That's where we'll begin. Come.' He darted through a doorway. Archer shrugged and nodded after him.

I looked suspiciously at the narrow door-frame as I stepped through it, but it didn't seem too weird, so I followed, curiosity again getting the better of me.

The room I stepped into was a logical progression from the first. Intricate, precision-made machinery predominated here too. I recognised nothing, but everything had a purposeful air. Gentle ticks, clicks, whirrs and clanks filled the air. Polished hardwood racks and shelves supported a plethora of gadgets and machines, with gleaming brass and copper parts rotating, ratcheting, descending and revolving. Here and there, inky nibs moved over slow-moving paper. Needles moved across etched scales and pointers flickered over dials and meters. A small window opened onto the cobbled close behind the shop, through which the feet of passers-by were visible.

'Please be seated. Be assured nobody and nothing will harm you whilst you are safely within my premises and I will do my best to answer your questions.'

I sat down at a large table and Traggheim placed three China cups and saucers on the table and busied himself carefully pouring boiling water into them through a fussily complex tea-strainer. 'Lapsang Souchong. Black tea from Mount Wuyi – the very best of the crop from Fujian province. Only the fourth and fifth leaves from the plant are dried slowly in a bamboo basket over a pinewood fire in the traditional way.'

Archer looked as though he had heard this many times before.

Traggheim added a slice of lemon to each cup. 'Nothing better to enhance the facultative mental processes.' He slid a cup towards me as though this would solve everything.

A sharp bark came from the street. Without looking round, Traggheim reached behind him and flicked open the window-catch in a well-practised act. To my surprise, Crockett slid between the window-bars and jumped to the floor, where he sat, wagging his tail. Traggheim let go of the window, which snapped closed.

'Crockett!' I said, leaning towards him. 'How did you...'

Archer raised a hand, stopping me short. He stared at the dog, who gazed back, tilting his head slightly. 'Ahhhhh,' said Archer. He and Crockett continued to stare at one another.

Confused, I looked at Traggheim and saw he was paying close attention to this exchange.

'Bit harsh, surely?' said Archer to the dog. 'I mean, he doesn't understand. Give him some latitude.'

I glared at Archer. 'What? I'm open-minded but he's just a dog and...'

Crockett, Traggheim and Archer all simultaneously turned their heads to look at me. There was a pause, then Archer asked, 'So what did you name him?'

This was a little embarrassing. 'Crockett. You know Davie Crocket, King of the Wild... front... ear...'

Archer looked at the dog. 'I see your point.'

Traggheim smiled gently. 'His name is Garm. He assists Archer with his work.'

A feeling of isolation washed over me. This was insane. Or a dream: deadly smoke with red eyes; golden glowing people; a communicating dog. I suddenly felt very weary and slumped down and put my head on my arms.

Archer grinned at Traggheim. 'Perhaps a drop of something stronger than your tea would be a sound idea?'

'Where to start?' Traggheim splashed something from a small bottle into my cup. 'There's a great deal you don't know about, so where to begin?'

'Hunted,' I said. 'He said I'm being hunted by the thing in the graveyard. Let's start there!' I looked from Traggheim to Archer and back again. 'WHAT is hunting me? And why? And... what the hell can I do about it?' I took a gulp of the tea, coughed, and croaked as it burned my throat. I peered into the cup. 'What the...?'

'Best not to ask, I find,' muttered Archer.

Ignoring the interruption, Traggheim fixed me with a stern look. 'Sceadhu are ancient creatures, though rare today. To tell truth, little is known of them, except that their appearance isn't random. Certain combinations of circumstances, emotions and human behaviours seem to combine and cause an... ah... influence, which they respond to.'

'And do what?' I asked.

'Kill. And worse.'

'Worse than killing?'

Archer leaned forward. 'There are many things worse than merely dying. A simple ending is one thing. A messy ending isn't nice. But Sceadhu can cause a drawn-out ending that leaves the soul screaming into infinity whilst they slowly feed upon it. Forever.'

I stared at him and drew a deep breath. 'I've never seen or heard of anything like this. Are you sure? How do you know this? Who the hell *are* you?'

'Traggheim has spent a lifetime studying matters like these,' said Archer. He glanced at Traggheim. 'Nobody has greater understanding. You can take it from me that what Traggheim says is always worthy of close attention.'

'Thank you, Archer,' said Traggheim. 'The praise of a daemon is a valuable and welcome thing.'

I pushed back my chair, slowly rising and backing away. 'Demon? You're an evil demon?'

'And so it begins, yet again,' growled Archer.

'SIT DOWN.' The flat of Traggheim's hand hit the table with a loud crack. 'Archer is NOT EVIL. Nobody and nothing is evil. Nothing is good. These things are all HORSE SHIT.' He took a deep breath and continued in a quieter voice. 'Kindly sit and listen to me.'

I slid back into my seat, keeping my eyes on them both.

'You, like so many, are the product of a system of confusion – a mass delusion, a confidence trick, if you like. All life exists on an ever-changing continuum. We all vacillate between perfection, abomination and the points between. One moment you stop a child from stepping in front of a car and the pendulum swings towards good, the next moment you want to wring the neck of the driver of the car for going too fast and the pendulum swings the other way. This is how things are, how they always have been and always will be.' He looked at me meaningfully. 'That individuals can be inherently good or evil is simply nonsense.

'Since time untold there have existed other human-like entities, who have sought to live alongside and amongst humanity, attempting to influence, help or use mankind for many causes and purposes – some malign, some not – depending on their own needs, wants and feelings. Angelii and daemons are amongst the most known and the most misrepresented.' He raised a hand to forestall the question I was about to ask. 'Yes, it was an angelus you saw at the kirkyard.'

'Prat,' muttered Archer.

'As Archer so kindly demonstrates, there is no love lost between them. However, I can appreciate Archer's strength of feeling–'

'Imagine a collection of pale, blond fools with a superiority complex and a tendency to make a pig's breakfast of whatever they do,' Archer interrupted.

'Succinctly put, Archer, though that is somewhat simplistic.' He looked directly at me. 'Many centuries ago, the angelii wove a complex fabric of lies, deceptions and misrepresentations and succeeded in subtly insinuating it into everyday human life. Imagine ahh…' He clicked his fingers, looking at Archer.

'Snake oil?' he suggested.

'Urban myth is, I think, the modern phrase. An urban myth occurs when a nonsensical fact is so widely accepted that the truth seems no longer to matter. The angelii achieved exactly that, but on a truly massive scale.'

Suddenly, it made sense. I clicked my own fingers. 'Organised religion.'

'Just so.'

Finally, I understood something. 'I've always felt there was something not right about that. So many rules and ceremonies, so many denominations, all arguing with each other and using religion as an excuse for all the bad stuff in the world.'

'Ahhh...no. That's nothing to do with the angelii. It's just humanity at their worst, I'm afraid. What I am speaking of is the myths that were interwoven into religious writings, describing the daemons as evil and servants of Satan, whilst the angelii are supposed to sit with God. In fact, neither performs any such role.'

I recalled the golden figure. 'But the angelus in the churchyard tried to save me?'

'I assume he attempted to banish the sceadhu?' Traggheim raised an eyebrow at Archer.

'He did. And of course it flattened him.'

Traggheim turned back to me. 'The angelii in the modern world have created a role for themselves. Based on the myths their kind have woven about them, they try to hold back anything they see as evil, and to save mankind from what they see as evil forces. Their philosophy is based on a nonsense and as a result their actions can be... problematic.'

Archer leaned forward. 'And as they equate daemons with biblical demons, not only do they get in the way, they actively cause problems. My kind exists to maintain balance in the world. There is an equilibrium that allows everything to function and life to go on. We prevent it from being harmed or destroyed by whoever or whatever may attempt to do so. The angelii are just an irritating obstruction to my work, making me more concerned about the presence of a sceadhu and why it's hunting you.'

'You and me both,' I said, pulling my mobile out of my pocket. The screen was blank, and I pressed the power button. Nothing happened. 'That's odd. It's dead.'

Traggheim stood up and peered at one of the many mechanical instruments. A long inky line wavered around a waxed paper cylinder where a pen connected to the instrument slowly moved over the paper. He pointed. 'Do you see this peak? This reading shows a massive surge in the background level of galdr near St. Giles, at about the time you two were skipping around with the sceadhu. Galdr is a form of powerful hidden energy. I suspect your portable telephone was damaged by that.'

'This day gets better and better.' I groaned, shoving the broken mobile back in my pocket.

'It's for the best,' said Traggheim. 'Electrical equipment is highly susceptible to manipulation. Having your whole life on display in your pocket makes you vulnerable to anything wanting to invade your existence. Look around you. All the instruments I use to monitor the city are mechanical. It would be infinitely simpler to use electronics to build these machines, but those who wish me ill would have invaded my workshop long ago, using the electrical currents for their own purposes.'

'Look up.' Archer pointed at the ceiling and I noticed for the first time there were no electric lights. Instead, bright white light from complex-looking, faintly-hissing lamps filled the room.

'There is no electricity in this building,' said Traggheim proudly. 'I won't allow my instruments and machines to be damaged or interfered with by any outside influence.'

Despite myself, I was intrigued. 'Old-fashioned gas lamps?'

'These are carbide lights. Water drips onto pellets of calcium carbide, releasing acetylene gas, which gives a clear, bright light, as you see.'

'When it doesn't explode, that is,' Archer remarked. 'Can we get back to the matter at hand?'

'Of course. We need to think about you, Mr Macleod, and what to do next.' He poked Archer in the chest with a thin finger. 'Archer, he needs to be kept safe whilst we look closer at what is happening and conclude a plan of action.'

'Are you sure that's a good idea?'

'He needs protection. He has not caused this situation, but he is the key to understanding it. You know where to take him for protection.'

Archer looked away, let out a long breath, and then looked back at him. 'Alright. I'll take care of it.' He sprang to his feet.

Traggheim stood and faced me. 'We don't yet know why the Sceadhu is hunting you. But I will do all I can to get to the bottom of it. And Archer will help keep you safe in the meantime.' He looked awkward. 'You can trust us, Drew. We will help you if we can.'

3. STENT

Stent strode along the wide pavement of George Street with the easy, economical stride of someone who has a long way to go and doesn't want to waste energy. His route followed the edge of the pavement, where fewer people walk, helping him make best progress between the locations on his mental list. He was slight, with a wiry, spare body and an uncontrolled shock of dark-blond hair. His beard was straggly, with a moustache overhanging his top lip. He had an untidy and scruffy appearance, but he was fastidiously clean. His well-maintained trainers and clothes, including baggy cargo pants and a loose blouson jacket, showed signs of wear but were free from dirt.

He moved from bin to bin, checking for useful yet clean stuff; you never knew what people would throw in a bin. He picked up cigarette butts not fully smoked from the steel tray on top, and put them in a leather pouch on his belt. These he would later take apart, forming the strands of tobacco into roll-ups, which he sold to the street beggars. He could earn several pounds a day doing that. Stent didn't smoke himself – why burn money?

As he passed each phone box and parking meter, he checked the coin return flap in case someone hadn't picked up their change. His eyes constantly scanned the pavement and gutter for dropped valuables or money. Edinburgh is a well-heeled city and Stent could earn a living if he kept moving, kept looking, kept thinking.

To Stent, living on the streets represented a life of dignity and freedom – but only if he did it his way. He didn't beg and he didn't ask for anyone's help. He looked down on street beggars, with their crayoned cardboard signs and pathetic messages of hope. He didn't despise them, he just knew he could do better – and made sure that he did. Keeping himself looking respectable meant he could pick up minor jobs, and keeping tidy and clear of booze or drugs made sure those jobs came his way. The rest of the time, he kept busy, very busy.

Stent glanced up at a church clock – he knew where all the clocks were in the city, using them to measure his progress – time was everything and efficiency mattered. He had twenty minutes to get to the meeting place; he would be there in seventeen.

On schedule, he turned off London Road and climbed a long flight of stone steps towards the meeting place on Calton Hill. He hardly broke stride to scoop a tarnished 20p coin from the ground, sliding it into his left jacket pocket and hearing a light 'clink' as it landed against others. People dropped small coins as worthless, but for Stent they added up, making him a few quid a week if he kept moving and looking.

At the top of the hill, there stood a group of monuments and memorials. This was tourist territory, often a good place to work, but today he turned towards the National Monument, a vast, unfinished Regency edifice of pillars and blocks. Something flapped gently on top of the pedestal of the monument. As he got closer, he recognised a familiar figure, reclining against a pillar and whistling a jaunty yet unfamiliar tune, coat dancing in the breeze. As Stent approached, he leapt down, landing lightly and reminding Stent of a cat.

He handed Stent a small leather pouch. 'As agreed. What have you to tell me?' He thrust his hands in his pockets.

Stent talked, telling the story of the streets, and what he had seen as he walked unnoticed through the city.

4. LIBRARY

Outside the shop I found myself once again hurrying to keep up as Archer's long legs ate up the pavement. Crockett (it was going to take a while for me to think of him as Garm) trotted along beside us. The little dog frequently stared to the left or right or glanced up, his sensitive nose constantly active.

'So, what is the story with the dog?' I asked, admittedly a little breathlessly.

Archer stopped and looked at me. 'You need to accept that some things around you are not as they have seemed to be. Things you have always accepted for what they are may be different. Most importantly, that things which seem harmless to you may not be. The world you know will never be the same.'

He looked down at the dog. 'Garm is not so much a name as a title. I don't know how many times he has died and returned in a new body, but it is many hundreds, each time adjusting his appearance and behaviour to allow him to move freely in the prevailing circumstances. In this city, at this time, a scruffy, confident terrier hardly receives a second look, unless he chooses to attract attention. Garm can go places and see things I cannot. He can sense things I cannot and keeps me informed.' Archer turned rapidly around a street corner and continued walking.

'So you're saying this dog was spying on me, whilst I thought he was a pet?'

'That is exactly what I am saying. Except one spies on enemies and I don't believe that is what you are.'

'Bloody hell, for a dog, he did a good job of taking me in. It sounds like he planned the whole thing.'

'When Traggheim's gadgetry detected signs of curious activity, I asked Garm to seek information. You're fortunate he found you and stayed close. Without word from him I may not have reached you in time.' He gestured impatiently. 'Enough explanations now. I need to get you where you can best be defended, whilst I lay some plans.'

I looked around nervously. 'Are we in danger from the sceadhu in the street like this?'

Archer strode away. 'Unlikely, with me here. But until I understand what's going on, I'll be happier with you somewhere secure.' He turned sharply into a children's play-park. 'And here is a good place to get you out of trouble.' He nodded to Garm, who immediately scampered away.

As we walked past the swings and roundabouts a familiar and horrible sensation came over me: the same nauseous feeling I experienced in the kirkyard; I stared wildly around for a sight of the sceadhu.

'It's followed us and is watching,' Archer growled. 'Come quickly, it's gained in confidence and I don't know why.' A massive steel grille blocked the entrance to a disused railway tunnel. Archer nodded towards it. 'In here.'

The massive steel bars included a gate, held closed with a solid-looking, rusty padlock. 'Have you got a key?' I asked.

'Not in so many words,' replied Archer with a scowl and a sideways glance. 'Breathe in deeply and hold your breath.' Before I could ask why, there was a vivid green flash and what felt like a massive invisible hand punched me in the back. A moment later, everything was normal again, except we were inside the tunnel, the steel bars behind us, and I was gasping for breath.

As my breath returned, I realised the nausea had gone, and I slowly straightened up. Then I saw Archer. He was squatting on the floor of the tunnel, looking pale, and was shaking. 'Give me a minute, would you? That's demanding at the best of times, but taking someone with me is a bugger.'

Outside, the sceadhu had gained form, the susurrating noise getting louder, but strangely, there was no sensation to go with it. I stared at the terrifying creature through the grille. Its crimson eyes flickered and burned and its billowing, smoke-like form ebbed and flowed but did not pass through the barrier.

Archer turned and looked at the steel bars. 'Ever heard of a Faraday cage?' Without giving me time to answer, he stretched an arm to lean on the damp brick wall of the tunnel. 'Metal blocks electromagnetic radiation. So does bedrock. A big grille like this, set into the tunnel walls, serves to hide us from anything that might seek us. The sceadhu can't follow. It suspects we are here, but it can't sense us.' He looked out through the bars. 'See – it's dissipating.'

Something small and dark swiftly flicked between the bars and looped round Archer. He scowled. 'Bat.'

I ducked away from the tiny creature and stepped back. 'Can it sense your weakened state and harm you?'

Archer stared at me. 'Why the hell would a bat do that?' He flicked a sleeve, which made it dance out of the way and flash back through the grille. 'Bats have nothing to do with the sceadhu. They're just nosy little bastards.'

He waved towards the dark interior of the tunnel. 'This is the Scotland Street tunnel. Cable-hauled trains once hurtled out of its mouth on their way to Leith. Scared the crap out of Robert Louis Stevenson. He whined on about the trains "shooting out of its dark maw with the guards hauling upon the brake." I must admit, it was pretty grim.'

I looked at the dank, rubble-strewn tunnel, barely lit by the orange glow of the street-lights in the play-park outside. 'Surely we can't spend the night in here?'

Archer grinned. 'To coin a phrase, "You ain't seen nuthin' yet". He pulled a long, slim taper from a pocket deep inside his coat, and rubbed the top between his fingers until it gave off a bluish-white light. 'Come on. You're going to like this.'

We stumbled through the tunnel by the light of Archer's taper, tripping over rubble, rubbish and pieces of rusted metal.

'What is all this stuff?' I asked.

'Since the railway closed 160 years ago, this tunnel has had many uses,' Archer replied. 'Mushroom farm, car storage, air raid bunker, you name it. But none of those people ever discovered its secret.' He stopped, facing a section of slimy brick wall that looked much like all the rest. 'The history books will tell you that three service tunnels linked this with Albany Street, above.' He grasped the brightly-burning tip of the taper in his fist for a moment. When he released it, the light had changed to a vivid orange. 'There were actually four.' With a flourish he drew the taper over the bricks, drawing a shape, the wall glowing orange where the taper touched it. A right-handed arrow formed, and with a start I recognised the shape I had seen created by those ants a few days before. Before I could say anything, the bricks shimmered and disappeared, revealing a stairway with a burgundy-patterned carpet leading upwards.

'Wipe your feet,' commanded Archer, stepping in. Fascinated, I followed, the bricks slipping back into place behind me.

At the top of a seemingly endless flight of stairs, we emerged into an immense room. I stopped, astonished at what I was seeing. Here, buried deep beneath the streets of Edinburgh's Old Town, and accessed via a sewer-like tunnel, was an extensive library. Dusty, leather-bound books and papers lay heaped on leather-topped desks. A large open fireplace faced a low polished table and burgundy leather chairs. Bookshelves lined the walls, floor to ceiling, crammed with worn, dusty books, tied-up bundles of papers, even scrolls. Tarnished brass rails enabled a ladder to slide along the walls, giving access to the highest shelves. The overall impression was of an Edwardian gentleman's club gone to seed.

Around the walls, lamps hung from ornate brackets, their pale-yellow light throwing multiple shadows around the room. 'Acetylene light here too, I see.'

'Actually, no. I don't have Traggheim's faith in violent chemistry. Camphene fuels these lamps. Not as good as the whale oil it replaced, but it suffices.'

I looked at the nearest shelf and read some titles: "Hesketh's Daemonologie"; "Ane treatys of ye unseen anes"; "The Bestyerie of Depths". I turned to Archer. 'You have an unusual home.'

Archer tapped the taper on the fireplace, which instantly erupted into life, becoming a welcoming fire. 'This is not my home. For millennia, deamons around the world have gathered information to help us in our fight against the darker forces and dangerous beings that surround you.' He shrugged. 'This is my library – simply a receptacle for all the current knowledge. This is our Internet. Tomorrow, we will begin researching what has happened to you. In the meantime, this is a safe place.' He gestured towards the chairs by the fire. 'Make yourself comfortable.'

I selected a chair and sat down. Meanwhile, Archer rummaged in an antique cabinet beside us and brought out a bottle and two glasses.

'Traggheim's smoked tea is all very well, but his cooking brandy is pretty rough. On the other hand, this is a very good Cognac. I laid in a supply in 1805 and it gets better every year.' He uncorked the bottle and poured a little into each glass. I filed away that reference to his longevity, adding it to my rapidly growing list of questions, but at that moment, it was simply good to relax in a place that felt safe.

I took a tentative sip, uncertain what to expect. The Cognac was warming and smooth in my mouth and a honey-soft aroma filled my nostrils. I grinned. 'Very good.'

Archer raised his glass to me and sipped a little. He rolled it around his mouth and gave an appreciative sigh. 'Like drinking the liquified breath of a small and very polite dragon.' He smiled reflectively. Then, as if recalling himself, he leaned towards me. 'So what is it you're not telling me?' Archer steepled his hands and gazed at me. 'Something is going on, something which has you as its focus, something we should all be worried about. We can only address what we understand, and that's what concerns me – I don't understand why you are the focus. So we are going to drink the contents of this fine bottle and you are going to tell me everything about yourself. Settle back in that chair, because we're going to be here for a long time.' Archer took another sip. 'Let's start at the beginning. Tell me about your family,' he said.

This wasn't a comfortable subject. 'My parents are both dead. I don't have any close living relatives,' I said.

'But who were they?' he asked. 'I cannot gain an understanding of what is happening without an understanding of *you*.'

'I grew up conventionally, I guess. A suburban middle-class family, nothing special. My father was a civil servant and my mother an academic, an archaeologist.'

'What sort of civil servant?'

That took me aback. 'He worked in an office nine to five for a government salary. Very boring. What more is there to say?'

'I don't know yet, but we shall find out.' Archer leaned forward. 'Drew, when I say I need to know *everything* about you, that is precisely my meaning. Now, where did your mother work and what research did she do?'

Gradually and skilfully he extracted from me details about myself, often half-remembered hazy recollections, that he somehow drew out. His questions grew ever more searching and increasingly personal, as he built a picture of my beliefs and politics, my feelings and emotions. To begin with, I resented Archer's intrusive questioning, but gradually as the Cognac rounded the edges of my objections and his quiet words relaxed me, I opened up to the daemon. Maybe Archer added something else to my Cognac. If he did, I didn't see him do it, but answering honestly and openly just seemed what I should do. Several hours later, after we'd drunk most of the bottle, we reached the present day and I described the strange behaviour of the ants and the jackdaw.

'Manipulative and negative forces often impact on animals. They instinctively resist and that can manifest itself in odd ways,' he said. Then he got to his feet. 'You need to stay here for now. There's a fold-down bed in the alcove in the corner. I'll return tomorrow.' Archer stopped and looked closely at my face. 'Get some sleep – you look like you need it. You're perfectly safe here.' With that, he strode across the room and out of the door, without looking back. Garm glanced at me, then went after him.

I curled up on the bed and tried to sleep, but my mind was in turmoil, trying to make sense of everything that was happening and the barking-mad circumstances I had fallen into. Why me? What could I possibly have done to make this happen and how would it end? I thought about Jamie and what he would make of all this. I resolved to get away and tell him about it at the first opportunity. He could be too relaxed about life, but his advice was usually right on the money. Eventually, exhaustion must have overtaken me. But my sleep was fitful and disturbed.

5. NIGHT

The vixen emerged from her den behind an overgrown gravestone and stood still, looking and listening, scenting the air. Only her nose moved. Satisfied, she set off across the cemetery, squeezing through a gap in the rusted railings. She followed a well-practised route that led to the streets where experience taught her there were likely to be good pickings. A car sped past, its engine growling to a light-drenched crescendo. She barely glanced at it, unperturbed and carried on, sticking to the shadows and avoiding the orange glow of the street-lights.

The scream of another fox pierced the night, and she paused before screaming herself, defending her territory. Her call startled a mouse in a patch of long grass, whose involuntary sound reached her at the same moment she scented its pungent odour and she leapt sideways, descending on it, allowing no chance of escape. A quick bite killed it and she ripped it open with her teeth before swallowing her catch.

Something larger moved in the darkness; a grey and white cat pressed itself low in her path and hissed at her. It had been stalking the mouse upwind of her and it resented her presence. But the mouse was gone, and the vixen knew better than to waste energy on something she couldn't eat and didn't need to fight, so she simply sidestepped the spitting animal and kept moving. She needed to eat more than one mouse if she were to suckle her cubs.

Further on, she found what she was looking for. A corner between two buildings provided shelter for drunks to eat their fish suppers and kebabs, dropping the wrappers before staggering homewards. She nosed in the pile of detritus, gratefully gulping soggy chips and other scraps.

A nearby scuffling sound made her start, and she pressed back against the wall, staring. On the other side of the street, a human figure walked purposefully, not noticing her. Her first reaction was to carry on eating, but instinct made her look again. There was something about this human, something that made her hackles rise. She crouched down, peeling back her gums to bare her teeth in a defensive threat. The vixen backed away as the human carried on walking. She didn't understand what it was about this human, but something was wrong, very wrong. All her instincts screamed at her to run, to get away from this threat. She involuntarily urinated in fear and panic, then sprinted away, terrified by something she couldn't identify but recognised as a danger too grave to face.

6. ALYSSUM

A faint sound awoke me, a tiny scratching noise. I shook my head, blinking. My brain felt like cotton-wool and my mouth had a sour taste. I looked around the room and saw a tiny mouse staring back at me from the top of a desk. It quivered slightly and then, almost too quick to see, bounced off the table and shot away, under one of the book-cases. This place might be sceadhu-proof, but clearly mice could find a way in.

I threw off the blanket and started looking around. I found a cut glass bottle of water and poured myself a glass, wandering along the bookshelves as I sipped. Many of the books were in what looked like Latin or ancient Greek and more were in languages I didn't recognise. I returned to the section of medieval books I had looked at the night before and lifted down "Ane treatys of ye unseen anes" onto a desk. It was a massive book, bound in verdant-green calfskin and bearing an aroma of dusty paper, leather and ink. I turned the thick parchment pages slowly. "Thee yvil anes and theyr ways" caught my eye. I gazed at a red and ochre inked picture of a skinny goblin-like creature with narrow, staring eyes and wrinkled skin, its glare a little too realistic for comfort. With a shudder, I turned a couple of pages and read another heading "Deammon's Seatt". Wondering if this might tell me something about Archer, I read on. "Amidst the cittie of Edinburgh thee hollow hills over thee Royal palays yf Holyrood Hows were aye thee home of deammons, Ane amongst them is calt Archer and abides theyr yet". I could hardly believe what I was seeing. The book was clearly at least 300 years old, yet Archer had seemed no more than thirty-five. How old could he be? I turned the pages, finding more weird drawings, many of which seemed far-fetched, accompanied by tantalisingly brief notes in the same archaic English.

A click and a creak made me start. I whirled round to find that a set of bookshelves had hinged open, revealing a hidden doorway.

Standing in the doorway was a youngish woman, looking directly at me. She had tied back her frizzy red hair in an attempt to restrain it. Bright eyes and an upturned nose gave her an irrepressible air, and she wore baggy, paisley-pattern dungarees, gathered at the ankles. An aroma had entered the room with her: a cacophony of scents I found difficult to place. But best of all, she seemed relatively normal.

'Err... hello,' I ventured.

She smiled warmly. 'Hello, yourself. I'm Alyssum. You look like Archer's put you through the mill. Was it the Cognac, by any chance?'

'Drew. Yes, it was,' I said, rubbing my forehead.

'I thought so. He Hoovers the stuff up and expects others to keep up. I bet he didn't tell you it's 60% proof!'

I shook my head – a that would explain why it was thumping.

'Would some coffee help?'

I grinned. 'Oh God, yes, please.'

She laughed. 'I'll see what I can do. Back in a minute.'

She soon returned, carrying a tray laden with a cafetiere, mugs, and a couple of croissants. I cleared some books from a table. The mingling aromas of rich coffee and flaky croissants made me realise I was starving, and I sat down.

Alyssum poured the coffee, and I sipped appreciatively.

'You look like you don't know what's hit you. Am I right to think it's not just Archer's Cognac that's messing with your head?'

I sighed with relief. Sitting with someone both sympathetic and normal, having a coffee and chatting, made me feel much better. Perhaps I'd dreamt the previous day, but a quick glance showed me I was still in Archer's library. 'I'm being hunted by a monster I didn't know existed. My rescuer is a demon, who laughs at angels and appears to live in some sort of museum.'

'It must feel like your world has turned somersaults. That explains why Archer has got you stashed down here. He left a note in my shop, asking me to look after you.'

'Your shop?'

'I'm a herbalist. My place is upstairs, and Archer uses it as a back entrance to his library. A few of his associates use the library and I monitor it in return for his protection.'

'Protection?'

'I'm a healer. As well as selling herbs and remedies to regular people, I know the ways to heal deamons and others like them. But being a healer makes me vulnerable, so a powerful patron like Archer is good to have. In the seventeenth century, I would have been called a witch. In the twenty-first century, I blend into the culture of "New Age" nonsense, which is handy!' She smiled engagingly. I warmed to her.

'He's an unusual character. He seems a bit…'

'Grumpy? Short-tempered? Downright cussed?'

'I was going to say prickly, but grumpy works.'

'He has a short fuse. Prickly or grumpy, that's his way. He carries a load of baggage. You can't live for hundreds of years without picking up some issues, but his heart is in the right place.'

The door banged open and Archer swept into the room and barked, 'You're up and about. Good.' He glanced at Alyssum. 'I won't be needing breakfast, thanks.'

Alyssum smiled sweetly at him. 'That's good, since I never offered you any.'

He continued, unfazed. 'I've endured Traggheim's peculiar taste in breakfast and we've been over what you and I discussed last night.' He pulled out a chair, hauled it round and swung his leg across to sit astride it. 'We both think your encounters with animals are important. The sceadhu are stupid creatures. If one is hunting you, then something else has given it cause to do so. Your ant and bird friends must be reacting to that – a sign there's a greater power involved here.'

I massaged my temples. Back to the madhouse already. I looked at Archer. 'What do you mean, "greater power?" Yesterday you told me the sceadhu was the stuff of my nightmares. Now you're suggesting its baby monster and mummy is out there somewhere.'

'That's actually a pretty good analogy, Drew.' Archer grinned. 'Not that they are in any way related, of course. It's a relationship of manipulation.'

'What did the ants and the jackdaw do?' Alyssum asked me. I described what had happened.

'Think of it as collateral damage,' said Archer. 'Traggheim has seen a lot of low-level galdr pulsing round the city over the past few days. He has hypothesised that this was an attempt to manipulate the sceadhu into manifesting itself against Drew. It's built up gradually, so as not to be noticed. Traggers thinks this may have resulted in some stray galdr impacting on wildlife. Colony insects like ants and especially clever creatures like jackdaws are susceptible. Hence, they reacted when they saw you.'

'What does the right-angled arrow mean?' I asked. 'The ants used it and so did you, when you opened the door to this place last night.'

'It's a generic power-sign. The shape doesn't signify. It's the making of it at all that is important.'

I asked the question I really needed an answer to. 'What do I have to do to make all this stop?'

Archer looked at me and slowly released his breath. 'There's the thing, Drew. You can't.'

There was a pause, then Alyssum put her hand on mine. 'Once you're drawn into this parallel world, there's no way out, the connection will never go away. It's like lighting the touchpaper on a firework – once you do it, there's no going back. But what Mr Tactless here omitted to say is that there are ways of living safely, of mitigating the dangers. It's like living with diabetes: you can live relatively normally, but you'll be aware of things being different and you'll have to take precautions against the parallel world taking control of you.' She grimaced and looked directly at me. 'It will not be easy.'

Archer broke the spell. 'But first we need to find out what is stirring up the sceadhu. And why?'

I was about to reply, when a piercing bright light lit up the room. A crystal ornament resembling a small sundial lay on a table, a bell jangling within it.

'The Tocsin!' Archer shouted, jumping to his feet. He turned to me. 'One of Traggheim's gadgets. When his instruments detect high levels of threatening activity, it sends a narrow beam of light to a mirror on Alyssum's roof, which reflects it down a vertical pipe to activate the Tocsin. Now perhaps we'll get to the bottom of what's going on.' He pushed me towards the door. 'I need you. No time to waste.'

Outside, it was dull and overcast as Archer and I emerged from the tunnel. The playground was deserted, except for a large ginger tom-cat, which raced past us. A moment later, Garm appeared from behind the battered roundabout, looking pleased with himself – and revealing the reason for its rapid departure.

'Focus, will you?' Archer snapped at him and I could have sworn the terrier shrugged. 'Go to Traggheim and find out what his machines are saying.' Garm turned and ran.

Archer reached inside his voluminous coat and withdrew a burgundy leather pouch with a drawstring opening, which he handed to me. 'Keep this close to you. If we're threatened, open it.' He set off across the playground, his long stride eating up the ground. He shouted over his shoulder, 'If you use it, make sure you mean it.'

I hurried after him, shoving the pouch in my pocket.

7. WERIGEND

Once again, Archer strode off without a backward glance. I'd put up with a lot, but now something snapped inside me and I ran after him and grabbed his arm, pulling him to a halt. The daemon looked at me in surprise. I don't think he was used to people doing that, but I'd had enough. I have a long fuse, but when it gives, it gives.

'Stop this now!' I spat at him. 'I'm not some pawn in your sodding game of dungeons and dragons. You expect me to chase along after you, without the faintest idea where we're going or why? Think again, demon.'

The surprise on Archer's face changed to anger, and his face darkened. 'Oh, the worm turns, does he? That's *daemon*, boy – never forget again. I saved your shabby, insignificant life and gave you my protection. And at this moment, I am attempting to understand why you're under threat.' His eyes flashed with anger. 'And you dare to lay a hand on me?'

'You don't own me,' I shouted back. 'I'm not your little dog to come running when you call.'

Archer glared at me coldly. 'I don't have time for your childish nonsense. Come now or face your fate alone.'

All my frustration, anger, and fear came together in two words. 'Get stuffed.'

'As you wish.' And in a heartbeat Archer was gone.

I stared at the space where he had been. The adrenaline dissipated as fast as it had come, leaving me cold and alone. 'Sorry. I didn't mean it,' I called, lamely. There was silence. I looked around the playground, but I was completely alone. Cursing myself, I started walking.

As I walked, I tried to work out what to do. My first instinct was to head for The Reekie Lum and see if Jamie was around. Jamie could be a clown, but he was a solid friend, and I desperately wanted to tell him what was happening. But how do you tell someone you're being hunted by a mythical monster? And what help could Jamie be, anyway, even if I could persuade him I wasn't off my head or high on something? Besides, I still didn't know why this was happening. I recalled what Alyssum had said: once in this world, there was no way out. Would it be fair to drag Jamie in too? I pulled out my mobile and looked at it, then remembered it was dead. Instead, as heavy drops of rain fell, I picked up my pace. I headed for my flat, the only thing I could think of doing.

'Big Issue, pal?' A tall figure loomed out of a shop doorway as I hurried past. My first instinct was to mutter some platitude and hurry on, but something made me stop. A skinny man with stained teeth and bad skin frowned at me. Under his baggy, grubby jacket, he protected a sheaf of magazines from the rain. 'Big Issue?' he repeated.

'Oh, yeah, ok.' I found a couple of pound coins in my pocket and handed them over in exchange, finding some comfort in the normality of simply talking to someone

'Thanks, pal.' He looked closely at me. 'You ok?'

'Fine... thanks. I just need to get home.' I stuffed the magazine in my pocket and hurried on.

A few minutes later, I reached my street and glanced carefully about. Nothing seemed out of place. The front door looked the same as ever. I wasn't sure what I was looking for, but I assumed there would be some sign if the sceadhu was there. I turned the key in the lock and slowly pushed the door open with my foot.

Inside, everything appeared to be as I had left it. Finding nothing amiss, I dropped my jacket on the sofa and went into the kitchen to put the kettle on. Whilst waiting for the water to boil, I sat down and realised how tired I was. I had slept little and felt exhausted. I leaned back, closing my eyes. Within moments my mind was ebbing and flowing between menacing sceadhu and a soothing daemon, who turned into a cartoon demon, complete with horns and pointed tail, that I poked at with a fork. The fork became a cup of smoky tea, thrust at me by Traggheim, but when I looked again, I saw only Alyssum's mischievous smile, her face rapidly turning dark and building into the sceadhu. It dragged me into its awful susurrating smoke-cloud as I screamed and scrabbled away in terror.

Waking with a start, I found I was still on the sofa, soaked with sweat, my eyes gummed up and my mouth dry as a badger's backside. I looked around the room, terrified, before realising I'd simply fallen asleep.

I heaved myself up and went to the bathroom to wash my face. My mobile was digging to my hip, where I'd been lying on it, so I dried my face, plugged it in to charge and picked up some mail on the doormat before heading to the kitchen to put the kettle on again.

I flicked through the junk mail, dropping it piece by piece into the bin. 'Crap... crap... rubbish... nonsense...' There was an indistinct murmur behind me. I spun round. Above the mobile was a wisp of dark grey smoke. Thinking it was on fire, I cursed and ran to pull the charger from the socket. But when my hand touched the plug, a sudden, violent force forced me away. Only then did I recall what

Traggheim had said about the danger of electronics. A chilling fear came over me as I realised what I'd done and what the smoke was. Nausea started in my stomach and I ran to the door, hauling at the door-handle, but it wouldn't open. Frustrated and scared, I kicked at the door. Then I noticed the entry-phone alongside, and knew I was wasting my effort: the electronic door control was being controlled to prevent my escape.

I turned back, gulping and gasping, trying to overcome the nausea. The shadow was building, forming a horribly familiar dark, billowing shape, which gradually filled the room in front of me, right up to the ceiling. The crimson eyes glowered at me from the depths of the shadow. Staring, appalled, I staggered to the window and tried to undo the latch. A tendril of shadow shot towards it and slammed the latch down. As the nausea grew, I felt myself becoming weaker and the dreadful, susurrating noise hammered into my head, making it almost impossible to think. Try as I might, I could not lift the window-latch, so I turned back to face the growing horror behind me.

Tentacle-like tendrils stretched towards me. Then something astonishing happened: such calmness crept over me that I wondered if death was what I deserved and must embrace. I sank to my knees, unable to resist the sensations which overwhelmed me.

As I folded sideways, I glimpsed my jacket hanging off the sofa and, with an effort, grabbed for it. The red pouch Archer had given me fell from the pocket, just out of reach. I stretched out my fingers and scrabbled on the nylon carpet until my fingernail caught in the seam. It flicked closer, and I closed my hand around it. I could feel myself fading and stuck my thumb into the top of the bag, forcing open the drawstring. A small brass object fell out, though I could barely see it through the waves of nausea, pain and self-loathing taking control of my mind. The object was teardrop-shaped, with a complex pattern of red, yellow and blue whorls and shapes enamelled on it. Around the edge were some etched words, but I couldn't make them out. With despair, I realised the object was not affecting the sceadhu. Exactly what I deserve, I thought. I was losing all control of my mind and body, and my thoughts wandered randomly. "If you use it, make sure you mean it". Who had said that? What did it mean?

Growing delirious, I saw myself as though I was no longer in my body. I lay on the floor of my squalid little flat, a writhing, pathetic, self-hating worm. Archer had called me a worm, and he was right: a vile and unwanted worm. Death was all I deserved.

A spark of anger formed inside me. Why should I die, I thought. The spark fired and grew. 'Stuff bloody Archer. Bollocks to him,' I muttered. 'Why should he be right? And why should this bastard creature finish me?'

Grinding and whirring noises came from the object and a smell of hot oil assailed my nose. I opened my eyes to see the sceadhu pulling away. The gadget's enamelled top had opened to reveal complex machinery inside: gears and cogs whirred round, springs flexed and a purple light appeared, building rapidly to an intensity that was painful to look at. The sceadhu recoiled from the light, which enveloped it, compressing its body to a fraction of its previous size. It screeched in pain, a rending, tearing scream that seemed to split my brain in two. I clasped my head in agony and blacked out.

As I came to, a steady, rhythmic sound was echoing in my head: loud banging. I tried to open my eyes and in a moment I was crouched on my knees, vomiting and gasping. There was a splintering crash as the door flew open, smashing against the wall. Vaguely, I realised that the sound had been persistent and violent knocking.

A small, slightly scruffy man barged through the doorway. 'Are you ok, man? It sounded like you wis dyin' in here.' I tried to pull away from him, but, 'It's ok, pal,' he assured me. 'My name's Stent. I know Archer. He's pure worried aboot you, man.' He took in the room. 'What the hell happened here?'

I spat to clear my mouth and looked blearily back at him, then at the room, attempting to make sense of what was happening. I tried to think how I could reply. 'Stent?' I croaked.

'Yeh. Stent, just Stent. Nane of that Christian name crap.' He peered closer. 'You sure yous ok? You're no' looking at all well tae me. I dinnae ken where Archer is, but he telt me tae find you and keep an eye oot, so here ah am.' He stepped past me into the kitchen, opened a couple of cupboards and found a glass. He filled it with water and handed it to me. 'Sorry aboot the door, but whitever was going down in here didnae sound good.' He frowned. 'It looks like a tornado went through and somebody set the remains on fire.'

I still didn't properly understood who he was, but he seemed to be on my side, so I took a deep gulp of the water. The cool liquid helped wash away the taste of hot oil and something else I couldn't define. I took another gulp and felt my senses returning. 'How did you know where I was?' I asked.

'Easy. You passed wee Jeannie, who was sheltering in the bushes, and further doon the road you bought a Big Issue fae Big Jim. They both telt me and I wis casting aboot when I heard the hullabaloo.' He looked past me towards the doorway. 'Good – the big man's here. This is all way above ma pay grade.'

I twisted round to see Archer filling the doorway, his hands thrust deep in his long coat and a strange look on his face. He was the very last thing I needed. I glared at him and struggled to get up.

Before I could say anything, Archer held out both hands. 'Don't. We were both at fault and I may sometimes be too quick to react to annoyances. Can we accept that for the moment and deal with the here and now?'

Reluctantly I nodded; inwardly I was relieved.

Archer's eye lit on the brass gadget, now lying in the middle of the floor. 'You used the werigend? It worked for you?' He looked closely at me. 'The werigend is one of Traggheim's better creations, but it requires a great deal of inner galdr to use it successfully. You defeated the sceadhu with it. Either you're bloody lucky or there's more to you than there seems.'

Behind him, Stent scuffed his feet. 'I'll be gettin' on then.'

Archer glanced at him. 'My thanks, Stent. Your particular skills were, as ever, extremely useful. No doubt you have a contact who can repair the door with no inquisitiveness?'

Stent nodded and left quickly.

Archer looked back at me and frowned. 'You're pale and exhausted, and I'm not surprised. The werigend draws its power from the user. It focuses and magnifies the inner strength and directs it towards danger. But it leaves its mark on the user. You'll need Alyssum's skills.' He stretched out an arm, pulled me to my feet, and steadied me as I wobbled. 'But I warn you – she's going to be furious with us.'

8. GARM

Garm trotted along the street, away from Archer. It wasn't at all bad, having the form of a small dog, he reflected. Whilst he wasn't all dog, he felt a sense of dogness: not only behaving and appearing like a dog, but allowing the form to dominate his inner self. He enjoyed the life. He could go where he liked outdoors, rarely getting so much as a second look from anyone. Getting inside was trickier, and often involved diving between people's legs and tripping them up. His powerful senses of smell and hearing were surprisingly useful. Sex was freely available and decidedly uncomplicated. Food was great too: finding pleasure in eating all sorts of disgusting rubbish was very liberating.

He kept up a quick, steady pace, unerringly finding his way across town, swerving now and again to keep clear of humans on the pavement. He found people rarely looked down and the price of not staying alert and nimble could be a painful kick where it hurt.

Although Garm and Archer couldn't converse verbally, they could hear each other's voices within their minds when close at hand, which was often useful.

A scent caught his attention, so he nosed into some bushes and through the tall grass behind them, sniffing where a fox had passed through the night before. He recalled his task and jumped over a low wall and into the alley behind Traggheim's shop. He jumped up at the low window and, falling back, allowed his claws to drag over the glass.

The window swung open and Traggheim said, 'Come in, then.'

He jumped inside.

9. ELEMENTS

Archer's warning was an understatement. Alyssum's fury was something to behold as she stood in front of Archer, squaring up to him. Her head was barely as high as his chest, but with her hands firmly on her hips, she glared up at him, eyes flashing with anger. 'What the hell were you thinking of? You left him alone! You knew he was at risk, you knew a sceadhu was hunting him and you left him alone. How stupid are you? Hundreds of years old, with great powers, and yet you behave like a testosterone-filled spotty teenager and run off in a huff.'

Archer took a step back from the furious woman. 'Alright, alright. I surrender. But when you've finished ripping me to shreds, could you work some of your herbaceous wonders on Drew?'

Alyssum's turned her fury towards me. 'And you! We sat down there in the library and talked about the risks you face, the world you have entered. Then what do you do? You wander off, straight into danger like an errant toddler.'

Behind her back Archer winked at me and I got an inkling of the relationship between these two unusual people. She shoved me roughly into a chair and lifted my chin so she could see my face. Her bright eyes looked deep into mine.

'Sorry,' I muttered, feeling like I was back in primary school.

'I should think so.' She smiled lopsidedly, her anger abating as quickly as it had come, and turned sharply to Archer. 'Go away and do whatever the hell it is that you do, before you cause any more trouble. Leave Drew to me.'

Archer held up his hands. 'I'm going.' He winked at me again, this time in full view of Alyssum, then made his escape through a large wooden door in the corner. 'I'll be downstairs in the library, Drew.'

'Coward,' Alyssum yelled after him, then turned to me, her face serious. 'If you've really knocked that horror into the middle of next week, then there has been an enormous cost to you. Your skin looks drawn and pale, your eyes are dull and there are dark patches under your eyes that weren't there yesterday. How do you feel?'

'I'm ok,' I replied, automatically.

'Crap.' She glared at me. 'Stop being so male and tell me how you really feel, or do I have to beat it out of you?'

I paused, surprised, then drew a breath. 'Knackered. Like I've had the stuffing kicked out of me.'

'You have. Your mind had to work harder today than ever before. I'll make up a mixture of herbs and extracts, which will help to rebuild your strength.' She moved to the large work-bench behind us. As she worked, I checked out her work-room. Jars of herbs, bottles of many-coloured liquids and dozens of small wooden boxes containing who-knew-what filled the shelves. Frames, hanging from the ceiling, suspended hundreds of bunches of drying plants. They filled the room with an array of scents, which wafted past me as Alyssum bustled about the room, opening jars and causing the ceiling racks to wave back and forth. The smell changed from savoury to sickly to pungent in just a few moments.

'You need to learn how to marshal your mental powers and apply them to the best effect. This world you've entered is all about your innermost strength. It's as much about emotion as it is about energy.' Alyssum looked over her shoulder at me. 'Whether you know it yet, you've already harnessed some powerful emotions to beat that horror.' She looked expectant for a moment, then shrugged slightly and went back to her work, added a green liquid to the stone bowl of herbs and mixing it vigorously.

I felt an urge to tell her everything, but something held me back. I was so weak and pathetic, I thought and remained silent, looking carefully at a shelf of bottles.

Alyssum carried on working and changed the subject. 'So where are your family?'

'I don't have any. My parents both died. There's just me.'

She turned to me. 'I'm sorry. That must've been hard on you.'

I shrugged. 'You get through it. What else is there to do?'

'You've a lot of emotions built up. There'll be anger, fear, bitterness and maybe a little hope. All of that strengthens you, but it also makes you vulnerable. Whatever you felt when the sceadhu attacked worked for you. The werigend focussed it for you, but it was your emotions that drove it and if you can learn to harness those feelings, you'll be better able to stay safe.' She handed me a glass. 'Pinch your nose and drink this. It won't taste nice.'

I looked dubiously at the glass. It had a swirling mix of violent colours, like a lava lamp gone badly wrong, which didn't make me keen to drink it.

'Stop being a wimp and get it down. That wretched daemon is bad enough. I don't need two snowflakes around here.'

Alyssum's mockery of Archer cheered me up enough to slug the glass back in one. Big mistake. My nasal passages seemed to fill with fire, whilst the taste encompassed everything horrible I had ever encountered on a base of pure kerosene. The texture writhed and rasped over my tongue and I spluttered, gasped and involuntarily gagged.

'No, you don't. This is going down and staying down, regardless of whether you want it to.' Alyssum grabbed my chin, pushed it up and rubbed my throat briskly, in what was clearly a well-practised manoeuvre.

I choked and wriggled, but I couldn't help swallowing. She let go, and I gasped, then glared at her. 'What was that about?' I spluttered. 'That's how you make a bloody pet swallow medicine!'

'Works well on humans too, doesn't it?' Alyssum replied, with a sweet smile.

'What was in that witch's brew? It tasted like Satan's backside.'

'Not a witch's brew. Witchcraft isn't real, you know.'

'What about all this?' I gestured about the room. 'If this isn't some kind of magic, what is it?'

'Oh, magic exists, though it's not called magic. It's much more limiting than you'd expect and few people have genuine powers. But what I do is simply put centuries of knowledge to use. Conventional human medicines are mostly derived from plants. In the parallel realm, plant extracts often work differently and more efficaciously. I can do things with plants that would give a G.P. a wet dream.' She surprised me by kissing me on the forehead before shoving me away. 'I'm finished with you now. Go on. I've got work to do.'

I thought it advisable to do as I was bid. Alyssum was clearly a caring woman with a core of case-hardened steel.

I opened the massive oak door and stepped through it.

It thudded shut behind me and I took a moment for my eyes to acclimatise to the dim light. I was standing at the top step of a wrought-iron staircase, spiralling tightly downwards within a narrow vertical shaft hewn from the solid bedrock. The walls gleamed with damp and a small gas mantle gave a dim yellow glow. I leaned forward and made out a series of similar lamps, all fading downwards in the gloom.

The clang of my feet on the cast iron steps echoed down the shaft. After descending what seemed like hundreds of steps, I found another heavy oak door, this one with iron studs and a large, round iron handle. I turned it and the light of the library flooded in. Archer and Traggheim, their backs to me, were peering intently at a massive, leather-bound book, held open at a page by strings of lead beads. Beside them, a large coffee pot bubbled atop a spirit burner.

'Ah, Mr Twist. Would you care for some more?' Traggheim enquired brightly.

I looked blankly at him and then at Archer, who shrugged.

'There's a winding stairway, down into the gloom,' the old man warbled in tremulous triumph. 'It's from a musical.'

'I have no idea where he gets this stuff,' said Archer. 'But I wish he wouldn't.'

Traggheim's indignant look made me laugh out loud, and he frowned at me. 'What are you reading?' I asked to distract him.

'Quite possibly your future, young man.' His reply sounded testy.

Archer scowled and waved towards the coffee-pot. 'We're researching some possibilities for the cause of the attacks on you, but don't worry about that now. Regardless of your wishes, you are now a part of this parallel realm. Your life will never be the same.' He paused and tilted his head slightly, his piercing eyes boring into me. 'I expected you to be unhappy about that, yet you seem sanguine?'

I shrugged. He had a point. 'What can I say? On the one hand, this is nerve-wracking, but if I'm honest – I feel alive for the first time in yonks.'

Archer glanced at Traggheim and continued. 'This evening's events suggest you may be capable of learning some skills that may help defend you from further attacks. If you focus and try hard, they may render you useful to me in my efforts to find out who or what is behind the attacks.'

I shrugged again. 'Sounds a good idea. Where do I start?'

Archer grinned fiendishly. 'Not so fast. First, you need to gain some basic knowledge.' He pointed across the library. 'Find McCrone's "Elements of parallel activity" in the far right-hand section, second shelf from the top, and start reading.' He waved again at the coffee. 'It's dry reading, best digested with a dose of caffeine.'

I poured a mug and selected another table to put it on, before sliding the ladder along its rails to the section Archer had pointed out. Climbing it, I ran my finger along the dusty shelf, until I found the book: a small volume, bound in cracked, dark-green leather. I climbed back down with it and settled into a chair. I glanced across at Archer and Traggheim, who had now resumed their murmured conversation, bent over their book once more. Taking a sip of the surprisingly strong coffee, I began to read.

"All creatures have the potential to develop inner power from their raw ability. A house-fly could become master of all, were it not for its lack, both of the intellectual capacity to develop its power and of the opportunity to learn how to do so. Any human being may become powerful. Many develop their inner power in tiny ways, for example, learning to manipulate others, to misrepresent facts and be believed, or to inspire and lead others to overlook their better judgement and risk their lives for foolish causes". I turned the page.

"Human beings have the capacity to develop their inner power to greatness, far beyond what any would believe possible. Inner powers may only be developed beyond the norm by long and demanding specialised training with one who has highly developed powers. With strong self-belief, intense application and great commitment, perhaps one human in a ten-thousand may become skilled in using inner power.

"How may inner powers manifest themselves? The individual drives the manifestation of inner powers by the person they are. One's skills may develop to a level of inspiration or even genius, techniques may enhance abilities to levels thought impossible, manipulation of both animate and inanimate surroundings become possible. There is much not understood about the workings of inner power and much which varies from what seems reasonable.

"Inner powers are finite and must be managed with care. Replenishment of strength requires time and the correct circumstances. In a weakened condition, the powerful may find their inner powers have unexpectedly waned. The wise preserve their strength carefully.

"For the powerful, training is a continuing process, to enhance, extend, strengthen and augment. Training others is a dangerous thing, only to be undertaken with great care and forethought. Permitting and assisting the development of inner powers by inappropriate persons not only poses risks for all, it creates a great danger for the trainer, whose own powers may become diminished because of their misapplication by the one they have trained".

I leaned back in the chair and looked at the fireplace, my eyes drawn to the dancing flames, as I reflected on

McCrone's words. Archer called across the room to me. 'What do you think?' He strode over. 'Your life is going to change and you must adapt to it.'

'This is dangerous?' I asked.

'Of course. Crossing the street is dangerous. But then buses don't turn you inside out with malicious intent.'

'But McCrone talks about risks for anyone who teaches the use of inner power. Are you sure you want to take me on as a pupil? Are you sure you want to take those risks with me?'

Archer shrugged. 'In this world, you take risks. Or you stand still and go nowhere. Here's your first lesson. What McCrone called inner power is properly called "galdr".' He rolled the R at the end of the word. 'Many things in the parallel realm have Norse or Anglian names, but McCrone was a prude, and he didn't like that, so he applied his own pompous names. Inner power!' He snorted and added, 'But don't expect me to be Miss Jean Brodie. I'm going to be a hard taskmaster. And make no mistake – if you don't do exactly as I tell you, I'll kick your arse into the middle of next week. We start tomorrow.'

10. GALDRLORE

I spent another uncomfortable night camped out in the safety of Archer's library and the next morning he virtually frog-marched me up Arthur's Seat. Effortlessly striding up the steep volcanic slopes, he soon left me behind. When I caught up, gasping and panting, Archer was sitting on the rocky outcrop at the summit and I flopped beside him.

Archer surveyed the vista of the city before looking sideways at me. 'Effective use of galdr isn't just brain-work, you know, it also requires physical fitness. You need to be fit, boy.' I tried to catch a breath to respond, but Archer continued relentlessly. 'Look at all of this, the entire city. Tens of thousands of people, thousands of buildings, all life happening in front of us. This is my chessboard. This is the world in which I work.' He paused, then glared at me. 'Crap about with it at your peril. And mine.' He stared at the city for another moment, then sniffed. 'Do you have the werigend?'

I pulled the werigend's pouch from my pocket and removed the brass gadget, laying it on the palm of my outstretched hand.

'The werigend will allow you to focus your galdr. It will allow you to make much more of the limited capacity you have. Use it. Think about it. Think about what you need to do and focus.' He pointed towards the Royal Mile. 'Do you see the traffic light facing us at the crossroads?' I nodded. 'Make it stay red.'

I stared at him. 'How?'

'Think boy, think. Use your head. Use your mind. *Force* it to stay red. Don't let it change. Don't *allow* it to change.'

I stared at the traffic light, concentrating hard. Nothing happened. The light continued to change through its cycle, unabated.

Archer sneered. 'Stop playing and try harder. It isn't enough to just want it to happen. You must be determined and you must force it to happen. You've got to pull from deep inside you. Make. It. Happen. For. You.'

'I don't understand. How do I do that? How do I make it happen?'

'From in here.' Archer poked my chest. 'For this moment, it has to be the most important thing in your life, the most critical thing, the thing that matters more than anything else in the world. And you have to force it, *will* it to happen. If you don't... nothing will happen.'

I tried again. I furrowed my brows, concentrated, and tried to do as Archer said. Suddenly, in my hand, the werigend gave a faint whirring sound and grew warm. Below us the traffic light changed from green, not to amber, but briefly flickered red, before returning to green. Suddenly, I experienced the mother of all headaches. I gasped, clutching at my forehead. 'God, that hurts.'

'Of course it hurts,' Archer said. 'This isn't a fairy story. You don't just wave a magic wand and have things happen for you. For everything you do using galdr there is a price. And you will bear the price. Train your mind. Be physically fit and learn to deliver galdr from within you to make things happen. The werigend will focus the galdr for you and accentuate it, but the power must come from within you. Now, stop whining and try again.'

We continued practising until I found I could hold the traffic light at red for a whole second, a blinding headache washing through me each time.

'Enough for now,' said Archer. 'But you can damn well run back.'

'What?' I said in horror.

Archer leapt to his feet and roughly pushed me. 'You need to get fit. Now run. And don't look back, because my boot will be close behind you all the way.'

For the following week, I worked like I'd never worked before. Three or four times a day Archer made me climb to the top of Arthur's Seat and there he stood over me whilst I tried to influence the world below us in some tiny way. When he got bored with traffic lights, we moved onto making birds fly in specific directions. Then we tried to make pedestrians sneeze and following that, the wind vanes change direction. After each session Archer made me run round Arthur's Seat and through the streets, until I hated him with a burning passion. But I recognised what he was doing; it kept a lid on my feelings and after a week I could just about make it to the top of the hill without stopping to get my breath. In the evenings, I studied McCrone and other books Archer kept thrusting at me. The more I read, the more apparent it became that this was going to be a complex, time-consuming, and demanding process.

I asked Archer about returning to my flat. He glanced at me and raised an eyebrow.

'Of course you can, you're not my prisoner. I assume you're comfortable with dying a horrible, lingering death?'

So for the time being, when I wasn't in Archer's company, I stayed in the library. He never seemed to eat and left me to sort out my own meals. Alyssum took pity on me and let me eat upstairs with her, provided I took my turn at cooking and washing up, but soon I was starting to climb the walls with frustration.

Between training sessions, Archer was constantly coming and going, pulling down books from the furthest shelves of the library and searching them, muttering and cursing under his breath. From time to time, Traggheim would arrive and they went into a huddle.

'He's really stressed about the Sceadhu attacks on you,' Alyssum commented over dinner. 'He feels somehow responsible, but until he identifies the source, he's going to get more and more scratchy and grumpy.'

'Don't I know it,' I said, ruefully. 'If I make the smallest of mistakes, I get it straight between the eyes. And if he decides I'm not trying hard enough, he flies right off the handle.'

'He's terrified something worse will happen to you before he can find the cause and deal with it. It's not just that he feels responsible for you. He feels responsible for everyone. He sees himself as a sort of shepherd, but he knows that if a wolf ever gets past him, the rest of the pack will be right behind and his entire flock will be doomed.'

As I walked back down the spiral staircase, I heard what sounded like shouting coming from the library. As I descended, the sounds resolved into Archer shouting. 'No bloody way. I can't collaborate with them. And you know I can't.'

'You can and you MUST, Archer,' Traggheim shouted. 'There is no alternative. How else can this be resolved? You have tried everything else, and I have no more ideas to offer.'

I pushed the door open. Archer swung round at the sound and hesitated. 'Damn it,' he muttered to Traggheim. 'You're right.' He barged past and swept through the tunnel exit.

Traggheim turned to me. 'I have never seen Archer driven to such distraction.'

'What was that about?'

It was Traggheim's turn to hesitate. 'Archer is going to have to swallow his pride and face up to something he loathes.'

'The sceadhu?'

'The angelii. Archer has much history with them, but they are sensitive to some things we struggle to gain a measure of. He will have to negotiate with them. And that will cost him a great deal.' He shrugged and fixed me with eyes that shone bright in his wrinkled face. 'Practise hard. He may need you.' Traggheim dropped into an armchair and stared into the fire, pulling slowly at his beard.

I had adopted one of the library tables as my own and I sat at it, opened a book, and began reading. I'd read the page several times already, but the turgid writing was difficult to absorb and Archer kept hammering into me that detailed recall was vitally important.

Half an hour later Archer swept back into the room and marched across to where Traggheim sat, dropping into the opposite armchair. 'It's done.'

I got up and walked across to them.

Archer silently watched me approach before turning back to Traggheim. 'Stent is carrying a message to the angelii. He'll send Garm with word of their response.' He turned to me. 'You are going to see the true face of the angelii now, how vile and manipulative they can be. If they agree to meet, then there have to be three of us – they will insist on threes. It's a superstition of theirs. You, me and the third had better be Alyssum. Stent is a good messenger, but this would ask too much, and Traggers here is too old.'

'As old as I feel,' muttered Traggheim.

'I don't like this.' Archer ignored him. 'I don't like it at all. This is as likely to make things worse as it is to help, but I don't know what else to do. There is a traditional meeting place, a place of truce. We'll meet them there. No doubt it will be at 3am, it always is.'

'The Grand Gallery at the National Museum of Scotland,' explained Traggheim.

We all jumped as an unearthly barking echoed around the library. 'Bloody dog,' Archer grumbled. 'The little fleabag can squeeze through the bars into the tunnel.' He opened the door and Garm trotted in. He gave Archer a meaningful stare and then wandered across to the fire and curled up in front of it, giving me a vague wave of his tail as he passed.

Archer nodded slowly. 'They agree to meet. And I was right: three people on each side, at 3am. Garm? I need you to check the lie of the land for me beforehand.' The dog sighed and then wagged his tail once against the floor, before gently farting and curling up again.

11. ACCORD

At the appointed time, Archer, Alyssum and I left the library via the stairs to Alyssum's shop, then made our way towards the National Museum. It was a damp, chill night and Alyssum shivered, pulling her jacket closer around her shoulders. I couldn't help looking behind, fearful of what might be there.

'You're right to be alert, Drew,' said Archer. 'The Sceadhu has been trailing us for several minutes, but it's giving us a wide berth.'

'Scared of you?' asked Alyssum.

'Hopefully. It's keeping out of sight. But they have a smell about them and it carries in this damp air.'

As we approached the National Museum, Archer nudged us both into a side doorway, shrouded in shadow. 'We'll wait here until the appointed time. We use the old entrance at the top of the big steps. Traggheim installed one of his gadgets years ago. The correct movement of the hand in the right place unlocks and opens the door. Quite handy, really. We used to have to bribe the night watchman, when there still was one.'

'Why not just use your galdr to get in?' I asked.

'And be weakened when I meet these bastards? I don't think so.'

We fell silent, and I kept a careful watch on the street. I breathed slowly, trying to detect the sceadhu's smell, but I couldn't make it out. After a few minutes there came a muffled 'wuff' by our ankles and we looked down to see Garm's black nose, gleaming in the sparse light, poking through an air-vent in the wall.

'They are here,' said Archer tersely. 'Let's go.' He strode up the imposing flight of stone steps leading to the entrance and made a complex hand-movement in front of the door, which unlocked and slid open.

We walked three abreast through the entrance hall and into a huge, open space. I glimpsed stars through a vast glass roof that was supported by massive cast-iron pillars. Scattered around the hall were large exhibits. A lighthouse lens, a dinosaur skeleton and a railway signal were nearest to us.

'I preferred it when they had goldfish pools in here.' Archer frowned as he looked around. 'Over there.' He nodded towards the end of the Grand Gallery, where a pale-yellow glow was illuminating the ornate, curving stone staircase. 'That's their piss-yellow light.'

'Play nicely, Archer,' whispered Alyssum, as we moved towards the stairs.

'They only turn it on for effect,' he muttered.

As we got closer, I saw three figures standing on the half-landing above us, apparently two men and a woman. All three wore loose white robes. They were tall, with blonde hair and milky complexions. The pale-yellow light bathed them, with no visible source.

'The one on the left is the one who tried to attack the sceadhu at Greyfriars,' I whispered to Alyssum.

'If they don't come down and speak to us face to face, I'll kick their smug arses off that landing,' Archer growled.

'And that will help, how?' I asked.

'You've been spending too much time with Mizz Herby here. Now shut up.'

The three angelii delicately descended the stairs and stopped at the bottom, facing us. The middle angelus stepped slightly ahead of the other two and his confidence suggested he was the senior. He looked directly at me, but spoke to Archer, never taking his eyes off my face. 'Demon, you asked for this meeting. Do you bring us a new disciple, or have you come to atone for your sins?'

Archer stiffened and Alyssum touched his arm. Like a snake seeing its prey the angelus' head snapped round to stare at her. He hissed, 'You dare to bring a hag to the place of truce?'

Fearing what Archer might say or do, I surprised myself by stepping in front of him and snapping, 'Watch your words. If this is a place of truce, then it should be a place of respect too. She's no hag.' The other male angelus slid rapidly forward in response, but the first one put a hand out to stop him, and his head snapped back to stare at me. Archer looked sideways at me with surprise on his face, but said nothing.

The lead angelus smiled thinly at me. 'Respect is important. As are good manners, when seeking an...' He paused '... accommodation.' He tilted his head. 'The woman is a hag, a witch, a mixer of herbs and a maker of spells. To bring her here is ill-mannered. But let us set that aside, for I sense there are bigger things at stake this night.' He looked at Archer, but it was the other male who spoke.

'What is it you want, demon? You come here with a human and a herb-grinder and you seek accommodation with us. Yet you have never given us reason to seek common cause with you. What is it you want from us and why should we wish to give it?'

Archer smiled grimly. 'We mustn't forget our manners, must we?' he said, quietly. 'May I introduce Mr Drew Macleod and Miss Alyssum Leadenham?' He glared piercingly at each angelus. 'They both live under my personal protection.' He paused and there was silence. 'Drew, Alyssum, may I present Brother Jophiel?' He nodded courteously towards the lead angelus. 'Brother Rillan, I have met before.' He looked at the female angelus. 'You, I have not met.'

She smiled bleakly. 'Sister Ashnil, demon.'

'Excellent,' said Archer. 'Let's be clear about our relative situations, shall we? You seek to protect mankind from evil. You choose to see my kind as evil, but luckily, your power isn't enough to do much about it. I seek to do what you fail to do, but you choose to see my work as tempting humans towards the evil you think you see in me. Agreed so far?'

Jophiel inclined his head slightly. 'Your words are as twisted as ever, but there is a germ of truth in what you say. What of it?'

Archer continued. 'It follows that as we both seek to protect mankind, albeit in different ways, there surely must be some common ground?'

Rillan snorted and opened his mouth to speak, but a sharp hiss from Jophiel silenced him. 'Let us say, for the sake of discussion, this is correct. I say to you again, what of it?'

'Brother Rillan. I believe you have met Drew before. In fact, I believe you tried to save his life.'

Rillan nodded. 'I did.' He looked at me. 'I am disappointed you have joined with this demon after bathing in angelic light.'

'That would be because you failed miserably, and I was the one who saved Drew's life, you smug–'

'Nice, indoor voices, Archer,' Alyssum said quietly.

Archer drew a breath. 'I apologise. The creature who attacked Drew was a sceadhu.'

At this, Jophiel turned to look at Rillan, who nodded. 'I believe so.'

'A sceadhu,' hissed Jophiel. 'What have you done, demon? What have you summoned?'

'Oh, get over yourself! I kicked its arse and saved his life. That's what I've done, and it's more than you could do, so don't even think about blaming me. Something more powerful is behind this, and I need to know what. You clowns may help prevent a catastrophe by sharing what you know, but as ever, your only interest is in playing your childish "us good, you bad" game.' He turned to leave.

'Wait!' Jophiel's voice had become sharp. 'There are... signs.' He paused, looking at me, then at Alyssum, before looking back at Archer. 'We will need a token of good faith.'

Both Rillan and Ashnil stared at him in horror. 'We cannot!' Rillan said.

Jophiel glowered at him. 'We can, and if I ordain it, we will.' Rillan lowered his eyes, his jaw set. 'But only if there is a suitable token. What can you offer, demon? How can you prove good faith to me?'

Archer gestured to one side. Daemon and angelus stepped away from the others and talked in low tones. Alyssum and I exchanged worried looks; this didn't sound good. The angelii stood in front of us, stony-faced.

Archer and Jophiel returned. 'It is decided,' declared Jophiel. 'This threat must be identified and addressed. I have received a suitable token. Sister Ashnil – I require you to scour the churches and meeting places of the city in search of information that will help identify the root cause of the sceadhu presence.' She nodded. 'Brother Rillan – you will liaise between both sides.' Rillan glowered, but nodded his acquiescence.

As we left the museum, Archer broke into a grin. 'Well, that worked out as well as it could have done. They agreed to help us and I succeeded in not punching anyone smug. I consider that a success.'

'But what was the token you gave them?' asked Alyssum.

Archer smiled grimly at her. 'Nothing much. Just my life.'

12. SHRUBHILL

'Don't tell me – crocodiles are part of all this too?' I asked.

Archer and I stood amid a massive derelict building, looking at graffiti on a brick wall. I'd been to the old Shrubhill tram depot before, it featured in all the abandoned building websites. The place had been lying empty for decades, its roof long since gone, the interior choked with weeds, rubble and a hundred types of abandoned junk, overlaid with the smell of decay. The huge brick walls had become a showcase for the local graffiti artists. I couldn't help thinking that Jamie would love this place. He was a huge fan of abandoned buildings and spent a lot of time searching websites for interesting and neglected places to poke about in.

'I'll grant you it's a very nice crocodile, but it's signifies nothing in the parallel realm.' Archer nodded at the graffito. 'It may have exceptionally large teeth, but I can promise you there are aglaecan with much better cause for nervousness.'

Voices echoed through the building and Garm broke off sniffing through the undergrowth, and growled. Archer smiled thinly. 'Excellent. I hoped some locals might show up. I can demonstrate a skill that may be useful to you.'

Before I could ask what he meant, there was a movement in the undergrowth and a teenage lad with badly bleached blond hair pushed his way through the brambles and staggered into sight, a rattle-can of paint in his hand. 'Oh! Alright pal?' He looked surprised to see me.

'How're you doing?' I muttered, then realised something. I glanced at Archer.

'No.' He grinned. 'He can't see me. Now watch this.' He touched my arm briefly.

Another couple of lads followed their friend into the space, and the first one looked back at us. 'Weird, man. There was a guy right there just now. '

'Now they can't see us.' Archer grinned again. 'Or hear us, for that matter.' He picked up a small stone and lobbed it towards them.

'What the fuck?' shouted the failed blond, as the stone skittered over his foot.

'Just loose stones, stop panicking.' His friend laughed at him as he muttered something and slowly wandered off through the rubble, picking through rubbish and eyeing up the graffiti.

'It's possible to be unseen and unheard with the application of a little galdr and some skill,' Archer told me.

I couldn't help myself. 'Invisibility? That's really cool!'

He sighed. 'No, not invisibility. They can still see and hear us, but we tweak their subconscious minds to tell them we're not here and their subconscious hides us from their conscious minds. It happens all the time. We just give it a nudge. The human brain is constantly interpreting what it sees and hears, making sense of all those neural impulses firing in from the ears and eyes, in the light of experience and knowledge. We just encourage that process to overlook us. I'm going to show you how to do it for yourself.' He gave me that hard Paddington stare of his. 'Use it to arse about with people and I promise you I will rip your head off. Understood?'

I nodded, now desperately keen to learn how to pull off this new technique. Although I didn't believe the actual threat, if I abused it, I knew he would make me regret it somehow.

We spent the rest of the evening practising this new method of manipulating people. To give me a target Archer "dumbed down", as he liked to call it. He allowed his mind to behave like a human's, so I could practise on him – a bit like a laptop reverting to classic mode. Not that Archer would have got the analogy.

As the shadows lengthened amongst the twisted metal and fallen masonry, I was just nailing it when the daemon broke off and stood upright. His head twisted from side to side, like a meerkat on watch, breathing deeply through his nose. I was about to crack a joke, then saw his face. It was a look I hadn't seen before and I didn't like it much. Garm's hackles rose, and he bared his teeth, backing towards us.

'What is it, Archer?' I edged closer to him.

'I'm not sure, but there's something nearby, something that shouldn't be here. Stay close and keep your hand on the werigend.'

I slid my hand into my pocket and felt the reassuring warm metal of the machine. 'What could it be?'

'I think it might be a shade, but there's something especially malevolent about it.' He clicked his fingers. 'Garm.' The dog ran off, heading for Traggheim's shop.

From my long nights of study I knew shades were essentially ghosts, and unlike most things in this mad world, they were not dissimilar to what we normally think of as ghosts, though not the cute Casper ones. According to McCrone, shades exist because they have an unfulfilled purpose, usually an unpleasant one. Their powers are very weak and they are usually unnoticed unless they find a way of building their galdr to where they can start harassing people by manifesting and scaring them. Clearly this one was different, but it didn't seem the time to ask questions.

After a while Archer relaxed, but his frown remained. 'Whatever it was has dissipated, but I still don't like it.'

Garm hurtled back into view and barked once. Archer nodded. 'I was right – Traggheim's instruments show a spike in galdr use in this vicinity in the last half an hour, with the mark of a shade and the character of movement.'

Unmoved by the significance of this, Garm sat down and began washing his genitals. I ignored him. 'What about us? We were using galdr. Surely that would show up?'

He gave a short laugh. 'I said a spike. Your efforts amounted to a slight rise in the background levels. I don't know how a shade has gained enough galdr to become active, but what concerns me is why and with what aim. I'm going to look about and see if I can pick up its trail. You go to Traggheim's and see if he can detect its direction of movement. Send the dog to me with any information.'

As I set off, he called after me, 'Go directly there and hurry. I'm not keen on this.'

When I got to his shop, Traggheim could offer no further information. Two cups of Lapsang Souchong later Archer arrived, but he had drawn a blank.

13. VIXEN

The vixen nosed her way slowly through the haphazard maze of rubble and brambles at Shrubhill, hunting for the mice and rats she knew abounded. Just one or two would give her the energy she needed to feed her cubs. They were growing fast and demanding more and more of her milk. She crept low, listening for the tiny sounds of her prey, and tried to catch their scent.

She sat upright and whined. Something was very wrong, but she couldn't understand what. Twitching involuntarily, she dug. The vixen didn't understand why she was digging, but simply knew that she must. She grew more and more frantic in her desperation to obey the sensation in her head that hurt her and forced her to act. She bit at the ground, clawing at the loose stones and rough earth until her pads and gums bled profusely, but still she dug, unable to stop.

Suddenly, she felt something hard. Bone, but old bone, without nourishment or value to her. The pain in her head waned and, panting, she nosed some of the spoil back over the skull. She lay back, catching her breath, and then licked her front paws, slowing the flow of blood.

After a time, she got up and limped off to her den, not wanting to spend any more time in this painful place.

Once there, she couldn't settle. Her two cubs were fractious, wanting food and play. All of her maternal instincts told her to respond to their needs: she should hunt and she should encourage them to explore and play. How else would they learn the skills they would need? But something held her back. Something wasn't right and she couldn't understand it. It frightened her, but she didn't know how to react to the strange sense of foreboding she felt.

Suddenly, she sat upright and growled. She shook her head, trying to fight the growing sensation within her as it rapidly became overwhelming, drowning out all other thoughts in an powerful deluge. Then the vixen knew what she had to do. She turned to her cubs. Without pause, she tore the throat from one and then the other, their fresh blood flowing over her muzzle. Her gleaming teeth tore their bodies apart and she gulped down the warm meat, crunching the bones, leaving just scraps of fur. She would need the energy for what lay ahead, and there was no time to hunt. She could no longer act according to will or instinct. Instead, she must do as the controlling sense in her mind dictated.

14. DWEORG

There's a limit to how long anyone can live in a library without going barking mad. Having Alyssum's company helped, but she liked her own space and, whilst I was welcome to visit her shop for meals and an occasional coffee, I could tell I was pushing my luck. Archer and Traggheim must have had the same thought, and they cornered me with their own solution.

'You can't return to your flat – that would be a gift to the sceadhu's organ-grinder, whoever that is,' said Archer. 'Your skills are developing, but until we've a better idea of what's going on, you need somewhere more suitable than this to live.' He waved vaguely around the leather and polished oak prison the library had become.

'What do you suggest?'

'We have the perfect solution.' Traggheim beamed. 'You can live in the rooms above my shop and workshop.'

'Won't I be in your way?' I asked.

'The rooms up there are rarely used. I'm much happier living in my basement.' The old man seemed to think basement-dwelling was normal, but I was learning to accept nothing at face value in this parallel realm.

'Traggheim's shop is well shielded from galdr and from electronics, so it's a perfect place for you to stay,' added Archer.

Traggheim was obviously excited about the idea. The wrinkles in his face creased into a delighted smile when I agreed.

And so I moved home.

'Come in, come in, Drew.' The little man ushered me through the machine-strewn shop. 'Let me show you your accommodation. I'm sure it is comfortable for you.' He led the way upstairs, to the top floor, and I had to avoid grinning at his apparent pride. It was as though he was showing me into a suite at the Dorchester.

'There's everything you should need. Here is a well-appointed kitchenette, gas, of course.' For which, read an old Baby Belling cooker and a small fridge.

'And these chairs I'm sure you'll find to be most comfortable.' He pointed out the threadbare chairs surrounding an old utility coffee table. The room was scruffy and dated but my flat was little better, so I would not be picky. Besides, his enthusiasm was infectious.

'Through there is a most comfortable bed-chamber for you. I, of course, have my accommodation in the basement, so we can both come and go as we wish.'

I wondered who had used the rooms previously. 'Who is the "associate" in your business name, Traggheim?'

'Hah! There's no such person. An artificial creation, to make the business name sound better. I think it works well, don't you?' He didn't wait for an answer. 'I will leave you to settle in, Drew. I have work to be doing.' He backed through the door, closing it gently.

'Thanks,' I called after him. 'Thank you.'

'You are very welcome.' His voice drifted faintly up the stairs.

I set my bag down and looked in the wobbly cupboard beside the cooker. Traggheim had thoughtfully stocked it with some staples, so I set about making something to eat.

Later, I went downstairs to Traggheim's workshop. His machines were fascinating, and this seemed an opportunity to find out more. Perhaps away from Archer, Traggheim might be more open about galdr-folc and the parallel realm.

'Can I come in?' I asked, seeing Traggheim bent over some intricate geared machinery, engrossed in what he was doing.

'Of course, do come in, Drew. How are you settling in?' He took off a pair of magnifying glasses and turned to face me.

'I'm very comfortable, thanks. What's that you're working on?'

He looked happy to be asked and set about explaining the complex mechanism that would drive an orrery – a machine that displays the movement of the planets. He soon left me behind, but he was enjoying himself so much I let him ramble on. After a time, he stopped and peered over his glasses at me. 'I'm so sorry. I'm probably boring you, but it's unusual for anyone to show much interest in my work.'

'No, no. It's fascinating.'

'Now you're just humouring me. Of course, this is just a trinket for the shop. My actual work is far more intricate.' He looked at me again, his eyes bright under a shaggy pair of eyebrows. 'I wouldn't inflict explanations of those machines upon you. It really wouldn't be fair.'

'What do you mean?' I bristled slightly, thinking he was implying it was beyond me – and it almost certainly was.

'Why? Because you're human, of course. You can't possibly comprehend dweorg-ware.'

'Dway-what?' I was getting that "Alice down the rabbit hole" feeling again.

'Dweorg-ware, the works of we dweorgs.' He paused thoughtfully and then added, 'Archer hasn't told you I'm a dweorg, has he?'

'Noooo,' I replied. 'With Archer, information seems to be rationed and issued on a "need to know" basis. What exactly is a... sorry, what?'

'A dweorg.' He pronounced it to rhyme with "stay, dawg". 'A dwarf in popular human culture, although that kind of thing is riddled with inaccuracy and stereotype, I find.' He laughed. 'I wish you could see your face at this moment.'

I apologised, embarrassed. 'Some of this is still sinking in with me.'

'Of course it is. It is a great deal for you to absorb in a short period. So let me help you if I can. First, some tea.'

The smoky flavour of the Lapsang Souchong was growing on me, which I think endeared me to him. Archer wouldn't touch the stuff and Alyssum preferred herbal teas, which wasn't a big surprise.

This time Traggheim made the tea in two huge enamel mugs. 'Workshop tea,' he announced with a wink. 'So, what to tell you about dweorgs? We are an ancient race, like many galdr-folc. The fairy stories are right, that we are happier below ground, or at least away from sunlight, but we don't turn to stone in the sun and we don't dig mines. We make things.' He said this in a hushed tone, as though it was almost a holy thing.

'Are you... excuse me... do you live long?' I was feeling my way in the dark, not knowing the social conventions and fearful of offending him.

'Not like the daemon, no. But two or three hundred years is quite usual, especially in Northern Europe, where we hail from.' He winked again. 'That's why German cars and Swiss watches are the best, you see.'

I looked around the workshop. 'I don't understand how all this is possible without electricity.'

'That's because your world is in thrall to the electron. Your species were too quick to abandon the potential of other technologies. Computers can be mechanical, you know. The attracting and repelling forces of magnetism, the way materials move and shrink with varying temperature. The way light can be bent, focused, diffused, and refracted. Oh, there are so many techniques, Drew.' He sighed contentedly, and I realised that technology, to Traggheim, was like a religion.

'But?'

'But all good things must end and my best work will not last forever. That any machines function at all is quite incredible. They are grinding and wearing away their moving parts all the time, reducing themselves to scrap metal. The true skill lies in delaying that process as much as possible. The ultimate goal is the infallible machine that never breaks down.' His face took on a wistful look. 'But that, of course, is impossible. Nature will take its course.'

Traggheim delighted in showing me some of his creations. His workshop was like a mechanical rainforest, with the sounds of wildlife replaced by a constant background cacophony of clicks, ticks, whirrs and buzzes. The scent of warm oil took the place of earth and foliage, and the room had a sense of safety and belonging. A series of slim belts crawled round various cogs and gears, powering the machines.

'This is the Geogaldrgraph.' A slowly rotating paper drum had a long row of inky needles, wavering and inscribing wobbly lines onto the surface. Small embossed brass labels showed the sensor locations. One said Castle, others: Holyrood, University, Greenside, Broughton, and so on.

'What powers these?' I asked. 'Presumably not electricity?'

'Oh, heavens no!' His face lit up with obvious pride. 'I have several mechanical power sources, all transmitting energy hydraulically to this room and others in the house. A turbine sits in an underground steep stream deep below us. A small wind turbine in the roof adds its contribution, as does a radiometer, which is moved by the light of the sun falling onto differently coloured vanes. And if they all fail, there is a gas boiler in the lower basement.' His sheer joy in his own inventiveness was infectious.

He showed me another machine. 'Over here is a galdr intensiometer, which shows the strength of the galdr being deployed at any time.' He whirled around to point to a further contraption, which sat on a polished shelf, with its gears clanking slowly round, pushing columns of different coloured fluids up and down a row of glass tubes.

'The McCrone's device displays the "marks" – the different constituent parts of the galdr in use. With some interpretation I can hypothesise the source of the galdr and perhaps its "character", that is, what it's being used for.'

'So you can see who is using galdr, what for and where?'

He gave me a slow smile. 'That is the goal. But there is a lot of interpretation needed. Do not think for a moment that we have an all-seeing eye into a lake, with a crystal clear view of all the fish. What we are looking into is a muddy pond, in which we gain glimpses of movement and must try to work out if we saw a tiny minnow swimming for its life, or a predatory pike, looking to devour its prey.'

*

Edinburgh was at the height of the festival, and the city was overflowing with people. I sidestepped gaudily-dressed leafleteers, each pushing their own Fringe show, and eased my way through the crowds of tourists, gathered round street vendors and acrobats on the Royal Mile. I stopped for a minute to listen to a comedian trying to enthuse people to see his one man show. But I didn't have time to waste and hurried on towards The Reekie Lum. I knew Jamie would be there and a catch-up was overdue.

After days and weeks in the company of Archer, Traggheim and Alyssum, I could use some "normal" company. They had become my friends – in Archer's case, that one challenging friend everyone has; the friend who, in any situation, will always find a can of worms and gleefully open it. But friends or not, I needed a break from them and I looked forward to seeing Jamie and talking about the real world.

As I'd hoped, he was finishing his shift. I waited as he chucked his apron under the counter and wiped his hands on his jeans.

'Oh, you're alive then, are you?' he asked. 'No answer to my texts or calls, not a squeak from you. Where've you been hiding?' Annoyed or frustrated, it was hard to tell which, but either would be unusual for my laidback friend.

'Grab a seat whilst I get the drinks and I'll tell you what's been happening.'

He grimaced and wandered off to find a table.

As I put the drinks down, I still hadn't decided what to say to him, but I had to tell him something. I thought about claiming I'd been shacked up with a woman, but knowing Jamie, he'd either see through me right away or grill me for the details, making me trip up and reveal the lie. Besides, Jamie was too good a friend to lie to.

I took a deep breath. 'I've been hiding out in an underground library after something tried to kill me.' As soon as I heard myself say the words, I already knew what the response would be.

Jamie didn't disappoint, choking on his beer as he burst out laughing. 'Pull the other one, Drew. I doubt if you could even find a library, let alone study in it. The death threats are a good touch, though.'

That was unfair – I love books and libraries. It's the academic use of them that turns me cold. Academics can suck the joy from anything. 'I should be so lucky,' I said. 'This is true, Jamie. And it's not an academic library, it's a library of–' I broke off, looking for a way of describing galdr that wouldn't include the word "magic". 'A library of unseen powers and hidden creatures.'

Jamie's laughing just got louder and people at nearby tables started looking.

'For God's sake, Jamie, I'm not kidding around here. Shut up and listen.'

His laughter slowed to a halt, and he looked carefully at me. 'Oh my God, you're serious, aren't you? Is this some sort of weird sect you've got yourself involved in? I mean, really Drew. "hidden powers" and "unseen creatures"? Are you having a Harry Potter moment?' His eyes widened. 'I'm not averse to a little mind-opening from time to time, but please tell me you've not been using magic mushrooms or something. That stuff can wreck your head.'

'No, I haven't. And if you shut up and think for a moment, you'll recall that this is me. Magic mushrooms, Reiki, chakras and all that nonsense are things I wouldn't touch in a million years.'

'Ok, that's true. You are basically pretty boring. But look, you're bugging me now. What is honestly going on? You're not really in danger, are you? Not in the middle of boring old Edinburgh?'

'Yes, I am. I really am.' I told him about the sceadhu attacks, about Archer and Traggheim and about Alyssum. I explained about galdr and how the parallel realm had sucked me into it and now I could never fully escape. When I finished, I sat back and took a long slug of beer, watching Jamie trying to process what I had said.

'Drew. I don't know what to say to you, but magic isn't real, nor is galdr or any of this stuff. It sounds a fair plot for a fantasy novel, but if you expect me to believe it, you're off your trolley. In fact, I think you're off your trolley, anyway.' I protested, but he held up his hand to stop me. 'No, Drew, just knock it off right now. I don't know what to make of this, but I'd say these people are using you or playing you for a fool. Tell me now you'll walk away from them. And I think you need to see someone – get some sort of help.'

'I don't need to see someone. What I need is for my closest friend to believe me when there's shit going on in my life and I don't know how to handle it.' I got up and stumbled away, furious with Jamie for refusing to accept what I needed him to understand and furious with myself for being stupid enough to expect him to.

Jamie called after me as I left the pub, but I didn't look back.

I wandered into Alyssum's shop and down to the library, where Archer and Alyssum were arguing.

'You can't simply say that people should avoid relationships,' Alyssum was saying. 'Contact with other people is as essential as breathing.' She saw me enter and tried to co-opt me into her argument. 'Drew, tell him I'm right.'

I wasn't in the mood to talk about the value of human relationships when my closest friend saw me as bonkers, rather than trying to understand.

'You're right, but you ignore the harm that relationships do,' replied Archer. 'Humans love to categorise, to put everything into pigeon-holes and label it in the simplest possible terms: this creature is good, that one is evil. This person is saintly, but that one is in league with the devil. You idolise or abhor, with no sense of the infinite variation that truly exists. It's a cult of labelling, a pathetic attempt to simplify the complex and classify the unclassifiable. And what is the result? Mob violence? Hatred and victimisation? Torture and murder? These and worse! There are days when I loathe humanity and all that your wretched, hating kind stands for.' He drew a breath, glaring at us. 'I loved someone once. A woman who tried oh so hard to make things better for people in her wretched community. A better, kinder person you would never find. But she was different. So, they killed her. They bloody killed her.' His voice dropped to a whisper. 'And it was my fault.'

Alyssum and I glanced at one another. 'Tell us,' said Alyssum softly.

Archer looked at her, his eyes damp. '1645. Her name was Agnes Finnie. She had the most beautiful blue eyes and hair like chestnut-brown silk. In an age when sickness and disfigurement were everyday things, that alone was enough to make people jealous. She and I shared some happy times together. But humans must look for someone to hate. And they picked Agnes.' His face turned desperate.

'She ran a small shop in Potter Row. Agnes was skilled at it. She stood up for herself and took grief from nobody. But she was warm-hearted and could never refuse somebody in need. Customers bought her wares and she let them pay her when they could. Or she would lend small sums of money to those who needed it. You might think people would be grateful and some were. But of course, not all. When she saw people spending money in the alehouse, instead of paying what they owed her, she'd challenge them. Drunks don't take well to that. So, there would be an argument. She'd try to threaten them, and they would react badly.

'Like you, Alyssum, she had skills with herbs and healing. When her neighbours were unwell, she'd try to help. So, if they didn't get better, their relatives would blame her. Do you know why? Because humans always revert to blame and hatred when life gets difficult. She was an unmarried woman with a strong character and a willingness to get involved with those who needed her help.' He shook his head.

Species guilt was new to me. Uncertainly, I asked, 'What happened to her, Archer?'

'She was different. So people who didn't want to pay their debts started spreading rumours. Families with loved ones sick or dying clasped onto those rumours and added their own. They called her a witch. They spat at her in the street and they shunned her. The rumours grew, and the hatred grew, and one day the pot of vile human behaviour boiled over.' Tears formed in Archer's eyes.

'What did they do to her?' whispered Alyssum.

Archer raised his head and looked at us. 'The seventeenth century was a period of horrific superstition. James VI was a twisted bastard of a king – his laws, his scribbling of vile hatred. He built a culture of witch-hunting and his idiot son Charles did nothing to change it. The Covenanters made it worse. They were a bunch of hard-faced shits. So, they came for Agnes. The City Guard was at the head of a screaming, shouting, hating mob, with a po-faced arsehole of a Presbyterian minister to give them superficial legitimacy. They chained Agnes up and dragged her to the tollbooth.'

I glanced at Alyssum, who was chewing on her lip, her eyes bright.

'I tried to rescue her but the iron fetters round her legs and her wrists meant I couldn't use galdr to remove her

– iron shields galdr. I bribed the guards, but to no avail. There I was, a being with great powers, abilities and knowledge, and I couldn't do right by a woman whose own community, whose own king's justice had abandoned her.

'They tortured a confession out of her. They called it pricking, and it was supposed to find the devil's mark, where that fool King James had said a witch could feel no pain. In fact, they stabbed her and stabbed her until she was a mass of wounds and in such agony she would agree to anything. Agnes admitted to being in league with the devil and as much other rubbish as they put in her poor, pain-filled head. That was all they needed to condemn her.'

Hesitantly, I asked the question I didn't really want the answer to. 'Did they... burn her?'

'Worse. They hung her at the front of the castle in the old medieval way, letting her slowly choke as she kicked and struggled on the rope. Then, whilst she still lived, they cut her down and tied her to a stake atop a bonfire and set it alight. She died slowly and horribly, writhing in the smoke and the flames.' He looked at us through bloodshot eyes and added bitterly, 'The crowd was screaming and laughing with excitement at the spectacle of that wonderful woman dying horribly.' He paused. 'That was all the justice she got from those shits and there was not a damn thing I could do about any of it.'

Without another word, Archer got up and stalked across the room. He left the library without looking back.

Alyssum and I exchanged looks.

'There's so much more to Archer than most people realise,' she said. 'He can be an arse at times, but he's genuinely warm-hearted within.'

'It never occurred to me he might actually love,' I said. 'What must it be like to live for hundreds of years, caring for people and then watching them die? And in Agnes' case, what a horrible way to go. No wonder he has a grouchy outer shell.'

15. WYRM

Despite Archer allowing me a glimpse of his private self, training and practising continued at full pelt. To get a little time to myself, I got into the habit of grabbing an hour each morning in a little place tucked away off the High Street. It was modelled on an American diner, all chrome and Formica, with comfortable booths to sit in. I was at my preferred table, with a clear view of the door, when a strong sense of warmth hit me. Not heat, but a feeling of inner happiness and love, which was odd, as Archer's unrelenting teaching style wasn't doing anything for my happiness.

The feeling intensified as the door opened and I tensed, unsure of what to expect. But it was a slight, feminine figure that entered the diner. She was dressed in a dark cloak with the hood shading her head and I recognised the sensual way she moved, almost gliding towards me. She pulled back the hood and a mass of strawberry-blonde hair flowed out. Sister Ashnil smiled at me.

'Can I join you?'

'Do I have a choice?' I refused to give in to the sense of fuzzy well-being she was enveloping me in. It was delicious, but clearly false. 'Can you switch that off, or is it just some sort of aura you carry about?'

She pouted and sat down, facing me. 'Give me a break, will you? I'm an angelus. We are all about love and compassion.' Nevertheless, she dialled down the fuzzy feeling.

'Just like the Tory party is about helping those who can't help themselves, but not when it's really needed. What do you want, Ashnil?'

'Cappuccino would be nice. And pancakes with ice cream and maple syrup.'

'That's not – oh sod it.' I waved to the waitress. Whilst Ashnil's coffee was being made, I studied her. There was nothing visual to suggest she wasn't human, except for a wholesomeness that seemed to say, 'I'm the girl next door you've always dreamed of.' The smattering of freckles on her nose set off her perfect teeth, but there was something else. She was almost too perfect.

'How are you finding training with Archer?' she asked. 'I imagine he's a bitch of a teacher.'

A good empathetic opening, I thought, followed by a heart-warming smile. 'He's an excellent teacher. We get on well,' I lied.

She giggled and put down her fork. 'Drew, that's just bullshit and you know it.'

Here it comes, I thought. The pitch for me to abandon the dark side and join the goody-goody crew. But it didn't come.

'I bet he's difficult to work with, but you know he's the best person possible to train you. He won't let up, and you need to train fast. There may not be much time.'

'Is that the official angelii line?'

'Good grief, no. Brother Jophiel would disapprove if he heard me saying something positive about a daemon, especially Archer. And Rillan would be incandescent. But the fact is, the world is changing and so is the parallel realm. Adapt and survive.'

That threw me off my guard. 'What's your point? That we should all be bosom buddies? There's an agreement, but nothing has come of it.' Or at least nothing Archer had shared with me.

'Jophiel will keep his promise. Rillan too, if only hoping Archer will slip up so they can claim his life. Until we know what you're facing, the most important thing is to prepare you for whatever comes. That's why I had to see you.' Ashnil took my hand in hers and looked into my eyes. 'You need to risk the wyrm. It's the only way.'

'The worm?' I didn't want to look a fool, but I'd really no idea what she was talking about.

'Not an earthworm, you wally! A wyrm with a "y". It's a bit like a mythical dragon, but far less physical and far more powerful.'

'And what is this wyrm going to do for me?'

'Well, he *could* kill you, but handled right, he could help you. And if you get him on your side, he has an unimaginable amount of power.' She started forking pancakes into her mouth again. For a slight girl, she could really eat.

'So what's he called and where do I find him? And if I do as you say, how do I stop this from ending badly? Or is that what you're hoping for?'

She dabbed her mouth with a napkin. 'He doesn't have a name. He's just known as the wyrm. And he lives under Salisbury Crags.' She nodded her head towards the royal park, close by.

'There's a dragon hidden in Holyrood Park?'

'Not in. Under. Anyway, you need to talk to Archer about it.'

That put me on my guard again. Why would an angelus be telling me to take advice from their favourite bad guy? My face betrayed my doubt.

'Drew, this is dangerous. I think it's a risk worth taking,

but if it goes wrong and you'd gone to see the wyrm on the advice of an angelus Archer would go raving bonkers with fury.' She smiled coquettishly. 'I'm sorry, Drew, but you're not worth starting a war over.'

As she got up, she briefly touched my face with her finger-tips. 'Speak to Archer.'

'What sort of idiot are you? You're seriously telling me you sat down and had breakfast with one of Archer's enemies?'

Stemming from an angelus, as it did, the wyrm plan was going to be a hard sell. I'd hoped to enlist Alyssum's help to soften up Archer, but that was a tactical error. As I sat at the table in her workroom, watching her stamping around the room, ranting at me, I couldn't help admiring her passion, whilst wondering if it might to lead to violence.

'Ashnil turned her charms on you, didn't she? She fluttered her eyelashes, wrinkled her pretty little nose and I bet you rolled over on your back for her to rub your belly, didn't you?'

I'd learned from Archer that the best way to handle a furious Alyssum was to keep my head down and weather the storm. Arguing with her would only generate a whole new round of fury.

'Why would you even think of risking your life on the say so of that bimbo?'

Archer had warned me that Alyssum's angry rhetorical questions were a savage bait. 'Never answer one – you'll be doomed to an extra five to ten minutes of banging, crashing and ranting.' So I resisted the temptation to tell her I only wanted to see what Archer thought.

The door to the library stairs cracked open and Archer himself tentatively looked at us. 'I'm reluctant to get involved, but what's the noise about?'

Alyssum drew a deep breath. Bravely, Archer hurtled

across the room and put his finger over her lips. 'Please, Alyssum. Let Drew tell me.'

I took my own deep breath. This was not the carefully planned ambush I had hoped to achieve. I was about to be caught between an angry Alyssum and a probably angrier Archer. Oh, well. I recounted the conversation with Ashnil for the second time and awaited the explosion.

It didn't come. Alyssum's foot was tapping with pent-up irritation and frustration as Archer gazed at the rows of herb jars, saying nothing.

After a moment the dam broke and Alyssum shouted, 'It's the stupidest thing I ever heard, Archer. You know it is.'

She broke off as Archer slowly stood up. 'You're right, Alyssum, it's bloody stupid. And that it came from one of those clowns makes me suspicious. But the fact is, she's right.' He held up a hand to hold back a renewed flow of anger from Alyssum. 'Who knows how long it will be before we can locate and hopefully deflect the threat to Drew? In the meantime, he is in danger and it takes too long to build skills by practise and teaching alone. Drew's galdr needs an accelerant beyond the werigend, and maybe this is it.'

'But, the wyrm? The bloody wyrm,' shouted Alyssum, tears running down her cheeks. 'It could kill him!'

Archer ignored her and crouched by my chair. 'Are you ready to take a risk, Drew?'

I gritted my teeth and nodded.

'You need to be certain. Absolutely certain. The wyrm is a fickle, self-serving creature, but his power is immense and, if he chooses to, he could help you beyond anything I can do.'

'The way I see it, I could try to get ahead with the wyrm's help and die, or I could just hope for the best and be just as likely to die, without having even tried. Game on – I want to do it, Archer.'

The door slammed as Alyssum ran from the room. Archer raised an eyebrow and shook his head. 'She worries about all of us, but I think you trouble her the most at the moment.'

'Buy why?' I snapped. 'Why me, for heaven's sake? I just don't understand why the hell I've been drawn into this. Why am I in a position for Alyssum to feel the need to worry about me?'

Archer looked away for a moment. 'You might well ask *why me*. I've lived more years than you can imagine, working away at a never-ending travail. Why and for what end I really don't know. I just know that it must be so and there is no alternative path. I'm afraid alternative paths are limited for you. But we must keep looking for the "why". For you, there must be a "why" and you're right to seek it.'

I stared at him. This strange person I'd become caught up with seemed to vacillate between extreme indifference and great insight. But his words didn't help me.

There's an Edinburgh tradition that the water of St. Anthony's Well in Holyrood Park has magical properties. People used to bring sickly children and ailing grandparents to be healed by the waters, and young couples used it, hoping to conceive a child. As with many traditions, there is a nugget of truth. According to a slim, worn book that Archer showed me, the well is also the route to the wyrm's lair.

Archer and I stood by the well in the damp chill of first light the next day. I shivered, wearing only a long shirt. Archer's book said my clothing should "reflect the air of a penitent". Archer snorted at that, but I reckoned it couldn't hurt.

The well was actually just a large rock with a shallow channel worn into it, through which flowed a trickle of water from a tiny spring.

'Keep your wits about you and sell nothing for nothing,' said Archer.

I nodded, stamping my feet to stave off the chill. I took a long strip of linen cloth and dipped it in the water, then tied it around my head, covering my eyes. Gritting my teeth, I put both hands into the water, as directed by the book. For a moment, nothing happened, then I fell forward as the rock gave way to nothing and I was tumbling into an abyss I couldn't see.

I hit solid ground and gasped, winded by the fall. As I coughed and tried to regain my breath, I sensed I was in a very different place. It was much warmer, for one thing, and the air was still, lending a deadened quality to the sound of my movements. I slowly unwound the linen from my eyes and blinked.

Two deep yellow eyes with vertical slits for pupils glowed in the darkness. 'Name yourself,' jabbed a harsh voice.

I fought back against a powerful urge to run like hell and found my voice. 'Drew MacLeod. I seek to add to my galdr powers.'

Slowly the wyrm became visible, glowing orange-yellow, with random tinges of green. The glow built until I could make out a slim body, not much bigger than mine, muscular and purposeful, despite its recumbent position. Disappointed by the lack of scales or fiery breath, I could see it was undeniably a dragon. Its tail swished and glided like an angry cat. Apart from its appearance, I had an overwhelming sense of being in the presence of something immensely powerful. There was so much galdr I could feel it physically and it wasn't a pleasant sensation.

'What know you of geology, Duh-rew Mac-loud?' The

worm spoke in a deep husky voice, its long, forked tongue licking its lips as it gazed at me with those unblinking, reptilian eyes.

Tricky. The wrong answer could bring a world of hurt my way, but apart from a vague memory of our geography teacher, Mrs Wilkinson, getting overly enthusiastic about glacial valleys, my knowledge amounted to very little. Luckily for me, the wyrm wanted to answer its own question.

'Hundreds of millions of years ago, volcanoes belched out vastnesses of molten rock, creating these very hills in which you find me in my fastness. Do you see, Duh-rew Mac-loud?'

This didn't seem the moments to mention Mrs Wilkinson's apparent love for magma, so I just nodded and the wyrm continued, appearing satisfied with this.

'The force you know as galdr is birthed in unimaginable quantity at such times and from this was my being created.' The terrifying eyes suddenly opened wide as its head jerked forward close to mine. Somehow, I resisted the urge to pull away as it stared into my soul.

'I am as old as the rocks. As old as the hills, older than all you know, Duh-rew Mac-loud. There is more galdr in the tip of my claw than you will ever experience, however long you practise.' The eyes continued to drill into mine and, try as I might, I simply couldn't look away. The wyrm was controlling me. Then it sneered and looked away, suddenly bored.

'I spare my energy on you only because I can sense you are from Archer.' It delicately scratched its leg with the tip of its tail. 'Why should I afford you my help?'

Archer had warned me about how to handle this. 'The skinny old git has galdr dripping from every orifice, but he gives nothing away willingly. Don't piss him off and don't take your eyes off him. He will make you do something in exchange. And don't expect it to be a pleasant experience – it won't be.'

I returned the wyrm's glare. 'I'm ready to return the favour in whatever way you require.' Behind my back I furtively crossed my fingers, hoped it didn't take the "whatever" too literally.

The wyrm slowly tilted its head, its eyes never moving from mine. 'You offer yourself as my play-thing?' A vicious smile played across its mouth. 'How do you know you won't regret this?'

'Perhaps I will, but my understanding is that you are known for fair exchanges and for leaving no mark on the world above us.' I squeezed the crossed fingers, praying it had no aversion to flattery. 'So whatever you want from me, I should be able to walk away from it.'

'Hah! Archer is teaching you well, is he? But don't presume to know the nature of all you meet from what you hear and see of them. Let me consider.' It closed its eyes. The tail continued gliding around like a probing, questing tentacle.

The wyrm's eyes suddenly snapped open. 'You may not like what I say, but don't trespass on my nature by presuming to negotiate or believing that you have some choice. When you came here, you gave away choice.'

Shit! Archer never told me this. My face certainly gave away my horror. This creature could do whatever it liked to me and there was nothing I could do about it? Shit, shit, shit.

The wyrm now had a sly grin on its face, enjoying what it evidently read in my face. 'I can never again leave this hill. The impact of my galdr would throw all balance from the world. I must remain here to shelter the world above from my power and might within the volcanic rock that surrounds me.' Its tail suddenly whipped towards me and wrapped around my legs, squeezing tight and pulling me closer. 'But I can travel with you, and I shall. A tiny part of me will become part of Duh-rew Mac-loud. I will see what you see and experience what you experience without leaving here.'

I pulled hard at the tail, struggling to escape from this nightmare in the making. 'No. Please! I can't live with you inside my head.'

'You can and you will. The decision is no longer yours, but I am not unfair: my presence will multiply your galdr.' It paused, then sighed and added, shaking its head slightly, 'I will not interfere. You will barely know of my presence except in that you will be stronger when it may be of help to you.'

Before I could respond, its claw ripped at my right forearm and I glimpsed sinew and bone, before a gout of blood welled up from the wound. An agonising pain swept over me. It felt like my right arm was on fire, the cave swimming before my eyes. Just when I thought I would throw up, the pain abruptly disappeared. Looking down, I saw the wound had instantly healed, leaving just a thin orange-green scar, recognisably the shape of a coiled wyrm. I stared at the scar and then at the wyrm.

'It is done. Leave me now. I thank you for a fair exchange, Duh-rew Mac-loud.' It turned away, rested its head on its shoulder, and closed its eyes.

16. PICTS

The National Museum of Scotland has a very different character in the daytime. With families wandering about, looking at the exhibits, the echoing central hall has an ambience that speaks of life and human achievement.

I climbed the stairs to the balcony cafe and swerved round a toddler, hell-bent on escaping its mother. She cast a wistful apology at me as she scooped it up, and behind her I spotted Archer languidly stretched out on a cast-iron chair that looked like it belonged in a French street café. Only Archer could get comfortable sitting like that. I bought two espressos and joined him.

'You summoned me?' I said, as I sat down.

'Yes, young Drew. I did, didn't I? We have things to discuss and sometimes it's more conducive to earnest discussion to do so away from the library.'

'You're still avoiding Alyssum?'

'No, actually. Or at least not at this moment,' he conceded.

A woman at a neighbouring table gave me an odd look, and I realised Archer wasn't visible to her; I must look pretty wacky, ordering two coffees and talking to myself.

'Will you knock that off please, Archer?'

'If it makes you happy, I shall make myself more visible. How do you feel?' he asked.

'Like there's a bloody dragon in my head.'

'Really? You can sense it?' He sat forward, fascinated.

'Not as such, no. But I can feel a reservoir of galdr that wasn't there before and that reminds me he's in there, watching. I suppose I'll get used to it. It's not like I can do anything to dislodge the invasive little scale-bag.'

'If you don't want a sudden migraine, I'd treat him with a little more respect. Have you tested your new powers?'

'Hell, yes. It's like driving to a garage and trading in a Ford Ka for a Porsche 911.'

'And just like any person who does that, you're liable to get over-confident and skid into a ditch half an hour later. We'll step up your lessons – you now need to learn how to use this additional galdr resource to defend yourself.'

My heart sank. I'd hoped for exactly the opposite. Maybe I should try to make best use of the wyrm's side of the bargain, but every day I seemed to be dragged deeper into the parallel realm. Where was this all leading? Archer wasn't in the mood to discuss my worries.

'For now, there's something else to discuss. Come with me.' He abruptly stood up and strode off towards the grand staircase.

I caught up with Archer in the Early Peoples exhibit, where he stopped in front of a massive Pictish carved stone – the Hilton of Cadboll stone. I knew a little about the Picts, though nobody really knows much about them. They were early residents of parts of eastern Scotland, best known for the enigmatic carvings they left behind.

'Bastards,' spat Archer, being more than a little enigmatic himself.

'The Picts? The museum? Schoolkids?' I hazarded, casting around for who was his target.

'No, the Ælves.' He pronounced it as rhyming with "calves". Oh help, I thought. Now it's the fairies coming after us, is it?

'What do you see in the stone?'

I looked at the printed descriptions alongside, then studied the carvings. 'Well, there are two distinct themes. There are those random-looking shapes the Picts are famous for: crescents, half-moons, complex patterns and plenty of animals too, but it says here nobody fully understands what they represent. The middle panel shows a Pictish hunting scene.' The carving showed helmeted figures on horseback, with dogs and deer. In the background, figures were blowing long horns.

'Not a Pictish hunting scene. The Picts carved these stones, but they depict ælves, not Picts. They're not hunting the hart – that's under their control, like the hunting dogs. They're hunting people.' He let that sink in.

'So you're telling me elves are real and they hunt people?' I asked.

'Not hunt. Hunted. All these symbols serve a purpose – to keep them down. The stone is over 1200 years old and there's been no sign of the ælf-folc regaining their power since then.'

'What stopped them?'

He smiled grimly. 'I did, with many companions, some of whom did not survive.'

'Just how old are you, Archer?'

'Let's simply say I was a younger person 1200 years ago and leave it at that.' He led me to another stone nearby. 'This stone shows the battle of Dunnichen, according to the label. It actually shows parts of our last battle with the ælf-folc.'

'Were they wiped out?'

'No, there will always be ælves. The buggers are as

inescapable as air or stone. But the stones hold them in check and their numbers are few. Or so I thought.'

Here we go, I thought – the reason for this little guided tour.

'I think perhaps the Ælf-queen may be the driving force behind the sceadhu and some of the other aglaecan activity Traggheim is increasingly detecting.'

I could tell from the look on his face this was bothering him a great deal. 'Archer, tell me why this is worrying you.'

We meandered through the museum's exhibits and Archer explained ælves are the true creatures of fairy tales. Not the cheesy-smiley Disney fairy-tales – the nasty, vicious ones that reflect our folk memories. When J. R. R. Tolkien wrote his books about Middle Earth, he described elves as a race of beautiful creatures, llnked to the ecosystem and sensitive to it and bound by a strong sense of morality and ethics. The true ælf-folc couldn't be more different.

'It's not that ælves are evil," he explained. "It's that they are horribly like an extreme version of modern humans in their attitudes. They care about nothing but themselves. All other creatures on the planet, including people, are there for the idle amusement of ælves. And ælves have galdr, plenty of it.

'Think of them like rats,' he went on. 'Rats are natural and there will always be some. But when people built homes and then towns and cities, rats gained the opportunity to flourish and spread. If you don't keep them down, they'll quickly become a problem. And they bring nasty hangers-on, like fleas, Weil's disease and bubonic plague. Now imagine rats with considerable arrogance and access to plentiful galdr, rats that are clever and manipulative, rats that don't just want the scraps. They want your soul, so they can play with it and they'll torture, maim, and destroy it simply because they can and because it gives them twisted pleasure.'

I looked at him. 'You're not making me happy, you know. If you're right and they're back and their queen has unleashed the sceadhu, then I have three questions – how, why, and why me?'

'In brief, I don't know, I don't know, and I don't know.' He grinned, but the worry-lines on his brow didn't dissipate. 'Somehow, they've breached the controls we put in place. The carved stones contained most of the measures to limit the ælves and many stones have been moved, like the ones here, or damaged, but they should still be effective.' He shook his head. 'Why? Because it's what they're programmed to do. It's in their DNA to push and push until they break through. As for why *you*, I have a theory about that. Up to now we've been considering your recent family and personal history and drawn a blank. Perhaps we need to go further back.'

A bitterly cold wind bit at my face and the wind hammered into me. I hunched into my coat and watched Archer standing next to me, oblivious to the weather, staring into the darkness.

'What is it?' I shouted over the noise of the wind, angling myself into it to stay on my feet. We stood on a slippery pinnacle of rock at the top of Arthur's Seat.

Suddenly Archer snapped out of whatever was attracting his attention. 'You know something? There was no Arthur, only Archer.' He grinned, rain running down his face. 'You asked how old I am. As old as anything made by man, and this is my HOME!' He stamped a foot and a flash of mauve reflected momentarily off the rain.

And then all was calm. I was standing in a velvet blackness, with a powerful smell of damp and dust assailing my nose. 'Archer?' I called.

'Here.' And he was right beside me. A slight flash of

mauve light and a candle sputtered into life, making shadows dance and jump around us. We were inside some kind of building. In the gloom, I could see it was a large space, with benches and tables, all with a thick layer of dust. Dried rushes crunched and crumbled under my feet.

Archer lit more candles and then a huge hearth, which lay in the centre of the building, illuminating woven wall-hangings, surmounted with spears and axes. Above us, rough timber beams, blackened with soot, had tattered banners hanging from them. I turned to Archer and his eyes were bright.

'This, Drew, this is my home. This is Archer's Seat.'

I could see his pride. 'Impressive,' I said, dutifully. In truth, it really was – it looked like a vision of Valhalla, with the drunken warriors missing.

He looked at me suspiciously, to see if I was mocking him. 'I grant you it has had better days. Many hundreds of years ago, I moved more openly than I do today and this was my hall.'

'Where exactly are we?' I asked.

'Under Arthur's Seat. Thousands of tourists pass overhead every day, unaware this is here.'

'They'd be even more startled if they knew the wyrm was dozing a little to the north.'

'His lair is much deeper,' Archer replied.

Something didn't seem right, and it suddenly clicked. 'How does the smoke get out unseen?'

'To be honest, it never really did. Some found its way through fissures in the rock, but this was always a smoke-ridden place. Back then, every dwelling was. This fire is only for show – it burns galdr, rather than fuel.' He looked a little downcast, then brightened up. 'Let me show you why I've brought you here.'

He crossed the hall to an iron-bound oak chest, almost black with age. He lifted the lid and took out a package wrapped in oilcloth and reverently unfolded it. With his sleeve, he swept the dust from a bench, blew away the last remnants, and placed down a large leather-bound book. The spine creaked as he opened it and I could see faded writing, beautifully symmetrical and neat on pages cut unevenly from vellum.

'I should keep this in the library, but it seems more fitting for it to stay here. This book is the "Annals of Dun Eidyn", as Edinburgh was called when the Angles ruled this region. It's written in the Northumbrian dialect of old English, but that doesn't matter. It's not the written contents we need – I can tell you all you could wish to know about those days. The book is also the repository of galdr annals, echoes of what occurred back then in the worlds of galdr-folc and aglaecan.'

He turned to me, his face filled with enthusiasm. 'I think we can use it to find out why you are being hunted and by whom.'

'How does that work?' I asked.

'Simple, really. Just sit down and read the book.' He pressed me onto the bench in front of it.

I looked at the book. 'But I can't read it – it's gobbledegook to me.'

'Ah, it's not the text you must read. Empty your mind, bring forth your galdr and move your eyes over the lines.'

I did as I was told. Initially nothing happened, then suddenly a big burst of galdr exploded in my head and I was no longer sitting beside Archer. I was flying, passing over wooded hills at incredible speed, twisting and turning through valleys and gliding over villages of rough huts, wisps of smoke rising from them. Occasional rough track-ways meandered along, outnumbered by the many burns and lochs which studded the landscape as I hurtled overhead, gasping for breath as the air rushed past my face.

I realised I was seeing the border-lands south of Edinburgh as they were in the time described by the book, but I had no control over the direction I flew.

Without warning, I stopped and descended into a clearing in the trees. A group of horsemen stood together at the edge of the clearing, looking around them, and it was evident they couldn't see me. They wore chain-mail, with woollen leggings and leather boots, cloaks wrapped around them against the cold. Swords hung from their waists and one also held a big war-axe.

One man looked familiar, and with a shock, I recognised myself. It wasn't me, but could have been a mirror image. He was taller and broader in the chest and a scar ran across his chin, but he was unmistakably very like me. He climbed off his horse and leaned against the trunk of a dead oak. My lookalike was better dressed than the others. There was gold gleaming on his sword-hilt. His thick cloak was a deep emerald-green, whereas the others wore cloaks which were drab or worn.

The group looked as if it were waiting for someone – or something – but my vantage-point was fixed and I couldn't change my position, so I settled down to await whatever transpired. The Annals had brought me here for a purpose and I guessed the lookalike was an ancestor of mine. Whilst I waited, I thought about how many generations of my family must lie between us. On average, a new generation pops up every twenty-five years, so this guy must be something like my great-great-great-grandad, with another fifty greats added in.

After a time, one man noticed something in the distance and pointed. I couldn't see what they were looking at, and I was too far back to hear what they were saying, even if I understood Old English. But it was clear from their behaviour that this was what they had been waiting for and my ancestor moved to the front of the group in anticipation.

A large group of figures on horseback cantered into the clearing – but these were not men. They had deathly pale skin, with long faces and prominent chins. Their large eyes were an odd shade of yellowish-green, and their limbs seemed too long for their torsos, making them look as though they were riding ponies. They rode horses, though, and two of them were riding stags with massive antlers. Their flowing clothes were shades of yellow and green, matching their eyes, but the most striking thing was the expressions on their faces, which looked hard, sneering and disdainful, making a shiver run down my back. I had little doubt about what they were.

My ancestor moved forward and bowed to one of the stag-riders, who I noticed had a thin gold circlet on her head. Presumably the Ælf-queen Archer had mentioned. A conversation ensued, with my ancestor doing most of the talking. He seemed to plead or request something and the ælf was slow to respond, staring at him. Then a horrible smile came over the ælf's face and she nodded once. She reached forward and touched him on the forehead, like a grotesque benediction. There was a flash of light and a sharp crack echoed around the clearing. I thought at first she had killed him, but he was still standing and was now smiling grimly. The Ælf-queen handed him a small object, then looked sharply, directly at me. She stared for what seemed a very long time, then the entire group turned simultaneously on their beasts and cantered back the way they had come, leaving the men standing by their horses.

What had I just witnessed? It was clearly some sort of exchange or pact, but it wasn't at all clear what. Then the world started spinning, rapidly getting too fast to see anything but a blur. But strangely, I felt nothing. I've never handled fairground rides well, but whatever the Annals were up to, my body was unaffected.

The spinning stopped. I was still in the same clearing, but it was summer, the afternoon sun shining through the trees. This time it was the ælves who were present, but they looked different. There were fewer of them and only one stag. Several of them were sharing mounts, and all were muddy and bedraggled. There was something else as well – the vitality and confidence they had displayed before had gone.

The Ælf-queen was angry and climbed off her mount, ranting and cursing in fury. Her retainers kept quiet, avoiding catching her eye. Her face was frankly terrifying and as she spat and swore the dead tree that my ancestor had leaned on cracked and collapsed with a flash of green light, an expression of her fury.

Then something happened which has lived in my nightmares ever since. She turned slowly and glared directly at me. Her eyes narrowed and slowly she hissed my name, her face the very epitome of hatred.

17. SHADE

The Annals didn't fly me back to Archer's Hall. Instead, there was a mighty thud in my chest, as though my heart had stopped, and in the blink of an eye, I was back in the hall, clutching my chest and trying to breathe.

'Come on, COME ON!' Archer shouted, with what I foolishly thought was concern for my life, but no – he wanted to leave.

'The tocsin has sounded.' He pulled me up, looked closely at me and said, 'You'll do,' as I breathed rapidly, getting back my wind. Archer grabbed my arm and instantly there was a green flash of light and we were back on the rocky slope. He coughed and spat, then grinned at me. 'Not as bad, now you've more galdr of your own.' And he stumbled and slithered down the slope. I followed.

The rain had stopped, but the ground was still treacherously slippery, and we both fell several times before we reached the tarmac road below. Once on firmer ground, I began to tell Archer what I'd seen in the Annals.

'You don't need to tell me – I already know.'

'You were there?'

'Think of it as looking over your shoulder. You've realised, I assume, that the dramatis personae the Annals showed you were an ancestor of yours and the Ælf-queen?'

'I figured that, but what was the transaction?'

'She gave him some sort of galdr gift, but it was only temporary, hence the token. That bound him to return it to her and, with it, the gift. But clearly he didn't.'

'She was certainly angry. And I'd swear that she could see me.'

'Yes, I didn't reckon on that. Ælves are immortal, but I'm surprised she could see across time like that. It's clear she holds you accountable for your ancestor's actions.'

'But that was over 1300 years ago and I'm a totally different person. She can't hold me responsible for that,' I protested.

He stopped in the road, the wet tarmac glistening under the streetlights. 'Oh, but she can, Drew. First, she's ælf-folc, so she doesn't feel any need to be fair or reasonable and she's frankly the bitch of all bitches. Second, haven't you connected the dots yet?'

I clicked my fingers. 'My galdr?'

'Just so. The galdr you have in you must be the residue of what she gave your ancestor. That's how you defeated the sceadhu. The werigend focussed it for you. We must find that sceadhu and finish it. She's going to hunt you until she gets that token back.'

'But I don't have it.'

'Do you really think she cares?' he scoffed. 'Though come to think of it, it is disproportionate. Knowing ælves it's probably a vengeance thing. Keep up – we've got work to do.'

Archer's ability to move his focus from my likely impending death to whatever was his immediate problem, without seeming too bothered, was disconcerting to say the least, but I was getting used to it. I was also surprised he was taking me with him – that was a first.

There were many questions I wanted to ask, but I knew

I'd get nowhere further about the Ælf-queen's token, whilst he was obsessing about something else, so I focussed on the immediate matter. 'Where are we going? And why?' Maybe if I asked him two questions, I stood a chance of getting one answered.

'Whilst you were skipping about the hills and winding up the ælf-bitch, the tocsin in the hall sounded and Garm showed up with news from Traggheim. He's as certain as he can be that a shade has manifested and it's a nasty bugger, so it's likely to be the one I felt last week.'

'Could this be linked to the Ælf-queen and the sceadhu?'

'Possibly, but I'm not sure how. Shades are notoriously fickle and self-obsessed. This one must have found itself a source of galdr from somewhere, to manifest enough power to make Traggheim's gadgetry react. Another concern is that, with this level of manifestation, it's liable to be noticed by the angelii and we could do without them getting in the way.'

'Now there's a truce, couldn't they be of some help? They have galdr powers, after all.'

'Don't make me laugh! Look, repeat this and I'll flay you alive,' he threatened, 'but they do some good, knocking out minor nuisances, but they expect too much of their limited abilities, over-reach and often make matters worse. Half the time, they're too busy trying to poke me with a sharp stick to pay attention to what really matters. Maybe the truce will help, but I will not be holding my breath, waiting for it.' He waved an arm as a bat flew close. 'Sod off, you little wing-rat.'

'What is it with you and bats?'

'I wish I knew. They're nosey little beggars and for some reason, I seem to fascinate them. Bloody irritating, though Alyssum thinks she might train them to be useful. Now, when we get there keep your hand on the werigend at all times – the wyrm-galdr gives you much more power than you previously had, but you don't yet have the skill to use it well and the werigend will help focus it and put it to use so you can save yourself.'

'I'll need to save myself?'

'Oh yes, Drew.' He grinned at me and picked up the pace. 'You're going to be the bait.'

I picked my way through the weeds and rubbish of the waste ground at Shrubhill and swore as I stepped into a deep, oily puddle. It was tempting to power up my mobile and use its torch. After all, I was trying to attract an aglaecan, but the thought of possibly attracting others dissuaded me – one shade was plenty to worry about.

The orange-yellow glow of reflected street-lights glistened on the surface of the puddle and I paused whilst my eyes grew accustomed to the gloom. The distant traffic noise only made me feel more alone.

Archer's glee at using me as bait was disconcerting, as was my suspicion that destroying the shade might just, if push came to shove, be more important to him than keeping me alive. Knowing he wasn't far away should have given me confidence, but it didn't. The tiny sounds made by mice and rats and the weeds moving in the wind didn't help, so I set off again, determined to find this wretched shade and play a part in flattening it.

But the massive figure that loomed up from a heap of bricks was far from wretched. He was a bear of a man, dressed in some sort of frock coat, with his shirt hanging open at the neck, and the thin light falling on his face was enough to convince me this was no mugger. It showed nothing but blind, savage hatred. The mouth was curled into a sneer and the eyes glowered from below his beefy forehead.

I summoned up all my galdr to counter him, but what came from him was not matching galdr, instead an almighty left-hander to my face, throwing me bodily backwards onto an old, rusty car wing. I scrabbled myself up and swung back onto my feet, slicing my fingers on the jagged metal. This wasn't what I'd expected. According to McCrone, shades have no physical presence in our world, so how was this possible? I shook my head to clear it and ducked another sledgehammer blow; it skimmed past my ear. Well, if this is the game, I'm better able to play it, I thought. But he was huge and powerful, so I'd have to keep moving and try to out-manoeuvre him until I had time to counter.

'You think you can win?' he shouted, bunching his fist and coming at me for another go.

'Who the hell are you, you big, ugly bastard?' I shouted back. If I could get him to lose his temper, that might help. He was already angry, but insulting him might get him to lose focus.

'Major Thomas Weir. And I'm here to take your soul, you wastrel.' He charged forward, but I guessed it was a feint and kept clear.

'A Major, is it? In whose pathetic army was that?' I jerked towards him and he stepped back slightly, the sneer growing on his face. I followed through with a punch to his neck. It was like hitting pig-iron. He didn't even flinch.

'Formerly the army of His Majesty King Charles II, but now my own. I'll send you straight to hell and as many more as I can, you diabolic.' He ran forward again and as I tried to duck under his arm, a rock shifted below my foot and his fist connected with my mouth, like a blow from a mash-hammer. I spat blood as he followed up with a savage kick to my knee that half-crippled me.

'What have I ever done to you?' I coughed and spat.

'What matters that? You will all go to hell. This city is

a riot of sinners, a hot-bed of Jezebels and betrayers of Christ and you're the first of many I will send to Satan.' He jumped forward, grabbed my hair with his left hand, slamming his fist into my face before shoving his knee into my stomach and throwing me to the ground – then stepping back to admire his handiwork. I'd been stupid enough to think I might hold my own with someone his size, but I was winded and dazed. My head span as he came in for the coup de grâce.

'You squander my galdr, Duh-rew Mac-loud?' whispered a voice in my head. 'You should know that shades lack physical form.'

I shook my head, desperately trying to clear it and, as the burly figure charged forward to finish me, I realised what the wyrm was saying. I grabbed the werigend in my pocket and summoned up all the galdr I could, projecting it forward. Almost at once, the charging figure faded and with it, all the pain he had inflicted on me. I rose and saw Thomas Weir as he really was: a slightly shimmering presence. The hatred was still there on his face, but a terrifyingly powerful feeling of galdr power replaced the towering physical presence. He had almost manipulated me into believing that I was being killed so that my body would follow my mind and simply die. The wyrm had saved me. Despite his promise not to interfere, he'd proffered the advice that saved my life. For now.

I was curious about this dreadful man, Weir, and what he wanted. He was tall, with a hawk-like nose and eyes that burned like black fire. Dressed as an eighteenth-century burgess, he held a long, twisted blackthorn staff with a silver head.

I tried to distract him, hoping the cavalry would arrive in the form of Archer. 'You're dead, so why don't you just fuck off?' Not my best opening gambit, but it worked.

A sarcastic smile crossed his face. 'My death was necessary. Yours is, as well. We are all sinners and we must all go into the arms of Satan, where we belong.' He spoke rapidly, with the energy and manic passion of a fanatic, his eyes staring wildly at me. 'I was executed at my own behest where you now stand. My sister too, and now we suffer in pits of brimstone – as we should.'

The mention of his sister and the sight of his unusual staff clicked a memory. 'You're Angelical Thomas!'

'Fools called me that, but they did not heed the word of the Lord.' He banged his staff down onto the bricks as I frantically dug through my memory for anything that could help me.

Angelical Thomas was the popular name of a renowned covenanting preacher who astonished those who knew him when, in 1670, he suddenly confessed to witchcraft on behalf of himself and his sister. He claimed they had taken part in incest, bestiality, devil-worship and black magic. Nobody believed him, but attempts to dissuade him failed and eventually the city had no choice but to find them both guilty. They strangled him, and he shouted his guilt to the very end. Now I knew for certain I was in the presence of a genuinely deranged personality and what was worse, he was stoked up with galdr, seriously angry and in front of me. I focussed my mind on a point between us and tried to visualise a barrier that could hold back both Weir and any galdr projections he might use. Immediately, the familiar headache nagged at me.

Weir sneered. 'You believe you can resist the power of hell?' He pushed back at my barrier and I could feel it starting to stretch and grow thinner. I dug deeper and tried to pull on the wyrm's galdr. It was frustrating to know I had that reserve of power, but I was struggling to deploy it and I felt the barrier give way.

A pale light washed over us and a voice behind me said, 'Step slowly back, but hold your wall as best you can.' Expecting Archer, I was taken aback to recognise Brother Jophiel as he edged alongside me and added his power to the barrier. I felt the pressure ease a little, then a bit more when Rillan appeared alongside him. I smelled a familiar light, sweet scent and Ashnil was to my left. As their galdr built, the barrier eased and became more rigid.

The shade glowered at them. 'Do not believe you can halt me. My task is to bring this city to Hell and I will not –' he cracked the tip of his staff on the ground '– be deflected by faux angels or by *you*, whatever you might be.' He pointed the staff directly at us and the ugly silver face on its top opened its mouth and vomited a stream of brilliant blue light, pushing back and weakening the barrier. The four of us stumbled backwards, fighting to keep the barrier up.

'Do NOT let him push us back,' hissed Jophiel. 'He must not win this fight.'

'You cannot win, you feeble and deluded creature,' snarled Weir. 'My galdr outweighs your pathetic efforts.' He shoved his staff again and the galdr flow increased, pushing us back again.

'I told you to see the wyrm for good reasons – can't you push back?' Ashnil was panting with the effort of maintaining her share of the barrier.

'I can't get it. The bloody lizard holds it back.'

'You must *make him* allow you to use it. You made a pact!'

Weir suddenly gave a deranged scream, and with a mighty shove of his staff, he forced the barrier to give way and collapse. I staggered back as he hurled a massive ball of galdr that threw Jophiel and Rillan off their feet.

As he turned his black eyes towards Ashnil and me, she grabbed my arm and hauled me behind an old skip. 'We have to stop him, Drew. He's insane and has gathered a giant horde of galdr. He could do anything!'

'Where the hell is Archer?' I hissed.

'Even he's going to struggle to deal with this monstrous creature,' said Ashnil, and we both ducked as a ball of white-hot flame struck the skip.

'You dare to doubt my ability?' Somehow Archer was crouching beside me.

'Where the bloody hell did you come from?'

He winked. 'You did well to hold him back as you did, but now it's time for the big guns.'

Ashnil raised her eyes heavenward as Archer rose and strode straight towards the shade. I watched in horror as a massive ball of white flame engulfed him, but when it cleared, he was still striding towards Weir, unmarked.

'Vile demon, you shall not stop me,' screamed Weir as Archer thrust his hand into the shade's chest. It shimmered and flickered as Archer twisted his hand left and right, muttering as he did so.

'He's trying to pull out the shade's heart!' Ashnil's excitement made her face glow in the reflected light.

'Surely a shade doesn't have a heart?'

'The heart is the metaphorical receptacle of emotion and self – it's where the soul resides in our imagination and so it matters even more to a shade than to us.'

Weir screamed and howled as Archer continued to twist and pull. Smoke poured from the shade's body until Archer began to shudder and stagger, still muttering determinedly as he worried at Weir's heart.

Suddenly, there was an explosion, and a cloud of smoke rolled over us.

'He's done it,' I shouted. But I was wrong.

The wind blew the smoke away from us and I saw to my horror that Weir was still there. It was Archer who lay on the ground, twitching, as Weir raised his arm to deliver the coup de grâce.

'No. No!' I ran towards them. Sometimes in life we don't think, we simply react, and this was one of those moments. In my pocket, my fingers found the smooth warmth of the werigend. I felt it respond to my touch, its temperature and the movement of its mechanism rapidly increasing. I wasn't sure what I was going to do, but I charged forward and emulated Archer. Thrusting my hand into the shade's chest, I felt his heart pulsing. It was rock-hard and cold as ice and I squeezed it and tried to pull, as Weir laughed manically in my face. With my other hand holding the werigend, I felt a flow of galdr move rapidly through my body, up my arm and punch through my fingers into the shade's heart. I kept twisting and pulling as hard as I could.

Weir screamed and spat. His huge hands wrapped around my head and he squeezed back, pouring his poisoned galdr into me. Pain like I had never known raced through my brain and I knew I was dying.

Suddenly a burst of galdr overwhelmed me and shot to my right hand. The pain subsided just a little. I felt the scar on my right forearm burn and realised the werigend had unlocked the wyrm's power, encouraged perhaps by the pain in my head where the wyrm's presence resided.

Now I was better matched with Weir and we tussled and fought, as I still tried to twist that cold, hard heart from his body. I recalled Archer had been chanting some sort of incantation, but I didn't know it and without it I wasn't sure if I could tear the creature's heart away. My head was screaming with pain and both my hands felt like they were on fire, but I kept twisting and pulling. I didn't know what else I could do.

Then a hand clasped onto my shoulder, gripping it tight and I heard Archer shout, 'Whinny and brig – brake and burn thy bane.' He repeated it and I joined in, guessing it would help. Together we recited the words again and again and, as Archer added his power, I felt a different sort of galdr flow through my shoulder.

The heart suddenly loosened and came away from Weir's body. With a huge rending sound, he was gone. My hand held what looked like a misshapen lump of granite. I fell to my knees, exhausted, gasping for breath, my head pounding and the wyrm-scar on my arm burning white-hot.

'That was well done, Drew,' said Archer, solemnly.

I stared at the stone in my hand until it sunk in – Archer had just praised me. Astonished, I turned to look at him, but he was already back to normal.

'We'll need to contain that,' was all he said.

Ashnil ran up and threw her arms around me. 'That was incredible,' she gushed, before she saw Jophiel and Rillan, dusting themselves off. She stepped back, primly.

Rillan glowered at her and I wondered if she had broken some angelus non-fraternisation rule.

Jophiel inclined his head respectfully to Archer and said, 'We would be honoured to dispose of that safely. Hallowed ground, I'm sure you will agree, would be the best place for it.'

Archer stiffened, and then the merest hint of a smile played at the corner of his mouth. 'Thank you. I concur,' he agreed, with stiff formality.

Jophiel kept looking at Archer. 'I shall probably regret this, but I return your token. Your life is not mine to take.'

Archer looked surprised, then nodded.

I handed Jophiel the stone heart, glad to be rid of the disgusting thing, and he wrapped it quickly in a piece of linen, avoiding touching it.

18. DWEORG-WARE

'May I present to you the one and only Mr Drew Macleod? Probably the only human daft enough to go toe to toe with a high-level aglæcan and come away in one piece!' Archer raised his glass, and the others cheered. Garm wuffed and then sank his snout into a glass Traggheim had put on the floor for him.

It felt like we had something worth celebrating, so Traggheim had delved into his mysterious cellar and emerged carrying several bottles of a pale-yellow liqueur. It had a light fizz, a subtle, hard-to-place, yet disarming flavour and a rather pleasant kick to it. I decided it was best just to enjoy it and not enquire too closely what it was.

I was enjoying watching Archer and Traggheim kicking loose a little. The old dweorg was already well-oiled and busy explaining something in great depth to Stent who, on his third glass already, was happy to listen to anything.

Alyssum sat quietly, holding her glass and taking small sips. I sidled up to her, and she gave me a mechanical smile.

'At present I'm not your favourite person, then?' I said, quietly.

She glared at me. 'As ever, your judgement is miles out, and this is neither the time nor the place to discuss my opinion of you.' She raised her glass. 'Congratulations,' she said drily and walked away.

'You've got some work to do there, pal,' muttered Stent out of the corner of his mouth. 'Don't muck it up. Take it fae me – some people are worth the effort.'

I silently added Alyssum to my mental 'to do' list.

Archer waved me over enthusiastically, pointing at his old friend. 'Traggers has an idea and I think it's worth hearing.'

Traggheim grinned at me. 'In vino veritas. Do you know what that means, young Drew?'

'In drink comes truth?' I hazarded.

'When he's rat-arsed he has good ideas.' Archer laughed.

Traggheim glared at him. 'A sip of this fine beverage of mine may have lubricated my brain a little, but I find it sometimes gets the, ah...'

'Juices flowing?' I suggested.

'Just so, just so. The juices are indeed flowing in my head this evening.' He smiled, looking satisfied with himself.

'Your idea?' I reminded him.

'Ah yes, my idea. I believe we need to monitor the activity of the Ælves, now that we know they are once more active and possibly planning to play an unwelcome role in your life. Ælf-galdr carries a unique signature, which can be distinguished with care. The high levels of galdr they employ should make it possible to pinpoint them from greater distances than normal. This is important, as they are rural creatures, so an attack may come from further away than we are accustomed to. I intend to investitit... investigunt.'

'Investigate?'

'Just so. Investigunt whether we can determine their activities from their galdr and thus divine what they are up to, the little tinkers.'

I looked at Archer. 'Little tinkers?'

He shook his head, grinning. 'If he can pull this off, it might tip the balance in our favour. These "little tinkers" make Thomas Weir's shade look like a cute little pussy-cat.'

The next morning, my head gave me an obvious message about Traggheim's patent liqueur and I was in no hurry to get up. When I finally surfaced mid-morning, I wandered downstairs, clutching a large mug of coffee, like it was a long-lost friend. To my surprise, Traggheim was hard at work in his workshop. Vast sheets of thick, cream-coloured paper covered every flat surface, and he was scribbling with great concentration. I looked closer and saw a patchwork of what looked like formulae, but using many symbols unfamiliar to me, interspersed with three-dimensional diagrams of complex mechanisms. Each looked as if it should have taken a draftsman days to produce and yet Traggheim was churning them out like a computer printer.

He paused and peered at me. 'Would you care for a hair of the dog, Drew?' He indicated a bottle of the fateful liqueur and I politely declined, wanting nothing more to do with the stuff.

'Ah well, I find it helps me to think, but in smaller quantities than last night, eh?'

I pointed to the snowdrifts of paper. 'What's all this?'

'This is a design for what I call my Hólmganga,' he said with obvious pride. 'If it works, and I'm confident that it will, it will help us understand what the Ælf-queen is doing at any time. Forewarned is fore-armed, as they say.'

'Why Hólmganga?' I asked.

'It's a Viking Scandinavian word for the settlement of a dispute, a kind of duel, where the disputants would repair to an island and fight for their honour. This machine will allow us to do the same, by equalising the Queen's unfair advantages.' He beamed with pleasure, blinking behind his glasses.

'How long will it take to build?' Given the apparent complexity, I assumed it would be weeks or even months.

'Oh, about a week. Less, if you help me.'

'I don't know the first thing about what you do, Traggheim, so I'm not sure how much help I can be.'

He regarded me, his blue eyes twinkling. 'You can pass a spanner, can't you?'

The next few days passed rapidly. Most of the time, I hadn't the faintest idea what Traggheim was doing, but it was fascinating to see a true craftsman at work. I watched as he drilled, cut, welded, shaped, bolted, screwed and adjusted a rapidly growing machine. Not only did all of this happen phenomenally fast, much of it was intricate and breathtakingly small. Traggheim wore big fold-down lenses over his glasses, but even with them flipped up, he was able to manipulate and work the most miniscule of pieces.

My contribution comprised passing tools, fetching materials, and maintaining a steady supply of chipped enamel mugs of tea and doorstep bacon sandwiches, which seemed to be his primary source of energy. He slept little and occasionally I dozed off and slipped away to recharge my batteries, astonished by the old dweorg's stamina.

As he worked, he talked out problems, using me as a kind of excuse to speak to himself out loud, which I think helped him. I certainly wasn't able to add anything useful to the discussion.

After a couple of days, I made an excuse and went out for a few hours. The gleaming machine was now the size of a small chest and contained layer upon layer of tiny, intricate workings. Yet still, according to Traggheim, the Hólmganga was nowhere near finished.

I stood in the quiet street, facing Alyssum's shop. From the outside, it looked like one of those health food and vitamin pill stores, but with everything made on the premises and a wholesome scrubbed-wood style, Edinburgh's better-off loved it. I clutched an enormous bunch of chrysanthemums and couldn't decide whether giving her flowers would help break down the barrier that had grown between us since I visited the wyrm, or whether it was just sexist and unimaginative.

That decision became academic when the shop door banged wide open and Alyssum stood with her hands on her hips, eyes flashing.

'You. Get in here and stop mooching about the street like a lovesick swain!'

'A what?'

'I don't know – it's what people say. Give me those.' She took the flowers and virtually propelled me into the shop.

'Only a man – no, only a man or a daemon, would stand around outside like that, instead of just finding some balls and getting on with it.' And she smiled, though a little grimly. 'Get your backside through there and sit down.'

I did as I was told, though this wasn't what I had planned. My carefully rehearsed speech of apology and reconciliation wasn't needed. Or was it? I felt like a mouse, being played with by a cat.

'Let's hear it then? You're obviously here with something to say,' she said brightly.

'Look, I came to clear the air. I know you were upset about the wyrm and I know you felt I shouldn't do it, but the fact is, it worked and I'm stronger for it. The shade would have finished Archer and I, if it hadn't been for the wyrm's power.'

She was listening intently, head on one side. 'Anything else?'

'Such as?'

'Oh, I don't know. Maybe an apology for not bothering to ask my opinion. Perhaps an apology for completely ignoring my advice when I offered it. And maybe an acceptance that dallying with that simpering angelus was a stupid and dangerous thing to do?'

'I did ask for your advice,' I replied hotly.

'No, you didn't. You told me what Ashnil had said and then announced you were going to do it. You just hoped I would smooth your path with Archer for you. What is it you see standing in front of you? A female object? A useful gopher? A woman to tend your cuts and grazes?'

'No! I have never seen you that way and I object to you portraying me as a sexist.'

'Oh, really? And how do you think I feel, to be marginalised as a woman?'

In truth, I didn't see Alyssum as anything but a clever, capable and resourceful woman, but maybe I'd focussed on Archer too much and allowed her to be eclipsed. I looked at her: the bright eyes, the button nose, the intensity and passion she put into everything she did. I couldn't help but like and admire her. That I'd clearly upset her, and she saw me as a sexist, bothered me.

'I'm so sorry, Alyssum. Remember, I'm still finding my way in the parallel realm, and it's hard to focus on what's important sometimes. But please believe me when I say that I really do value your opinion and I value your friendship.'

She stared at me for a long moment. Then suddenly she stepped forward and slapped me – a powerful blow, hard enough to make my ears ring. I opened my mouth to ask what the hell that was about, but the words didn't come out. Instead, she grabbed me and kissed me firmly.

She released me and stood back. 'Now you know where

you stand, Drew Macleod.' A mischievous smile played across her face.

'I do?'

'Probably not. You've got a cock, so that means you're probably even more confused than ever. You should probably get used to it.'

'But we're friends again?'

'Of course. We never stopped. It was just that you needed a bit of adjustment.' She kissed me again, this time on the top of my head. 'Now, I've lots of work to do and you have a dweorg to fetch and carry for, so get gone.'

As I left the shop, she called after me. 'Thanks for the flowers. Next time, cook me a nice dinner.' I reflected Alyssum was a unique, terrifying and thoroughly nice person.

19. HÓLMGANGA

The Hólmganga was a work of art. If it never functioned at all, but simply sat on the table in the middle of Archer's library as an ornament, it would be a thing of wonder and beauty. Polished brass gears and cogs slowly rotated, mechanisms ticked and whirred, springs stretched and relaxed. Wherever you looked, there were tiny parts moving smoothly and purposefully. A warm ruby-red glow radiated from somewhere in the centre, making it appear alive.

Archer, typically, focussed on practical matters. 'Does it work, Traggheim?' he asked with just a hint of a mischievous grin.

Traggheim drew himself up to his full height, the top of his head no higher than Archer's chest. 'Have you ever known anything I make to fail?' he asked haughtily.

'No, but the first time must surely come!'

Before Traggheim could indignantly respond, Alyssum punched Archer's arm. 'Stop it.' She glared at the daemon, who looked aloof, though he surreptitiously rubbed his arm.

'It's beautiful, Traggheim, and I'm sure it'll work very well. Ignore this tactless oaf,' she said.

The old dweorg was a sucker for Alyssum and he beamed back at her. 'Yes, well, shall I demonstrate it for you?'

'That's why we're here,' replied Archer, subsiding as he got a sharp glance from Alyssum.

'The Hólmganga draws galdr from those around it, those who are well-disposed towards it. We all fit into that category, so it can utilise tiny amounts of our galdr. The machine is so efficient that the amounts it uses are too small for us to notice and it can store the galdr for use when nobody is near. It means that even at full operation it will not impact on us.' He peered over his glasses at us, as though expecting an interruption. When none came, he continued.

'I have engineered the Hólmganga to sense the miniscule waves of radiation generated by the use of galdr, in much the same way as some machines in my workshop. However, there are several critical differences.'

'Do we need to know...' Archer subsided at another glower from Alyssum, muttering under his breath '...all the tiny details?'

'Yes, you do, Archer, or how will you understand it properly?' Traggheim heard him. 'Ælves, unlike other aglæcan or galdr-folc, use galdr constantly to maintain their appearance. They are profligate and this helps us as it creates a constant signal we can monitor. Their galdr has a unique and, one might almost say peculiar, signature, which the Hólmganga can use as a sort of hook, to help it focus on our target.'

'So, how is this different from your other monitoring machines?' asked Archer. Despite himself, he was obviously fascinated.

'Well, I told you before that the strength and constancy of ælf-galdr would allow us to monitor over a much greater distance, but perhaps more importantly, the peculiarities of their form of galdr means that the machine can interrogate and interpret the galdr traces it intercepts.'

'In what way?' I asked.

'Let me show you,' the dweorg replied with pride. 'Tell the Hólmganga to show you the Ælf-queen. Be aware that it will need additional galdr to display your answer. As you're asking, it will draw it from you. Don't fight it – let it have what it needs.'

I looked at Archer. He nodded. Remembering myself, I looked at Alyssum, who smiled. I emptied my mind as much as I could. Then, looking at the machine, I said, as clearly as I could, 'Show me the Ælf-queen.'

There was a pregnant pause. Then I felt a prickling at the back of my neck as the machine drew some galdr from me. Slowly the top of the machine folded upwards and out, to create a flat oval plate intricately engraved with a pattern of whorls and shapes. We all leaned forward to look at the plate when a flickering blue light formed on top of it, slowly brightening and expanding into multiple shapes. Gradually, the shapes resolved into an image of the Ælf-queen. With her were two other ælves, talking animatedly to her, though we could hear nothing.

'That's incredible,' breathed Alyssum at my shoulder. 'This is what she's doing at this very moment?'

'It is,' replied Traggheim.

'Unfortunately, none of us has the skill of lip-reading,' commented Archer drily.

Traggheim's bright eyes twinkled with delight. 'My dear Archer, it's muted! Drew simply needs to tell the machine to increase the volume!'

I did so, and we listened to the singsong voices of the ælves, as they continued their discussion.

'Does anyone speak ælvish?' I asked.

'A few words,' said Traggheim.

'As little as possible,' was Archer's response.

'They're talking about a cousin of the Queen's, who they

fear may not be loyal. They're arguing over whether to buy him off or wipe him out.'

We all turned slowly, to stare at Alyssum.

'Not just the wee wifey then, am I?' she said happily. 'As well as treating cuts and bruises and baking amazing brownies, it turns out I understand one of the most complex languages ever devised. Who'd have thought it?' She gave us a triumphant grin, her arms folded.

'I never thought that–'

'Of course you're more than–'

'Alyssum, you're much more–'

She cut us all off. 'Yeah, yeah, yeah. So the important thing is, how are we going to use this machine? Watching the queen is one thing, but we need to gather some intelligence you can use.'

Over the ensuing days, we gradually worked out a system for monitoring the Hólmganga. Alyssum moved into the library, as she was the only one of us who could understand the strange, high-pitched speech of the ælves. During the day I had to serve customers in Alyssum's shop: Traggheim would have freaked them out and Archer's impatience and indifference would have bankrupted her business in a day, even if he could have been persuaded to help. To begin with, I frequently had to gallop down the spiral staircase, to ask a question on behalf of someone who wanted to align something or enhance something else – all of it made-up nonsense, in my opinion. After a few days, I came to understand that the range of herbal remedies she sold was actually quite simple to follow. As she said, 'It's the galdr-healing that needs actual skill and knowledge, this stuff is just pandering.' Thankfully, I wasn't called upon to get involved in any galdr-healing – not that she'd have let me, anyway.

Alyssum turned out to be an impressively well-organised spy. As the days went on, heaps of loose-leaf notes piled up around her, each page noted and cross-referenced in index books, which she constantly updated and amended. A decent spreadsheet would have been so much easier, were it not for the risks of using electronics.

For my part, I maintained a flow of coffee and meals, and in the late evenings we plundered Archer's drinks cabinet. Gradually Alyssum became the acknowledged expert on the Ælf-queen and her court.

'How is it you speak Ælvish?' I asked one evening, idly swirling a generous measure of Archer's finest brandy around a balloon glass.

'I had no choice, really. Regular medicine originated from the Arabic world, if you ignore the fatuous concepts of "balancing humours" and treating sick organs with plants that look like them, which the Western world clung to for centuries. In the parallel realm it was the ælves who, long ago, developed the techniques of galdr-healing, identified which plants have enhanced effects for galdr-folc and worked out how to use them. The only way I could fully develop my skills was to immerse myself in their writings.'

'But surely there's a difference between reading a language and hearing it? When I dabbled in Norwegian, it was easy to recognise many of the written words, but hearing them spoken was much harder.'

'Ælvish isn't like most human languages. It's very intuitive and made up of many sounds. Written ælvish is essentially spoken ælvish, written phonetically. The only way to make sense of it is to read it aloud.'

'Where did you study?' I asked, curious.

'Right here. My mother was a healer too, and we come from a long line of what would've been called witches a few hundred years ago. I never knew my father and my mother died when I was twelve. Archer adopted me.'

I stared at her, gob-smacked. 'Archer's your stepfather?'

'I suppose so, in a sense, but he arranged for a galdr-touched family to take me in for a few years and he was more of a mentor than a stepfather. He made sure I received the training and education I needed to follow in my mother's path. That's why he deserves my loyalty. Even though he's a bit of an arse sometimes.'

Gradually, a picture built up of the Ælf-queen and her subjects. She didn't seem to have a name as we would understand it. She was clearly a spiteful creature, perhaps more so than her kin, and that was saying something. Often they spoke obliquely, making it hard to identify the subject of discussion in her court, but Alyssum's burgeoning library of notes and indexes filled in some gaps. Inevitably Archer had mocked her organising until she banished him.

The Hólmganga fascinated me and I spent as much time as I could, sitting with Alyssum, watching the three-dimensional figures shimmering and moving around their little platform, like actors on a stage. Alyssum sometimes simultaneously translated, so I picked up a few of the simpler, frequently-used phrases.

Once the Queen spat out a sentence including what sounded like "Aah-churr". I looked at Alyssum and she nodded vigorously. But it turned out to be a reference to his part in her downfall a millennium and a half ago and not to him as a current foe. There was frustratingly little information about anything outside the ælvish community, and I despaired. What had seemed a promising tool seemed to be of little help. I wondered if she was perhaps aware of us, remembering how she had stared at me when the Annals of Dun Eidyn took me to see her. But Traggheim was adamant that this was not possible.

Eventually Alyssum picked up snippets of information that seemed to have some relevance and she summoned a council of war to tell Archer, Traggheim and me what she had found out.

'There are three major themes slowly emerging,' she began. 'Aside from the vast amount of data I have on their back-biting and nasty internal politics, the queen makes Joseph Stalin seem like a balanced and sensible leader.'

'Who?' queried Traggheim.

'I'll explain later,' I promised him.

Alyssum continued. 'The first theme isn't surprising, as they are desperately keen for the Ælvish Kingdom to re-ascend and gain the power they had before Dunichen.'

'Nothing new in that, surely?' said Archer.

'Yes, and no. There's a sense of expectation, almost an innate belief that this is genuinely going to happen. It could just be an ælvish arrogance thing, but it seems like more.'

'And the second theme?' asked Archer.

'This is clearer. They have been steadily beavering away to manipulate people to destroy or remove the Pictish stones, to remove the limitations the stones put on them. The Queen calls them something like "Bastard-stones of the daemons".'

'That'll be you, Archer,' I put in.

'I'll accept that as a badge of honour. It fits though, doesn't it?' he said. 'I was assuming people had randomly destroyed stones or moved them to museums, but the old bitch and her acolytes have been twisting people's minds to make it happen.'

'This makes sense, Archer,' said Traggheim. 'This is the type of devious long game we should expect from ælves.'

'But I should have seen it coming.' Archer banged his hand down on the table, causing the Hólmganga to jump slightly.

Traggheim frowned, and I could see he wanted to remonstrate with Archer, but bit his lip instead.

I turned back to Alyssum. 'What's the third theme?'

'This is the hardest one to make sense of. She's been laying plans for some sort of visit or travel.'

'Do you know where she's going?' snapped Archer.

'No, it's not her – someone is coming to visit the court, but the way they speak is so imprecise I can't make sense of who or why, but it matters to them.'

I turned to Archer. 'Could there be a potential ally or collaborator who might meet with her?'

Archer rubbed his chin slowly. 'It would be surprising, though there are many creatures who theoretically could. She may break down the controls we surrounded her with, but anyone thinking of allying themselves with ælves would take enormous risks. Not only of being cast out by all galdr-folc but also the dangers inherent in dealing with ælves – double-crossing and back-stabbing is a way of life for them.'

'It's not a potential ally,' said Alyssum flatly.

'How can you be sure?' asked Traggheim.

Alyssum pointed to the Hólmganga's platform. A human figure lay sprawled face-down in front of the Queen. A retainer grabbed the prisoner's hair and pulled it back, so that the Ælf-queen was looking directly into the face–

The face of Jamie Renton.

I blinked. It couldn't possibly be him. How could Jamie come to be a captive of the ælves? He had laughed at the possibility of the parallel realm. It must be someone who looks like him, I thought...

Then the truth dawned on me and I felt sick. 'This is my fault,' I whispered.

As I stared, unable to believe what I was seeing, the Queen spat some venomous words at Jamie, and his body convulsed in agony, as though a massive electric shock was pulsing through him. His scream went straight to my heart, a sound that would live in my nightmares for the rest of my life. I couldn't believe what I was seeing. Jamie, daft as a brush, but always there when I needed him. Nobody could deserve what I was watching happen to him, but especially not Jamie. And worse, he could only possibly be in this position because of me.

Seeing my face, Alyssum put her hand on my arm. 'You know him, don't you?'

Instead of answering, I bolted from the room, retching.

20. ACCORD

I've heard it said there is a fine line — a very fine line — between everyday normality and mental illness, and that it only takes the right spark to nudge us over that line. For weeks I had been existing in a world that was utterly alien to me, living in fear of my life and trying to understand how to survive in my new environment. So perhaps it was inevitable that I lost all control of myself when I saw my best friend enduring physical agony at the hands of a creature that personifies cruelty. And it was my fault.

I can't remember much of the next few hours. I do recall ranting, screaming, crying, and breaking things. Eventually I must have exhausted myself and calmed down enough for Archer and Alyssum to get me to the flat above Traggheim's workshop and put me to bed.

In the morning I awoke with a very peculiar taste in my mouth – a combination of extreme sweetness and smoky flavour, with more than a hint of bitterness. Alyssum was sitting at the bottom of the bed, reading a small, leather-bound book.

'You're back with us, then,' she said, moving closer and looking at my eyes.

'You doctored me with something, didn't you? That's why I've a weird taste in my mouth.'

'Guilty as charged. I'd do it again, so sue me.'

'My closest friend is being tortured by those freakish monsters and I'm lying in bed, thanks to you.' I pulled back the covers and gasped as waves of pain and nausea swept over me. 'Ugh! What've you done to me?'

'Not me, this is all your doing. Now lie back.' She shoved me back into bed. 'You've been living on your nerves and developing galdr skills far faster than your body can cope with. Last night's extravaganza of fury and frustration was the unavoidable culmination. The remedy I gave you simply forced your body to re-boot itself.' She poked a finger at me. 'I'm a healer, remember? Healing people is what I do.'

I sank back onto the pillows and waited for the room to behave itself. 'So, what now? I have to do something. What's happening to Jamie Renton is my fault.' I swore again. 'And I'm lying in bed.'

She smiled. 'One – you'll be able to get up in a few hours. Two – only a complete idiot marches into battle without a plan, and three – we don't yet know where he's being held. So hold back the testosterone for a bit and start using your brain. I'll tell the others you'll be open for business this afternoon.'

As she went through the door, she turned with an oddly warm expression. 'By the way, you're truly magnificent when you're deranged. Even Archer was a bit impressed.'

I made a half-hearted attempt to throw a pillow at her, but my aim was poor and she was long gone by the time it landed.

I lay back and pinched the bridge of my nose. Alyssum was right, of course, as she so often was. I couldn't hope to rescue Jamie alone. I desperately hoped that we could do something for him. But why did the Ælf-queen take him? If this was a kidnapping, hoping to regain what she had lost to my ancestor, then Jamie was in deep trouble, as I didn't have what she wanted. But surely the first thing would be for her to make contact? One thing bothered me though: why was she torturing him? She might want me to know he was being tortured to encourage me to play ball, but she didn't know she was being watched. Was she trying to extract information from him? If so, what? He knew even less than I did about the missing artefact, but, of course, she wouldn't know that. Also, as Alyssum said, we didn't even know where they were. I punched the mattress in frustration and tried to think through what I knew and whether there was anything that could help. But no inspiration came.

We met in the living room of the flat; none of us felt like being near the Hólmganga and the need for us to meet was too urgent to wait for me to feel less knackered. Archer greeted my shame-faced apology with joviality. Traggheim and Alyssum were more empathetic. Garm, curled up on a threadbare sheepskin rug, lifted his head, briefly stared and growled softly before going back to sleep. I had absolutely no idea what that meant and I didn't fancy asking Archer.

Curiously, Archer had invited Stent to join us, without saying why.

Traggheim hefted a large calfskin book onto the table and poked at it with his bony forefinger. 'Here, I think, may lie the answer to what this whole matter truly concerns.' He looked around the room, then his eyes fell on me. 'The token your ancestor received from the Ælf-queen we know to be at the heart of her cause for pursuing you, Drew.'

I pulled the book towards me. Embossed on the spine in tarnished gold letters was the title "Ælvish creations and methods". I looked at Traggheim. 'But whatever it was, I don't have it.'

'Ah, but perhaps you are wrong.' He held up a hand to forestall my protest. 'This tome is a study of what we know about ælvish technology and I suspect the token was and probably still is, protected by a galdr-shield – an ælvish device which cloaks an item of value with the physical characteristics of an everyday object and,' he leant forward, 'it can reinvent itself to suit its surroundings, by reflecting the previous generation. It may appear to be some worthless keepsake from one's recent forebears, when it is in fact an ancient and valuable artefact–'

Archer cut in. 'I asked Stent to, shall we just say, "gain access", to your flat and search for anything you could have inherited.'

'Sorry, pal,' said Stent. 'But the big man said how urgent it was.'

I didn't care. If Traggheim was right, this could be the breakthrough that led us to Jamie. Stent pulled several objects from his pocket and laid them on the table. We all leaned forward, and I felt a sudden flash of galdr.

'Only the ælf who created the shielded object can sense it,' said Traggheim. 'Or the person for whom they intended it.' He glanced at me. 'Or their rightful heir.'

'Do you sense anything?' asked Archer.

I nodded and stared at the three objects in front of me – all I possessed of my parents, other than some books and a dwindling bank balance. I felt a twinge of regret that I didn't have more to remember them by. Just a Bakelite engineer's compass, an odd tool for measuring distances on maps and a battered die-cast toy motorcycle and sidecar, which I knew had been my dad's when he was a kid.

I touched each but felt nothing specific, so I concentrated, staring at each one, until gradually the compass glowed faintly orange. I pulled the werigend from my pocket, but before I could use it, the compass changed its form. Slowly, like molten lead, it flowed and reshaped itself, gradually becoming something totally different.

'A bloody stone? Was that the best the Ælf-bitch could come up with?' growled Archer.

But it wasn't just a stone, it was a beautiful piece of polished basalt. I picked up the carved oval and found that it fitted perfectly into my palm. As it did, I felt the heat associated with powerful galdr. The tiny carvings were incredibly complex. I turned the stone over, marvelling at its beauty.

Alyssum put a hand on my arm. 'This is what your ancestor bargained for and never returned. Put it down now.'

I tried to put the stone back onto the table, but somehow it resisted. It belonged in my hand and I didn't want to let it go.

'Drew.' Alyssum put her hands on my cheeks and pulled my face round so I was looking into her eyes. 'Drew, you must put it down.' She continued to look into my eyes until I slowly, reluctantly managed to put the stone on the table. Archer and Traggheim both breathed out and Alyssum squeezed my wrist.

'It's lost none of the power your ancestor wanted it for,' said Archer. 'And it will try to keep hold of you if it can. I strongly advise you not to let it.'

'Pure heroin in a rock,' put in Stent.

I stared at the stone, fascinated by the power it exerted and its long history in my family. Down the centuries it had passed from generation to generation, changing form from one apparently innocuous item to another, finding its way down a millennium and a half to me. I turned to the others. 'So now I know why I was pulled into the parallel realm. This stone was in my possession all along and the Ælf-queen wants it back. So why don't I simply give it to her? She'll release Jamie and call off the sceadhu and anything else she's unleashed and we can all get on with our lives.' As I was saying it, a small voice in the back of my head was pointing out that this life was more exhilarating, lively and engaging than anything I'd ever known. I shoved that thought to one side.

They were all silent. I looked at each of them. Stent shrugged. Traggheim was taking a deep interest in a broken waistcoat button. Archer was looking at me but saying nothing and even Alyssum seemed lost for words.

Something pushed at my ankle and I looked down to see Garm, who growled softly and slowly shook his head, causing his ears to flap. Then I understood.

'I get it. It really isn't that simple, is it?' I said.

Alyssum answered first. 'You didn't really expect it to be, did you?' she asked with a gentle smile.

'Ok, so tell me the worst.'

Archer raised his head, frowning. 'If we set aside for now the vengeance for which the Ælf-bitch is renowned, that stone isn't some pretty little gee-gaw. Consider how long ago it held enough power to help your ancestor to risk dealing with the Ælf-bitch when people knew all about ælves and what bastards they are. Fifteen hundred years later, it still holds vast power – you can sense that yourself. We must not allow the Ælf-queen to get it back.'

'With or without it, we've got to find Jamie Renton and get him out of her clutches,' I said, louder than I'd intended.

'Even I wouldn't deny that rescuing your friend is a priority. But defending this stone is another,' said Archer.

'Before we can do anything we need to know where the ælves have got Jamie,' said Alyssum. 'How do we do that?'

'And how're you gonnae walk in there, against a powerful enemy, without getting blootered tae hell?' asked Stent.

Traggheim coughed and looked pointedly at Archer.

'I know, I know Traggheim.' Archer grunted. 'We're running out of options.'

'How did you defeat the ælves at the Battle of Dunnichen?' I asked. 'Surely they must've been powerful then, from all I've heard.'

'Ha!' said Archer. 'That was a very different time. Back then I was one of many daemons and it was their help and the support of dweorgs and many others that enabled us to overcome the Ælf-bitch and her clan and hole up their remnants behind a network of galdr-stones. Never more!'

'They're all dead, Drew,' said Traggheim gently. 'Down through the centuries, one by one, the daemons have been lost.'

'All of them?' I looked at Archer, who was bristling, and more defensive and angry than I'd ever seen him.

'All but two, so far as we know,' the old dweorg replied. 'Archer, and a renegade called Obadiah.' He glanced sideways at Archer, who snorted.

'No hope of anything but trouble from that quarter,' he snarled. 'This is my fault, my failure. I should have recognised what the Ælf-bitch was doing and put a stop to it. Now it may be too late.' He leapt to his feet and paced round the room. 'What can I do? I cannot allow them to spread their vileness across the face of the earth once more. They have captured and are torturing an innocent human. But I can no longer call on the depth of help I once had. Damn it!' He punched the wall, then rubbed his knuckles. 'The bloody angelii. For once, they might be some sort of use, but where the hell are they? They undertook to look for the source of this problem, yet Traggheim got there first.'

'They were a help to me at the tram depot,' I said. 'Let me talk to Ashnil.' I saw Alyssum's face darken and quickly suggested she come as well.

'I'll get word to her,' said Stent, before Archer could object.

'It's a good idea, Archer,' put in Traggheim. 'There isn't time for a formal galdr-moot and there's no choice but to talk to them.'

'I know, I know. Whilst you're doing that, I'll give some thought to a strategy. We need to replace some of those stones, and fast. But it be easy.'

I reckoned taking Alyssum with me to meet Ashnil was the best thing to do. Without her there, the others would think I'd been hood-winked or influenced by some sort of angelus juju. And it would save me another round of Alyssum's full-throttle disapproval. But this would not be easy at an emotional level. I was going to be stuck between two women, both of whom I liked a lot, neither of whom I truly understood and one of whom hated the other. Could it be that Alyssum was jealous? I thought of her more as a sort of big sister figure, but she'd definitely shown signs of warmth towards me recently. Was that just friendship or her healer's bedside manner, or was there something else? As for Ashnil, once she turned off the warm fuzzy angelus stuff, she was a genuinely nice girl, with a feisty attitude that I quite liked. But she was an angelus. I did not know how biology worked in the parallel realm. Besides, my priority was to get Jamie out of the hell that I'd caused him to land in.

When Ashnil glided into the diner, I sensed rather than saw Alyssum stiffen and braced myself. Alyssum was too polite for overt fireworks, but I could be in for a session of the non-verbal aggressive square-dancing that women are so good at and which leaves me miles behind.

Unexpectedly, Ashnil was straight to business. 'Jophiel's gone off at the deep end,' she started, sitting down facing us. 'As you know, he ordered Rillan to liaise with Archer. But Rillan disagreed with Jophiel's decision to co-operate and ignored the order – I've never seen Jophiel so angry. I don't know what will happen next, but he's instructed me to apologise and promise that we'll do better.' She put a hand on mine. 'We know about your friend, Drew. I'm really sorry.'

I glanced sideways and could almost feel the blast of cynicism Alyssum was giving off.

'He must be rescued from the Ælf-queen,' Ashnil said.

'We're working on it,' replied Alyssum coldly.

'Do you know about the stones being moved?' asked Ashnil.

We both nodded.

'Then you know how grave it is. This isn't just about your friend – it's a much bigger problem that we know Archer cannot face alone.'

Alyssum sniffed and Ashnil turned to her.

'We know Archer doesn't trust us and nor do you. And we understand why. Jophiel insisted I make it very clear we won't make the same error twice.'

'Sorry?' I said. 'What error?'

'Fifteen hundred years ago, our angelus forebears refused to take part in the suppression of the ælves. It was a foolish decision and not one we intend to repeat. Please, Alyssum, you must help convince Archer that there must be a full alliance. I know he thinks we're useless and feckless, but we must work together. We don't have his powers.' She smiled at me. 'Or yours now, Drew, but we do have other abilities that can help, and we are determined not to repeat the error of Dunnichen.' She kept looking at me. 'Archer and the daemons almost lost the Battle of Dunnichen because my forebears didn't play their part.'

'How do we know we can trust you now?' asked Alyssum. 'Words are easy.'

'I've brought some information. We offer you this gift without need for restitution or debt,' Ashnil said formally.

'What's the information?' I asked.

'We know where the ælves are holding your friend.'

There was a pause whilst we processed this. Then I gasped, 'Where? Where do they have him?'

Ashnil glanced towards Alyssum. 'Before I tell you, I want you to promise me something.'

'What the hell? What happened to "no restitution or debt",' I demanded. 'Jamie is being tortured by those monsters. Whilst we sit here chatting, he's in agony and you're playing games? Where the hell is he?'

Alyssum held up her hand. 'Stop, Drew. I think I know what Ashnil's going to say. She's right.'

Ashnil gave her a quick smile and took both my hands in hers. 'Drew, if I tell you where Jamie is being held, promise me you won't try to do anything on your own? You're not powerful enough. You'll just get yourself killed and probably Jamie too.' She gazed at me and out of the corner of my eye I could see Alyssum nodding in agreement.

'Ok, ok, I agree.'

Alyssum kicked my shin hard under the table as Ashnil continued to look at me.

I sighed. 'All right then, I promise.' I had no choice, caught in a pincer movement between these two strong-willed and determined women. 'So where is it they have him?'

'The Goblin Hall at Long Yester.'

I stared at Ashnil, trying to make sense of what she said. 'Goblins?' I asked tentatively.

'I've heard of the Goblin Hall,' said Alyssum. She looked at Ashnil. 'Do you mind?' Ashnil shrugged and Alyssum continued. 'So Yester Castle is an old ruin in the woods, near Haddington. There's not much left, but what it's famous for is a massive underground vault. In the fifteenth century nobody in Scotland knew how to build like that, so a Dutch mason called Gobbelin did the work and the locals heard his name, added two and two to make five and the vault has been called the Goblin Hall ever since.' She looked at Ashnil. 'Is that about right?'

'The locals call it the Goblin Ha' in Scots, but what worries Jophiel is that it is apparently a very strong defensive position. It's a strong underground structure, approached through woodland, which gives the ælves an advantage. And that's not the only problem.'

'Oh?' I asked.

'Rillan is dead-set against any kind of alliance with Archer. After his failure to follow Jophiel's instruction, they're heading for a big clash.'

'What would that look like?' I asked.

She looked scared. 'Jophiel could cast him out.'

'Let's hope it doesn't come to that,' I said. 'So, how do we get Jophiel and Archer together quickly?'

21. STRATEGY

Yester Castle, or what remains of it, sits on an overgrown hump between two wooded burns. I knelt behind a rotten log and peered through the undergrowth at the decaying remnants of the stonework above ground. Of course I shouldn't have been there, I'd promised both Alyssum and Ashnil I'd stay away, but my mind had revolved endlessly round and round the twin facts that I was warm and safe in bed whilst Jamie was less than twenty miles away, suffering in ways I could only imagine. As dawn crept in, I packed a rucksack and rationalised what I was doing by pretending I was only going to reconnoitre the castle. In truth, if a chance arose, I was sure as hell going to have a go at rescuing him.

It took several hours to work my way into the woods. My skills with a map and compass were rusty at best, but using an electronic GPS would've been like gift-wrapping myself for the ælves. I took my time and used the contours and winding burns to edge through the damp, mossy wood. I avoided the tracks and paths, as the Ælf-queen's look-outs would watch those. During my travels abroad, I did some outreach work with a tribe in Belize and now I mentally blessed the elderly hunter who had amused himself by teaching me to creep slowly through the undergrowth without making a sound. Eventually I found my target and, slowly pushing the map into my pocket, I folded myself into the angle of a fallen trunk and settled down to watch and wait amidst the scents of leaf litter and crushed wood sorrel.

The small noises of the woodland gradually became clearer: scurrying in the long grass; the flutter of a wren's wings as it hunted through a mossy bank; the occasional buzz of a passing insect. I made myself as comfortable as I could and it would've been relaxing, were it not for the knowledge of ælves nearby and that they probably had a sensory advantage over me. Worse, I really wasn't sure what I was watching for, but I hoped I'd know it when I saw it –something that didn't fit in, perhaps. I assumed the ælves would have cloaked the Goblin Ha' with galdr, so nothing obvious would be visible to the naked eye. I kept the werigend in the palm of my hand, relying on it to give my senses a boost when required, and hoping that the wyrm's galdr would be available if I needed it.

Whilst I watched, I thought through last night's events, starting with the incredible arrival of Jophiel, invited into Archer's library. The two of them had spent a long time closeted together, whilst Alyssum and I sat in her workroom, debating what was being discussed and whether the two could manage to, as Alyssum sardonically put it, 'Play nicely together and use indoor voices.'

'Do you think they'll come to an agreement?' she asked me.

'You know Archer better than me, but it's been clear from the moment I first met him he hates angelii with the heat of a supernova. But...'

'But?'

'I can't help thinking the one thing in Archer's mental superstructure that might trump it is his commitment to protecting mankind from the threats they don't know about... What?' Alyssum was giggling.

'Sorry, Drew. It's just funny to hear you talk about "they".'

'I know. A few weeks ago, I was one of them, blithely unaware of what was going on around me.'

'No, you don't understand.' She gave me a coy smile. 'It's just that it's really nice to have you committing to being a part of the parallel realm.'

'It's not like I have a choice, is it?'

'No, but the few others I've heard of going through the sort of thing you've been through – I mean, being brought into the realm unexpectedly and against their will – they fought it and refused to accept their new reality. You're different.'

I thought for a moment. 'I guess I was ready for something more than the life I had.'

'No, it's not just that. I know you'll scoff at this, but it was your destiny, Drew. The moment your ancestor failed to return the stone, it became inevitable that this would happen and somehow the galdr-forces made sure you were ready for it.'

'The galdr-forces? When you say it like that, it sounds almost like you're describing deities.'

'Perhaps I am. Nobody really knows the source of galdr or what guides it, so maybe there are sentient forces behind it.'

At that moment, the door banged open and Archer barged in. 'Right, we have an agreement. Garm!'

The dog leapt up from his cosy place by Alyssum's fire.

'Fetch Stent and then get word to the other angelii to come and meet us here.'

Alyssum bristled.

Archer shrugged. 'Alright, then. Tell them to come to the

Scotland Street tunnel and I'll let them in that way. Where's Traggheim? Drew, could you rootle the old bugger out, please?'

22. BETRAYAL

I doubt if the old library had ever seen so many people at one time. Usually there were only two or three of us rattling around in the palace of mahogany, leather and brass-work. Now it seemed full, with Archer and Jophiel presiding over the throng. Traggheim was clearly revelling in the occasion. Ashnil looked worried and Alyssum had made a point of speaking to her. Rillan sat alone, with a scarcely-disguised scowl. The presence of three other angelii made me wonder if part of the reason for Archer's antipathy towards them could be their numbers, compared to the decline of daemons. Garm completed the gathering, making one of the angelii wrinkle his nose and edge away from Garm's unique aroma. All the angelii looked ill at ease, glancing apprehensively at Archer and Traggheim. Alyssum and I, being human, didn't get the same level of attention.

Archer stood up slowly, pulling at his ear-lobe, and I realised he wasn't entirely sure of himself.

'Thank you for joining us,' he said. 'I'm proud to say that Brother Jophiel and I have agreed we shall all work together to deal with the crisis facing us, and that bygones shall remain exactly that.'

I sneaked a look at Rillan and saw him staring fixedly at the ground.

Jophiel added, 'We're not accustomed to co-operating with demons, hags and others, but co-operate we shall.' He glared at each of the angelii in turn, resting his gaze on Rillan. So that was their cards marked.

Archer explained the strategy they had agreed to rescue Jamie and curb the Ælf-queen's growing power. First, Stent would mobilise his friends and followers from the city streets and either move stones back into place or replace them. 'Stent is certain they can meet the challenge and I have faith in his ability to lead them to success.' Archer glance round, checking for dissent.

'The Picts really went to town on the original stones – they had something to celebrate. They are mostly grander than necessary, so smaller carved stones can replace the ones which have disappeared over the years. We've worked out the patterns required and Stent knows someone who can carve them.'

Jophiel cleared his throat. 'The angelii will make a full-throttle approach to the stronghold where the ælves are holding their victim. Our aim is to distract them sufficiently to allow the demon Archer to rescue their hostage.'

'Do we know yet what it is they want?' asked Traggheim. 'We know they want what Drew has, but they haven't made contact, have they?'

'The quicker we act, the better the likelihood of catching them off-guard,' said Archer. 'We won't wait for them to act.'

As I thought about the plan and the unprecedented co-operation between Archer and the angelii, I felt a twinge of guilt at not playing my part, but hopefully I could lend a hand when the time came.

The day dragged slowly, with no sign of life in the ruin. Figuring that I was going to be there for some time, I set about quietly collecting material to make my vantage-point more secure and better camouflaged.

Suddenly, something changed. At first I couldn't work out what, then I put my finger on it. All the small sounds had stopped, birds were no longer singing and now there was simply silence. I watched carefully. In my hand, the werigend grew warm, and I felt the slight vibration of the gears and workings within it beginning to move. Then I sensed it – a hint of galdr. But it wasn't the galdr I was used to. I could almost taste a difference in it – a sort of earthiness, in some ways like the smell of a newly-dug garden. This must be ælf-galdr. I hadn't been able to sense it when I saw the ælves in the medieval clearing, presumably because I hadn't really been there, although the Ælf-queen had certainly sensed me. I focussed hard on the galdr and a fast-moving, shimmering light faded in on the track. Within it, two tall figures loped along and I recognised them as ælves as they disappeared through the shattered doorway of the old ruin.

I was both excited and dejected in equal measure. I now knew that with some effort I could see the ælves, despite their galdr-cloak, but rescuing Jamie from this holdfast would be near impossible.

Over the ensuing hours, there was more movement of ælves in ones and twos, in and out of the castle. Perhaps this increased activity meant Stent's efforts to replace the stones were already having an impact. Surely it was too soon, though, and the angelii shouldn't be starting their assault yet either. I was sure the ælves would react to that in numbers and I wondered how many were in the Goblin Ha' itself.

'Arsewipe!'

I nearly died of shock at that one word, whispered into my left ear. I leapt back to see Archer crouched beside me, scowling.

'What the– How?' I gasped.

'You really thought you could sneak off and do some damage by yourself? You fool. Have you learned nothing from me?' he hissed.

I could only avoid his gaze.

'I ought to leave you to your fate and let the ælves take you to pieces – slowly. And believe me, they would.' He paused, then smiled that sardonic smile of his. 'You are so utterly predictable, Drew. Don't you think it was bloody obvious you'd do something like this? So much so that I simply built it into the plan.'

Now I didn't just feel a traitor, I felt a stupid one. 'How did you find me?' I asked.

'It's easy with the right help.' He turned to one side. 'Isn't it?'

An answering faint 'wuff' came from within a pile of twigs and leaf mould and a black nose poked out.

'I know you're good at this woodcraft stuff, Drew, but Garm's a lot better,' he whispered. 'Now, let's see what's going on, whilst I decide whether to grass you up to Alyssum.'

Archer and I sat in silence, watching the castle ruin and waiting for the ælves to make a move.

I glanced at my watch. 'Surely the angelii should've started their diversion by now. Why aren't we seeing any kind of response?'

'I don't know, but I don't like it. If the angelii have betrayed us...'

'I'm sure they haven't,' I interrupted. 'It cost them too much to meet with us and come to the library. They're committed now.'

He grunted. 'Is that your brain or your trousers speaking?'

It was my turn to grunt.

'Garm – see what you can find out,' whispered Archer. There was a slight rustling sound as the dog edged away through the leaf litter.

'Drew?' Archer said quietly. 'Would you really have given them the stone?'

I should have realised Archer would see through me. 'I don't honestly know. It's here in case I need it as a bargaining tool, but I'd have to be really desperate to give it up to them.'

'I'm glad to hear that from you.' He sighed. 'But these aren't straightforward decisions and I don't judge you. The stone is yours, you inherited it. I can't stop you from trying to exchange it for your friend. But...'

'It won't work. I've realised that,' I said.

'Hmm.'

A few minutes later, Garm returned. He and Archer stared at each other and I felt the warm tingle of the galdr as they communicated silently. Archer swore.

'What is it?' I asked. 'Has something happened to the angelii?'

'He says they are two short – Rillan and another aren't with them, but the rest are almost here. Sssh.'

I gripped the werigend tighter as I sensed the ælf-galdr again. Two groups of ælves, in quick succession, dashed into the ruin.

'What does that mean?' I asked Archer. 'Are they falling back on the castle?'

'Makes little sense. They haven't even resisted the angelii. We counted on the angelii being too weak to break through easily and more ælves being sent to reinforce a defensive line. They've fallen back without even making contact. Why draw the angelii back to their base? The Ælf-bitch is a better strategist than that.' His brow furrowed as he tried to make sense of it, then he kicked the log angrily. 'We're in trouble, Drew. They know what we're doing. It's the only explanation. Otherwise they'd try to knock out the angelii away from the ruin. This is a trap. They know we're coming.'

As Archer spoke, I felt a burst of ælf-galdr hit me, like a powerful gust of wind. Alarmed, I looked at Archer, who was slowly standing up, staring towards the castle. I followed his gaze and was horrified to see the Ælf-queen and about twenty of her followers moving down the slope towards us.

The Ælf-queen exuded an overwhelming confidence, but whether this was because she had the advantage or because it was her nature, I wasn't sure. Either way, it was unnerving. She stopped and raised a hand, signalling her retainers to spread out behind her.

'Aaah-churr,' she called out, in her peculiar singsong voice. 'I know you are here. Sshow yoursssself.' Her speech, heavily accented and drawn out, was difficult to understand.

Archer stepped forward. I stood up as well, but Garm growled softly and stayed down amongst the leaf-litter.

'I see you, Aaah-chur.' She spat noisily and deliberately on the ground. 'And you ass well, child of your forebearss.' She stared at me and it felt like her eyes were boring holes through me. She gestured suddenly then, and her retainers parted to reveal Jamie, hanging lifelessly from the arms of the two of them.

Archer stepped sideways, to block me from doing anything stupid.

At another gesture from the queen, the retainers threw Jamie to the ground. He lay there, unmoving.

'I have hiss soul. Return what wass stolen.' My jaw dropped as I realised what she was saying.

A noise beyond them drew everyone's eyes as Jophiel, Ashnil and two other angelii deliberately moved into sight, their pale-yellow glow evident.

The Ælf-queen laughed in delight. 'Angels! You are too late. Much too late.' A flash of brilliant white light, like a nuclear explosion, obscured everything and for a few seconds I could see nothing.

Archer swore, and I dropped to the ground, still unable to see anything and expecting an attack of some sort.

As my sight wavered, I saw Archer looking down at me. 'You can get up. The bastards have gone.'

As my eyesight returned to normal, I could see he was right, but Jamie was still there, like a broken doll on the ground. Ashnil and the other angelii were running towards him.

I galloped up the slope to my friend, slipping and tripping in my haste. When I got there, he was lying in Jophiel's arms. His eyes were open, but they were unfocused and he was unresponsive.

'I'm sorry, Drew. She was telling the truth,' said Ashnil. 'Your friend isn't here, it's only his body.'

23. BLOODCAP

At Alyssum's insistence, we took Jamie to her shop. 'I'll have access to everything I might need to help him,' she said. 'But I can tell you now, Drew, it won't be enough.' She squeezed my hand. 'I can heal his body – repair the awful things they did to him – but you must accept I can't bring back his soul.'

'So he'll die?'

'Not as such. It's a bit like a coma. He'll be able to breathe and to eat and drink with help. But he's like a house with nobody home: the heating will still work, but there's nothing going on inside. I'm sorry, Drew.'

I could hardly believe what had happened to Jamie because of me. He didn't deserve any of this.

Alyssum threw me out so she could work on Jamie unhindered. I knew Archer and Traggheim were at Traggheim's shop, so I went there. If anyone knew what to do, surely it would be them?

I found them working their way through a bottle of eighty-year-old whisky which Archer had unearthed from somewhere, and I collapsed into a chair to join them.

'I know what you're going to say, Drew.' Archer splashed a substantial measure into a glass for me. 'There's nothing to be done that I know of. The Ælf-bitch has bound his soul into a vessel of some kind, which she'll be keeping close.'

'So, although he's with us, she can still continue to torture him to her heart's content,' I said bitterly, taking a deep slug of the whisky without really tasting it.

'Actually, no. Without a body, there is no way she can interact with him, so to him it will be as though he's in a deep sleep. He's saved further torture, at least.' Archer shrugged.

I turned to Traggheim. 'Surely there's some kind of machine you could make?' I waved at the collection of instruments gently ticking and whirring on the shelves beside us. 'You're an expert in galdr engineering. If anyone can do it, you can.' But I already knew what his answer would be.

Traggheim spread his hands in resignation. 'Don't you think that if I could do something, I'd already be in my workshop?' He looked more dejected than I had ever seen him. 'If we had the vessel, then perhaps something could be done – though that would be more in Archer's line of work than in mine. But the Ælf-queen has it in her fastness.'

'Not only do we not know exactly where that is,' said Archer. 'But the level of defence it will have is massive, so stealing it away from her would be incredibly hard.'

'We must do something,' I insisted. 'I have the carved stone to give her in exchange. Once Stent has the Pictish stones back in place, that will keep her down, surely?'

'I hope so,' said Archer. 'But to hand her back more power would be foolish, when the fate of many could be involved. We treat that as a last resort.'

'Surely we've reached the last resort?' I said.

'Possibly. It will be weeks before Stent's work is complete.'

'I'm going to go and help,' I said. 'At least I can do that

much for Jamie.' We fell into silence for a while, each of us staring into our glasses, reflecting.

Suddenly, a loud knocking on the front door made us all jump.

'Who the hell's that?' said Archer.

I got up and answered the knock. Ashnil stood on the doorstep, wearing the formal white robes I had seen her in at the museum, and it was obvious she had been crying. To my surprise, she fell into my arms.

'Ashnil, what is it?' I asked, as she folded her arms round me, her head against my chest.

I'd never seen her vulnerable like this, but after a moment she sniffed and pulled away, wiping her face. 'Is Archer here? I need to talk to him. And to you too.'

Upstairs, Traggheim leapt to his feet when he saw Ashnil. Acting the perfect host, he ushered her to a seat and poured a drink.

Ashnil took a gulp of the whisky, grimaced, then looked straight at Archer.

'What has happened now?' he asked grimly.

'Jophiel has cast out Rillan.' She gulped. 'That's how the Ælf-queen knew to expect us at Yester. Rillan betrayed us to her.'

I was gobsmacked. 'Why on earth would he do that? An angelus betraying us to them? It makes no sense!'

'Actually, I think it does,' said Archer slowly. 'Rillan opposed the alliance, didn't he? Is that what made him do this?'

She nodded, tears rolling down her cheeks. 'He and Jophiel had a huge argument about the alliance. He refused to accept that we should combine forces.' She sniffed and Archer handed her a large, burgundy-silk handkerchief. She accepted it daintily and blew her nose. 'Jophiel forced him to agree to accept his authority – him and Eleleth, who supported Rillan. They didn't come to Yester, and when we returned, Jophiel confronted them. They admitted passing word to the ælves. Rillan said we wouldn't have achieved any more than we did, anyway.'

'In that, he may have been correct,' muttered Traggheim.

'So Jophiel has cast them out?' I asked. 'What does that mean in practice?'

Ashnil's eyes widened, and she chewed at her lip before answering. 'It's terrible, Drew. There was a vicious and humiliating ceremony where they were stripped of their powers and rights, then physically beaten and thrown into the gutter.'

'I'd say they got what they deserve.' I glanced at Archer, who got to his feet and stared out of the window.

Then he turned. 'They deserved worse, much worse, than that. But justice isn't the actual issue here. Rillan and his sidekick are now out there, with hearts filled with hatred and heads filled with vengeance.'

'They've lost their powers,' I pointed out.

'Their powers were feeble to begin with, but there are others out there who will gladly help them restore and develop them for the right price.' He scratched his head and scowled. 'Two more aglæcan to be watched out for.'

'Rillan's not an aglæcan,' protested Ashnil.

'He is now,' said Archer. 'Your master just made him one, him and his sidekick.'

Traggheim leaned across the table and put his big, scarred hand on Ashnil's tiny white one, concern in his eyes. 'Ashnil,' he said, gently. 'Just who was Rillan to you? Personally?'

She wept again. 'That's just it – I don't know. I truly don't know.' She wiped her eyes again with Archer's handkerchief. 'Part of me is glad he's gone, because I didn't like him. He's arrogant and selfish and he has fixed and old-fashioned views. He's the opposite of who I try to be.'

'And the other part of you?' asked Traggheim. 'Was Rillan chosen?'

She nodded, dissolving into tears again.

I looked at Archer, catching him rolling his eyes.

After my first proper encounter with the angelii at the galdr-moot I'd spent some time in the library, attempting to speed-read a massive, turgid book called "Engel Lore", which explained in mind-numbing detail all that was known about angelii in 1872.

It seems they live in close association with organised religion, from which they can extract much of their galdr. The reformation and the sixteenth-century rise of Protestantism had fuelled their growth. The change from worshipping as instructed to vernacular bible-reading and religious teaching brought with it a change from superstition to fervent belief, generating galdr they could use. According to Archer, the twentieth century rise in what he referred to as "happy-clappy-ism" had further aided the angelii by providing a fertile ground for them to operate.

Archer had led me to think of the angelii as parasites, drawing their power from the passion of people's beliefs, but "Engel Lore" showed a different side – that the angelii didn't harm or debilitate anyone but tried to use their galdr-powers to protect people from aglæcan.

The chapter on the reproduction of angelii had struck me as thoroughly strange. As human-linked galdr-folc, they can have children with humans, though the progeny will be prone to galdr and usually end up entangled in the parallel realm. But for new angelii to be born required two angelii from different backgrounds to be brought together formally – a sort of arranged marriage between strangers, except it was less a marriage and more of a merger – and their souls combined to become one, sharing two bodies. No wonder Ashnil was so upset and confused. She'd lost her fiancé, but a fiancé she didn't like, didn't get on with and for whom sharing her body would have become a very literal thing.

I realised Ashnil was looking at me. She gently pulled her hand from Traggheim's, smiling wanly at the old dweorg as she did so. 'I'm so sorry that we have betrayed you, Drew.'

'You didn't betray us, Rillan did,' I said. Then a thought struck me and I looked at Archer. 'You're remarkably sanguine about this. Why aren't you crashing about, blaming the angelii for all the world's woes and threatening to find Rillan and tie knots in his entrails?'

Archer glowered at me for a moment, and I heard Traggheim snort. Then he grinned. 'I appreciate your concern, Drew. I'm a little surprised myself. But recent events have shown me that being intransigent doesn't help us. Don't get me wrong, I still think angelii are irritating, piss-yellow wimps...' He broke off and smiled at Ashnil. 'Present company excepted, of course. But perhaps when aglæcan are knocking at the door I should accept that they can be *our* irritating, piss-yellow wimps.'

I looked at Ashnil. 'I'd accept that – it's as good as you'll get from him.'

She giggled. 'With Rillan's poison out of the way, we might see daemons as allies and not as overbearing, intolerant, smug, sledge-hammer to-crack-a-nut thugs.' She smiled sweetly at Archer, and Traggheim coughed loudly, to cover what I'm sure was a laugh.

Archer stared at her momentarily before breaking into a grin. 'Touché,' he said.

A commotion outside interrupted us.

'Hell's bells,' said Archer. 'Can't a daemon enjoy a well-earned drink without constant interruption?'

He recalled Ashnil and apologised, but she just grinned at him.

The noise grew louder, resolving into shouts and curses, interspersed with barking and growling.

'On second thoughts, this is exactly what I want.' Archer jumped to his feet and rushed out of the room.

I looked at Traggheim, who shrugged. 'Anything is possible with Archer.'

A moment later he was back, pushing in front of him a dishevelled, stout old man. Garm was nipping at his heels.

'Thank you, Garm. There's a time when duty become devilment,' said Archer, nudging the dog with his foot. 'That moment is now.' Garm sat back on his haunches, looking disappointed.

'What the bloody hell is this?' demanded the old man, glaring round aggressively. 'Yer mutt should be locked away.' He was a curious-looking character. I'd have put his age at well over seventy, yet he was vigorous. At about five feet tall, he was dwarfed by Archer standing over him, and dressed as I imagine a Victorian mole-catcher might, with the addition of a shapeless red-brown felt hat, which made him resemble a garden gnome which had deteriorated a bit.

Archer bowed formally to the little man. 'Please accept my apologies for my method of achieving your company. Garm lacks subtlety, but he is quick and effective. I am Archer.'

The little man's eyes opened wide, his anger vanishing. 'Archer, ye say? The daemon?'

Archer nodded.

'Then let me shake yer hand, sir!' He pumped Archer's hand vigorously, beaming at him. 'Where's me manners? Me name's Harkin. Harkin Red.'

Traggheim stood up and bowed. 'Harkin Red, I am Grosscott von Traggheim and I welcome you to my premises. Please be seated whilst I pour you a drink.' Traggheim clearly had no more idea than I did what this odd man was doing in his shop, but he would not let that impede good manners.

Archer looked at him, embarrassed. 'Apologies, old friend. It made sense to ask Garm to bring Harkin here once he found him.' He introduced Ashnil and me and then explained. 'It was through the offices of Harkin here that Jophiel discovered it was Yester Castle the ælves were using to hold Jamie Renton. They needed a forward base and Yester was it.'

'Bastards.' Harkin spat. 'Begging your pardon, miss.' He winked conspiratorially at Ashnil. 'Those ælves threw me out of my home.'

'Harkin is a Bloodcap, a red cap,' said Archer to the rest of us. 'Like all his kind, he dwells in a ruined castle and guards it.'

'Not that I guarded it well from them ælves.' Harkin growled. 'A poor day for me.'

'No fault of yours, Harkin,' soothed Archer, and I wondered what he was up to.

'Red cap?' said Traggheim. 'Is it true–'

'No,' snapped Harkin. 'I don't dip my cap in the blood of my victims. I don't *have* victims, 'cept the odd mouse or rat. The hat's a tradition, that's all.'

Archer coughed. 'I'm glad you're here, Harkin. I hope you can help us.'

'Help the daemon who cleared out them ælves back in the day? You can be sure I will.'

'I was hoping you could tell us what you saw of the ælves. Perhaps you can help us understand better what they are doing. You know, the Ælf-queen deprived our friend of his soul?'

'Aye – that I do.'

'When you were in her captivity, before she threw you out of the castle, what did you see of her and her retainers?' asked Archer.

'I was tied up in my own castle. Trussed up like a piglet for market, they had me. But I've eyes in my head and I saw what went on. She's a nasty piece of work, that queen of theirs. Not regular nasty, she's got a whole special sort of nasty all to herself.'

'We've seen that for ourselves,' said Ashnil, drily.

'You mean that lad? That was an awful thing to happen to anyone. Even the other ælves are sorely afraid of her.'

'The Ælf-queen?' I asked.

'Yes, that's her. Taller than the rest, with eyes that burn like the coldest ice and a heart to match. I reckon they'd turn against her if they dared, but they daren't. She has more power than the others put together and gives herself no limits.'

'Did anyone else come to the castle?' asked Archer.

'Only one that I saw – and that was curious. Not what you'd expect, even for those ælves, who are a long way from civilised, by any measure.'

'Who was the visitor?' I prompted, getting a sense that Harkin enjoyed the sound of his own voice.

'A vixen. A mangy-looking one at that.'

'A fox?' asked Tragghcim.

'Yes, a fox, but not a well-fed Yester fox, living off the fat of the land. I reckon this animal was a city fox, used to eating rubbish and taking the knocks of life in a busy place. Shifty and furtive she was, even for a fox. And she spoke.'

'Spoke?' I exclaimed, louder than I'd intended.

'That's what I said – she spoke. She and that Ælf-queen spoke long into the night. But I can't say what they were talking about, seeing as I don't know the ælvish tongue.'

We all exhaled at once, realising we would not get details of the conversation. If only this had happened after

Traggheim built the Hólmganga, Alyssum could have translated the entire conversation for us.

'Strange name too, for a fox, and a female one at that,' continued Harkin, unbothered by our reaction. 'Ob-something. Let me think for a moment.'

All colour suddenly drained from Archer's face. Traggheim had noticed it too.

'Archer?'

'Obadiah,' said Archer, slowly.

'That's it,' said Harkin, oblivious. 'Couldn't understand a word of their talk, but that queen, she greeted the fox by that name.'

'Oba-bloody-diah?' Archer spat. 'You're certain, Harkin? It couldn't be another name?'

'No, Archer, Obadiah is the name. I heard it as clearly as the dawn song of a Jenny Wren.'

'Oh, this just gets better and better.' Archer pushed his chair back from the table and started running his fingers through his dark hair.

'Who is Obadiah?' asked Ashnil. 'Why is a fox so important?'

'Only the worst person possible to gang up alongside the Ælf-bitch,' said Archer bitterly. 'The fox is a shell. He's using it to keep himself hidden.'

'So who is he?' Ashnil persisted, but Archer stood up and kicked his chair away violently. 'Fuck!' he shouted and stormed out of the room.

'I hope I didn't speak out of turn,' said Harkin, who had blithely missed all the signs leading up to Archer's explosion.

'I'm sure you haven't, Harkin,' said Ashnil, looking at Traggheim and I.

'This is the renegade daemon that you and Archer were talking about, isn't it?' I asked Traggheim.

'It is, and it's the worst possible news,' the dweorg replied. 'Don't worry about Archer. He'll be back, calmer, once he's broken something.' He looked thoughtful. 'Or challenged some poor drunk to a bare-knuckle fight.'

'What's so awful?' I asked. 'I get that a daemon on the other side unbalances things, but why is this so bad?'

Traggheim gave a grim smile. 'Drew, Ashnil, Harkin – Obadiah is not an ordinary daemon, if there is such a thing. He has used methods of building his powers that any right-thinking creature wouldn't consider for a moment, methods that transcend galdr-lore and are well beyond sane comprehension. He's a foe of immense stature, who hasn't been heard of for many years. We hoped he was gone forever, but…'

'Any good news?' I asked, in a doomed attempt to lighten the mood.

'Not really,' said Traggheim. 'You see, he and Archer have history together. With them it's very, very personal.'

24. FIERDWIC

There's something about terriers and cars. If they're on the outside, they want to chase and bark at them. If they're inside, they use it as a platform to bark at everyone else. Driving to Stent's camp, I had to cope with Garm, amusing himself by bouncing around, barking at every passing vehicle. Meanwhile, Harkin, sitting in the passenger seat, was fascinated by this strange and swift mode of transport, though he did stop short of calling it a horseless carriage. I suppose there isn't much call for transport when you live in a ruined castle in the woods. Whilst answering Harkin's extensive questions, I was privately considering Jamie's reaction to the impact Garm was having on his alleged classic car. If he ever recovered.

The worn plastic and faded-leather interior of the Carpy was a familiar experience, with a rather odd aroma, which Garm was not enhancing. But after weeks in the world of dusty dark wood, leather and brass-work that comprised Archer's library and Tragghéim's workshop, the familiarity was welcome. The car was Jamie's pride and joy and whenever I borrowed the old heap, you'd have thought he was lending me the latest executive model. With a pang of sorrow, I reflected that this time he couldn't do that.

I had pulled the fuse from the car's audio system, depriving me not only of a chance of decent music, but of sat-nav.

Eventually Garm got the dog stuff out of his system and, having worked out where the warm air emerged, curled up in the passenger footwell, heaving Harkin's feet aside to make space for himself. Archer had insisted Harkin join me for my expedition to help Stent, giving the impression he expected Harkin and Stent to keep me out of trouble. Long-winded he might be, but Harkin was stolid and reliable and, thinking he might be a useful ally in a tough spot, I didn't argue. Harkin himself seemed ready to do anything that Archer asked of him.

'There's a smell,' said Harkin now. 'Like nothing I know. It's clean and sweet. I like it.'

And there, I thought, is how mankind became enslaved to the modern world of chemicals and plastics. 'It's the stuff Jamie uses to clean the car.'

Harkin's gaze dodged from side to side, taking in the rapidly passing world. Until today, he'd thought cars were some sort of pimped cart or carriage and given them no thought. Now he was actually in one, he was having a ball.

'I'm surprised you can smell anything over the stench Garm gives off,' I went on. I was being polite – Harkin didn't exactly have the scent of a rosebush either, ruined castles being a bit lacking in the bathroom department. 'How long have you lived at Yester?' I asked him.

'Don't rightly know. Our life is different to yours, lad. We react to things happening. Sometimes I'm there, but not so as you might know about. Other times I'm there in body and soul. Time means different things to different galdr-folc.'

I tried to digest this. A life involving powering up and down like a laptop would presumably lead to time being stretched and compressed. I tried to think how else to measure the passage of time. 'The first people you saw, then – how were they dressed?'

He reflected. 'The first human folk were workmen robbing stones from the castle ruin. They dressed roughly. Practical-like.'

Not much help, I thought. Working clothes have always been simple and practical, untouched by fashions. 'Did you see anyone in charge?'

'There was a man who turned up on a white horse from time to time. Too high and mighty to lift a finger. He had a daft-looking, long and curly, hair-piece, a fine long deep red coat and silk stockings instead of leggings. That seems like last week to me, but I reckon it was some way back, in the way you see things.'

'Well, that sounds like the seventeenth century to me. I looked up Yester Castle. It was abandoned that century, so I guess it would make sense that they'd be taking the stone to build the new house.'

'Bastards. Destroying the place, they were. I did all I could to scare them away. It worked sometimes.'

It occurred to me that right there was the probable source of the "Goblin Ha'" legends. 'So that would make you about 350 years old, Harkin – if you were born about when the castle was abandoned?'

'Not born, lad. We form naturally. None of that messy stuff you humans do.' Harkin winked. I wondered how much human canoodling in the ruins he had witnessed over the years.

'Here's another question: you travelled to Edinburgh to see us–'

'Not that I had much choice!' Harkin glared briefly at Garm, snoring gently in the footwell.

'But are you not tied to the castle?'

He considered that carefully before replying. 'It's like an

itch. I belong to the castle and it belongs to me. When I'm there I feel settled, but when I leave there's a sort of feeling, dragging me back. The longer I'm away, the stronger it gets. Like when you really want a good smoke, but you've no 'baccy for your pipe. Eventually it gets to you, so you just have to do something about it.'

'Where on earth do you get tobacco from?'

He winked at me again. 'People visit the castle to stare at the ruins and scare themselves in the Goblin Ha'. They don't always take away what they bring with them, lad. Sometimes old Harkin relieves them of useful things like a bit of tobacco or some coin to buy it at the village shop.'

I visualised Harkin queuing up in the local "Happy Shopper", and realised there was much more to him than met the eye. 'Have you travelled far from the castle?'

'Now and again, I've been to look at what's out there. I know my way around the land of the saltire for certain, though maybe not the far north. Looked across the border in Northumberland too.' Harkin gazed around now, with interest. 'This is a place I've known before. I might know some people that might be of a help to us in what we need to do.'

I pressed him for more details, but he grunted something about resting when the chance came along, and settled back in his seat, pulling his cap over his eyes. Soon he was competing with Garm in a snoring contest.

Eventually, after a few false turns, we reached our goal. As ever, I was missing my iPhone. Harkin might have an itch dragging him back to Yester but I had an itch for some information technology. But when you can't use sat-nav, the Ordnance Survey is your friend, and after several wrong starts, I found the location Archer had given me, deep in the Pentland Hills.

The directions were to turn off beside an old stone bridge and follow a track for a few hundred yards (I'd persuaded Archer to stop referring to distances in furlongs, but I reckoned the metric system might be a step too far). Archer had assured me that Stent would be waiting for us. How Stent was to know when we arrived wasn't clear, and I hoped he didn't have to wait around too long.

We bounced up the track, with an occasional thud from the car floor, making me wince and worry about damaging the Carpy. A steel farm gate drunkenly blocked our way. It was chained and padlocked, as well as having a remarkable amount of hairy baler twine in several colours, tying it in place. As we couldn't go any further, I looked about, wondering how to seek out Stent, when I heard his voice behind me.

'How're you doing, Drew, pal?'

I spun round and narrowly avoided being floored by a massive slap on the back from Stent, who was grinning like a Cheshire cat to see me.

'You're a sight for sore eyes and nae mistake. And Garm, ya wee reprobate!' He bent down to pat Garm's flank, the only affection Garm was likely to tolerate without teeth becoming involved. 'And who's this?' he asked, as Harkin clambered awkwardly out of the passenger door.

I introduced them and watched, fascinated, as they did a kind of verbal square-dance, politely assessing each other's places in the parallel realm without giving too much away too soon. They reminded me of a couple of Ozzie backpackers meeting in Princes Street.

'So where's your camp, Stent?' I asked, not looking forward to reversing back down the track.

'Right here!' He beamed, waving at a patch of scrubby woodland beyond a ditch and dry stone dyke.

Harkin was ahead of me. 'That's a grand bit of enchantment, Stent,' he said.

I looked at Stent, who was laughing at my confusion, since I knew he had no galdr-skills.

'Traggheim worked one of his bits of mechanical magic for me.' He pulled a small cut glass bottle from his pocket and held it up. Inside I could see the plethora of tiny brass cogs, springs and levers that were Traggheim's trademark, all illuminated with a dull cherry-red glow.

'How the hell did he build it inside there?' I asked.

'Been asking masel' the same question. I think he does it just because he can, the old show-off.' Stent pressed down on a small plunger poking through the cork and the little mechanism started working. A moment later, the woodland briefly blurred and then came back into focus, to reveal a railway sleeper bridge across the ditch, wide and strong enough to drive the car into the clearing beyond.

'That's no' a bad trick, is it?' said Stent with pride. 'It shields us from galdr-folc, as well as regular people, so we've a secure and secret base to work from. Archer said we should call it a fierdwic. I think that's just a fancy name for a camp, though.'

We all piled into the car and I drove cautiously over what turned out to be a solid surface. As the clearing opened up, I was amazed at what I saw. Knowing Stent for a resourceful and practical man, I'd expected a well set-up camp-site, but not what lay in front of me. At the rear, a well-worn VW camper was parked up, a striped awning stretching across in front, and I guessed this was Stent's abode. Alongside was a semi-circle of six Arctic-standard tents, and in the centre a large fire-pit smouldered, warming enough rough-hewn benches to seat at least a dozen people comfortably. On the other side of the VW was a marquee, with a couple of propane cylinders outside, betraying its purpose as a kitchen. Felled timbers had been used to construct an open-fronted workshop, with a turf roof and walls on three sides made from what looked suspiciously like wattle-and-daub. Inside, two Asian men were hard at work, chipping at stones with mallets and chisels.

As we parked up and climbed out of the car, several other figures emerged from the tents.

Stent made the introductions. 'This is Jake the brick.' He indicated a wiry man with tousled sandy hair, who had just emerged. Jake shook my hand and damn near broke it, grinning as he did so.

'And that's why he's the brick,' said Stent, in what was obviously a regular party-piece. 'You'll maybe ken wee Jeannie?' He nodded towards a short, fat woman with eyes like bright-blue pebbles in a wrinkled face. They peeped out from under long mousy hair that was piled into an untidy bun. I looked at her for a moment before realisation dawned.

'There it is,' she said. 'Takes a moment to recognise folk away from where you know them. You always get your "Big Issue" from me.'

'What're you doing here?' I was astonished.

'Stent asked me,' she said simply. 'And when Stent asks, you know it matters, so here I am.' She turned to him. 'There's a big pot o' stew nearly ready and Hamza's got some bread on the go as well, so there'll be plenty.' To me she added, 'Hamza'll say hello when he's time – he takes his baking real serious and won't leave it 'til it's done, but his sourdough loaf is really something.'

'Cheers, Jeannie,' said Stent. 'Drew, these two are Jackie O and Jackie No.' He pointed at the two masons, who both wiped their hands on dusty aprons, before shaking hands shyly. 'You've never told me where you got those names, lads.' They had the burly figures and ready grins of Sri Lanka, so I guessed had probably found it easiest to adopt names Brits could pronounce. They both nodded and went straight back to their work, with the steady, economical movements of lifelong craftsmen.

'Bit shy,' whispered Stent. 'But brilliant masons. No' much call for it, though, not if your skin's the wrong colour and your English is rough round the edges. What kind of world is it where skilled people can end up on the streets?' He shook his head. 'The others'll be back later. Could you use a drink?'

He didn't have to ask twice. As we walked towards the camper, Jeannie came back out of the kitchen, whistled, and threw a massive bone in the air. Garm hurtled towards her and leapt up, catching it neatly, before dragging it under the camper.

With the kettle whistling on the gas hob, Stent set about telling us what he and his team had been doing, pausing only to pour three massive mugs of industrial-strength tea and put them on the fold-down table in front of us.

'It took a bit o' work to get this camp set up, but Archer gave me a bag of cash to buy gear and it's amazing what these guys can do when you give them a purpose and a sense o' worth.'

'Tramps?' asked Harkin.

Stent bristled, so I interrupted hastily and explained Harkin's background.

'A Bloodcap, eh? I'd heard of redcaps, but I didn't realise they were real. You'll be a handy lad to have around. These folks are off the city streets, Harkin. We live in an age that casts good people aside with no support, no money, and nowhere to live. I'm ok – Archer gives me work and whenever I can I pass it onto them. They're our eyes and ears on the streets and the money Archer gives me for them helps keep body and soul together.'

I listened intently. This was a new side of Archer for me.

'I won't hold wi' drugs, though. Drugs cloud the mind and mess with the memory. A wee drink's ok, but alcoholics are nae good either. I try to help those ones kick the drugs and booze if I can. Anyway, this lot've worked hard for me and, as you can see, we're well set up here.'

'Do any of the locals suspect anything?'

'The gamekeeper's been touched by the parallel realm and has seen enough of the ælves tae want tae help us. He's a good man and willnae give anything away. Traggheim's wee machine keeps us hidden fae casual dog-walkers and the like, as well as fae any aglaecan that come looking. By the way, Drew, Archer said you'd be able to recharge it with galdr. Said you've tae act like it's an ælf you want tae see implode. That'll do it, apparently.'

Nice to be trusted by Archer, I thought. 'I'll have a go at that later for you.'

He nodded. 'Aye, you'll be keen to know about what we've been up to.' He reached behind him for a rolled-up map, pushing our mugs aside to make room to unroll it. 'This map has all the stones marked on it. Red means it's gone, black is still there and yellow means we don't know and need to find out.'

I gawped at the map. It's well-known that Pictish carved stones are widespread, but the map showed hundreds upon hundreds. 'Where on earth do you start?'

'Aye, well, Archer gave me a list of priorities. Seems some of these stones are more powerful than others, so we're dealing with them first. The rest act as a kind of back-up. To strengthen the effect.'

'Surely people notice when you pitch up with a bloody great carved stone and start erecting it in their field?'

'Tactics, Drew, tactics. It's amazing what we can get away with if we wear Hi-Vis jackets, especially if I stroll about with a clipboard and do nothing. For the more obvious ones, we hae tae be canny – burying a stone at night is easy enough.'

'Won't people notice the disturbed ground?'

'They might, but burying a dead badger over the stone will gie their nosiness a bit o' discouragement.'

We all laughed at that. In the midst of everything, there was something comforting about Stent's confidence.

'What about the ælves? Any sign of them yet?'

'Now that's something I'll admit I'm nervous about. Eventually, they're going to notice the effect the stones are having on them and they'll maybe come looking, but so far, not a squeak from the nasty buggers.'

'Alyssum is keeping watch on the Hólmganga, whilst she's nursing Jamie. She'll get word to us if there's any sign of trouble.'

'How's the lad doing?' asked Stent.

My heart sank. 'She reckons he'll be physically fine, but unless someone comes up with a way of getting his soul back from the Ælf-queen, then he might as well be dead, for all he'll know about it,' I said bitterly.

There was a pause. 'Aye,' said Stent quietly. 'That's nae good.'

Harkin cleared his throat and looked at each of us. 'I've been thinking about how I might help. I want nothing but harm to the ælves, after what they did to me and my home. And what they did to your friend is just wrong. Anything you do that hurts them is good medicine by my measure and if you're setting up to put that queen of theirs back in her cage, that suits me just fine. I'm by your side through whatever comes.

'It seems to me you have two problems that maybe I can help you with, and I'd like to do just that. First, having the lass Alyssum watching the Ælf-queen from a distance is well and good and all power to her, but it's going to take time for her to get word to you here and that might be time you need. I said earlier I'd spent some time around here and I made some friends – good friends – folk who might watch for news that might warn us when the ælves are up to no good.'

Stent looked at me momentarily. 'That sounds good, Harkin. If Archer sent you, I'll trust you and your help's welcome tae me.'

I nodded. 'We'd be mad to turn it down. Thanks, Harkin. But what's the second thing?'

'Drew, lad.' He paused and looked at me searchingly. 'I know you probably think I'm just a Bloodcap – a narrow-minded, old-fashioned creature, forged in and tied to a ruin and lost in this world.' He held up a hand to stop my protests. 'It's not just how I seem, it's how I am, Drew. But old country galdr-folc know things and do things that keep us hidden and help us make our way in this modern world of yours.'

'Your friend Jamie – I feel a kind of kindred spirit with him. We were both imprisoned and tortured at Yester by that scum-washed harridan of a queen. So I'm determined to help recover his soul, and I think I know how it might be done.'

I knocked over my tea in my haste to ask for more details. As Stent and I mopped it up, before it damaged the map, Harkin explained.

'There's this woman I know. Lives in a hidden spot in the hills. Odd sort of woman for round here, but she's settled. I reckon if anyone knows how to get this Jamie's soul back, it's her. The Harbinger, she's called, because she has skills in prediction. If she has a real name, I've not heard her share it. She's powerful. Really powerful. I'd like to see if she'll help.'

'Harkin, that's fantastic,' I gushed, drunk on the news.

'The sooner the better.' I paused. 'That is, if you think I should come?'

'Haud on a minute!' cut in Stent. 'This sounds good, but how do we know she will not be on their side? And if she isn't, why should she risk poking the wasps' nest by helping us?'

'She walks her own path, that one. A rare one for that. She wouldn't help the ælves any more than she'd help Archer or anyone else. But she cares about what's right and what's wrong. If an ailing aglaecan turned up on her doorstep, she'd help it the same as she'd help us – if she believes help is needed and deserved. But take her for granted and hell mend you; she has a caring heart and anger like the fires of fury. You should come with me, Drew, because you're a direct link to your friend and your telling of the tale may persuade her to help.'

'Stent, I really think it's worth the risk,' I said to him.

'I cannae stop you, and I can see why you want to do this, but if this goes wrong, we might just end up with you two in the same boat as Jamie.' He shook his head, frowning. 'Or worse, if she gets her hands on that thingy in your pocket.'

'Harkin knows his way about and we'll take great care, Stent. But I don't think there's a choice, I have to try.' I turned to Harkin. 'It'll be dark soon. Better we leave in the morning?'

'I reckon so. And there's something else, Drew.'

'What?'

'She cooks food like you'll taste nowhere else. Even if she won't help, she'll feed us well!'

As the light faded, one of the two Jackies started a diesel generator, powering floodlights in the workshop so they could carry on working into the evening. I wandered over and asked if they minded me watching for a bit.

'No trouble,' said the nearest Jackie.

I watched as he gently tapped his chisel with a wooden mallet, slowly cutting along a curved line marked on the smooth surface of the stone. He was carving an intricate pattern of interlaced ribbons. Around it were some of the famous stylised Pictish animals; I recognised a dolphin and a dog, amongst others. Each stone had carvings which were important and added power to the stone, whilst others were deliberate distractions. Stent had showed me a massive leather-bound book, brought from Archer's library, containing the original patterns for all the stones, painstakingly inked by hand onto the parchment. The Jackies used this to trace from.

'Doesn't it bother you, having to use an English name instead of your own?' I asked. 'Would you rather we use your own name?'

He shrugged and grinned. 'You try? Real name Hewasandatchige Bandaratilleke.'

'He-was-sandat -' I stuttered and stopped.

He laughed long and loud. 'Life too short!' He handed me the mallet and chisel and nodded at the stone. 'You try it.'

I took them gingerly and gently tapped the chisel as he showed me, terrified of destroying his fine work.

'Stop being wimp – hit more,' he encouraged, his brother laughing in the background. I did as I was told and slowly made a little progress, following the line in the stone.

After a minute, he gently took the tools back from me. 'Good, but too slow for urgent work.' And he carried on working contentedly, making another stone to contain the ælves.

25. HARBINGER

We left early the next morning, taking with us a package of food thrust into my hands by Wee Jeannie.

'You be careful, both of you,' she said, concern showing on her face.

'We will, I promise. And thanks for this.' I pointed at the food.

'Aye well, Hamza likes to make plenty. He reckons people work better with full bellies, and he's right at that.' She leaned closer. 'I think he's sweet on me. At our ages!'

'You're as old as you feel, Jeannie, and you've enough energy for someone half your age.'

She giggled and pushed me away.

As we walked to the car, Harkin stopped and looked around at Stent's fierdwic. 'You've more experience than I do about people, Drew, but it seems to me these people are... what's the word? Energised. Don't you think?'

He was right. Stent was a charismatic leader, who cared deeply about the people who followed him, but I'd felt it too – a sense of common purpose, driven perhaps by being given a second chance.

I'd planned to leave Garm with Stent, which was foolish. Garm goes or stays where he chooses and he chose to accompany us. Some animated growling and bared teeth made that clear. As I opened the door of the Carpy, he hopped in and took up station, standing on the passenger arm-rest, with his head out of the open window.

We parked on a muddy patch off the road and I laced up my hiking boots. Harkin eyed them thoughtfully, comparing my Gore-Tex and synthetic fibre boots to his stout leather ones and his time-worn leggings. Whether he was envious or contemptuous was hard to judge, and he was too polite to say.

'This way.' He pointed to a birch-lined gully, winding steeply upwards and fading into the hill-mist above us. Despite his short stature, he had a steady, powerful gait, so I had to work hard to keep up with him. Garm, of course, bounded up the slope as though it didn't exist, sniffing and peeing freely as he went. We stepped from rock to boggy ground to tussock grass, as the gully zig-zagged upwards. It was good to get out in the fresh air of the hills. The peaty, mossy scent of the moor, combined with the cool, moist air as we ascended into the mist, created an otherworldly sense of seclusion and safety.

Suddenly Harkin grabbed my arm. 'Down,' he hissed, and we both dropped into shelter between a clump of bracken and a large rock. He nodded towards Garm, a short distance ahead. He was stretching, low to the ground, sniffing and baring his teeth.

'Not a word,' breathed Harkin in my ear. 'We aren't alone.'

I reached slowly into my pocket for the werigend and found the smooth, comforting warmth of the brass. To my surprise, it was already working. I could feel tiny movements of the mechanism through my finger-tips.

We lay rigid, listening for any hint of what had spooked Garm, whilst water seeped through my trousers from the mossy ground. Eventually the dog started edging forward, sniffing the air, before rising and trotting forward to a bend in the gully.

'A false alarm?' I asked quietly, but Garm turned and raised his lips momentarily, displaying his teeth in a simple message – whatever it was, he had definitely sensed something. So we edged our way up the gully, ready to drop into cover at the first sign of trouble, letting Garm warily lead the way.

Harkin mouthed, 'Ælves?' and I shrugged. We knew we were in ælvish territory – the danger of running into them was something we'd discussed the night before. The warmth of the camp-fire and the companionship of Stent's crew now seemed a long way off. What if there were ælves? What else could be out there? There were aglaecan I still knew little about. I gripped the werigend tightly and hoped the wyrm would feel helpful.

We crept on slowly for what seemed like hours. Gradually the terrain changed as the gully shallowed and the birches gave way to stunted rowans and bracken gave way to heather.

We stopped to catch our breath and Garm crept ahead to scout, giving us a disdainful look as he did so.

Harkin murmured in my ear. 'I wish we could see further than this wretched mist allows, but with luck, it may mask any sound we make.'

'Or that anyone else makes,' I added glumly.

He nodded towards the rowan I was leaning against. 'Do you know the power of the rowan? The witch-tree? It wards off evil if you keep it close–' He started. 'What was that?' And looked wildly around. The mist made it hard to judge where the sound had come from, but I'd heard it too: the hard thwack of an impact.

We stood, straining to hear, and wishing Garm was still beside us. Then, from ahead, a scream pierced the mist, followed by an explosion of growling and ripping sounds. We ran towards the sound and an incredible sight came into view: Garm, who seemed to have grown larger and more muscular, held an ælf on the ground, gripping it by the throat and shaking it like a rag-doll, as the ælf screamed again and again. Garm had a lime-green arrow protruding from his rump and blood streaked down his leg. Three more arrows whistled past Harkin and me, one of them lodging deep into my rucksack. In the mist, I could see the dim figures of two more ælves, one of them aiming an arrow at the dog.

'Garm!' I shouted. He looked up, saw the danger, and jumped back. The ælf on the ground dragged himself upright and staggered toward his companions, who kept up a covering fire of arrows, whilst we took shelter behind a shallow rock.

The clink of a loose stone made me look behind us and, to my horror, two more ælves were looming in the mist. 'Shit, we're surrounded, Harkin,' I shouted, pressing myself lower.

Harkin rolled around the rock to gain the cover of a crease in the ground. As he rolled, he pulled something from his jerkin pocket and I saw it was a slim wooden tube, which he put to his lips. With a loud hiss, he blew some kind of projectile at the new ælves. Whatever it was, they didn't like it and both dropped into cover. As Harkin reloaded his blow-pipe and fired again, I turned my attention to the original ælves, who were keeping up a steady rate of fire, now they'd hauled their injured comrade into cover.

I glanced over my shoulder and could see Harkin was keeping his two ælves' heads down, so I focussed on the group in front. In my hand I felt the werigend whirring and I pushed up a galdr-shield. The first couple of arrows plink-ed off it and fell to the ground, but maintaining it against a galdr-rich foe was taking too much energy. I needed to be proactive if we were to get out of this. I released the shield and concentrated as hard as I could to create a beam of galdr and project it forward. A brilliant yellow light shot from my hand, making the mist sizzle, but it faded before it was more than half-way towards them. Their response was a cackling laugh and two more arrows, which thwacked into the ground beside me, too close for comfort.

I seemed to hear Archer's voice in my head, reminding me of the days on Arthur's Seat, working on my galdr-skills. 'Stop arsing about, trying to be clever. Do what you know and do it well.' *Do what you know.* Holding the werigend tight in one hand, I pressed my knee against the gnarled root of a rowan and threw a ball of blue fire at the ælves. That got their attention, smug bastards. Whether it was the rowan, the werigend, or just sticking to what I knew how to do, wasn't clear, but it was working. I followed up with another, then a third with a tidy left-hand curve, which produced a satisfying scream of anger.

'Good shot, Drew,' called Harkin, reloading his blow-pipe with what looked like a dart. He rolled onto his belly to get a better aim and a moment later, another scream told us he'd hit his mark. 'Where's Garm?' he asked, sliding another dart into the blow-pipe.

I looked around and saw him crawling towards us, panting, the arrow still in his rump. He seemed to have reverted to normal. 'Got him,' I said to Harkin, pulling his little body towards me.

'Right, I reckon if we give both groups a scorching at once, we can retreat west.'

'Which way's west?'

'That way.' He waved to the side. 'Do your fire thing, Drew.'

I did as I was bid and threw three balls of blue fire in quick succession at the ælves, but they seemed to have gone to ground. Beside me, I heard a couple of hisses as Harkin gave his pair a parting gift.

'Go.' He panted, leaping up and zig-zagging through the heather. I hoisted Garm under my arm and followed suit. Thankfully, the ælves didn't follow.

Harkin and I staggered to a halt and collapsed into deep heather. The wiry growth was surprisingly comfortable and kept us off the damp ground whilst we regained our breath. I could feel Garm's warm body inside my jacket.

'I think we've lost them,' I said.

'That's not all we've lost,' said Harkin, as Garm's nose forced its way out of my jacket. 'I've no notion of where we are and less idea of how to find our way in this damned mist.'

I lifted Garm out and checked him over. The arrow seemed to have caused a flesh wound only, but he bared his teeth as I gently touched it.

'Leave it be,' said Harkin. 'The Harbinger's the best one to deal with that. If we ever find her,' he added.

Garm growled softly and pushed out of my arms. He stretched experimentally, whimpered as his muscles tensed around the arrow, then took a few steps and scented the air. He turned and tried a different direction, then a third, the fur on his forehead furrowing.

'I don't think he'll gain a scent in this moist air,' Harkin said.

'I've learned there's more to Garm than either of us understands,' I said. 'If he gives us a direction, I'm for following it.'

Garm turned and stared at me. Then he set off through the heather, limping as he went. We got to our feet stiffly and followed, fearful of losing him in the mist. How Garm found his way, I do not know. For all I know he could have been leading us in circles, but I didn't think so. His stamina was astonishing. At one point I offered to carry him again, but a curl of his lips showed his dignity had already been sufficiently compromised.

After about an hour of slogging through the wet heather, a faint light glowed through the haze, rapidly resolving into a warm glow from the windows of a small, white-painted cottage, nestled in a fold of land.

I was cold and hungry, so the thought of a warm fire and the Harbinger's famous cooking made me pick up the pace a little.

Harkin grabbed my arm and muttered, 'Remember what I said about her. She's not on our side – she's on nobody's side. She'll only help if she thinks we deserve help. So be cautious of what you say.'

26. STANLEY

Ahead of us the cottage door was open, an elegant black woman in the doorway. She wore a green and blue scarf around her hair, and her arms were folded under a substantial chest.

'Waal, look who we have here,' she said in a voice that sounded like molten honey. 'Harkin the Bloodcap, I not seein' for a long time. And you brought friends.' She gave me a broad smile, but when she looked at Garm, it was a slight bow.

'Come in, come in. Tell me your news and your woes and the Harbinger will do what she may to make 'em better.'

She ushered us through the door and I stopped in my tracks, astonished. I whirled round to look back through the door and saw the misty heather outside. But we weren't in a Scottish cottage, it was a palatial Caribbean house. Tall, salmon-pink walls had contrasting sky-blue fret-work. Large windows had half-closed louvre shutters through which I glimpsed palm trees beyond a balcony outside. We were in an entrance hall, with doors off to several other rooms. Intricately painted bannisters enclosed stairs around two sides and led to an impossible upper storey.

I realised the Harbinger was laughing at me and I

apologised. 'I've never seen anything like this.'

She closed the door behind me and shook her head. 'Oh, but you have. This is jus' a bigger and better version of Archer's library, Mr Macleod. I jus' do it with much more style than he.'

I wondered how she knew who I was, but anyone who could create this paradise inside a tiny cottage had a lot of power and she clearly wasn't called the Harbinger for nothing.

She led us into a room furnished with comfortable-looking cane furniture. As we sat down, the sound of birdsong drifted in through the window. The air was still and sultry, and I rapidly set down my rucksack and peeled off a couple of layers.

'I find a Haitian climate conducive to shakin' off the cold of the Scottish winter,' she explained. Her eyes fell on my fallen rucksack and she plucked the ælvish arrow from it, frowning. 'I heard you boys'd been getting into some trouble on my hill. First thing we mus' do is fix his wound.' She knelt beside Garm and asked formally. 'May I?' Garm, who must have been exhausted, fell into her arms. She gently lifted him and carried him out, saying as she went, 'I'll return shortly. You two relax meantime.'

'This is incredible, Harkin,' I said, gazing around us.

'It is. She's powerful – never doubt that.'

The door creaked open and a teenage girl came in backwards, expertly nudging the door with her hip. As she turned, we could see she was carrying a silver tray with glasses and a pitcher of something that clinked with the movement. She wore a dress the colour of sunshine and had braids that swayed as she bent to put the tray on the table. She gave us a shy smile and poured two glasses. 'This is Mamma's fruit cordial, made to her recipe,' she said. 'It's real good.'

We thanked her, and she flashed us another smile. 'This is Mamma Harbinger's home. We're happy to have you visit us,' she said, before leaving us.

The cordial was incredible. I could detect hints of papaya and pineapple, with a remarkable depth of flavour and something warming too. I stopped and put the drink down. 'She wouldn't drug us, would she?'

Harkin laughed. 'I'm sure she could – and many would. But not the Harbinger.'

She had either re-entered the room noiselessly or had somehow materialised beside me. Either way, I jumped when she spoke.

'Your caution does you credit, Mr Macleod. You've entered a world where you must have your wits about you. But Harkin tells the trut'. Nothin' will harm you here.'

I felt myself turning red, but she laid her large hand gently on my arm and the depth of her smile seemed to make an apology superfluous.

'Your friend is resting in comfort. I took the arrow out an' bound his wound. It was in the flesh only – he gon' be fine. Now we mus' address your troubles, Mr Macleod. May I call you Drew? I tink we're gonna get to know one another.'

'Sure,' I said. 'What should I call you?'

'Those who get to know me call me Mamma. If you're fine wit' that, so am I.' She didn't wait for an answer. 'The ælves, Drew. What do you tink about 'em?'

'Their queen has a long-term grudge against me and has done something terrible to my friend. That's why we've come to you.' In the background, I saw Harkin wince.

'I know all about dat. Is not the question I ask you? What do you tink about the ælves? Not their queen. Them – all of them.'

My response could be my one chance to recover Jamie's soul, and I pondered. 'They follow their queen, but I don't know if that's from choice or repression.' I thought for a moment. 'It wouldn't surprise me, from what I know of the Ælf-queen if they have no choice but to follow her bidding. To be honest, I don't know what to think of them as a race. As a culture, they have been cruel and destructive over many centuries, but I can't truthfully answer your question without knowing more. I won't judge anyone without evidence – that would surely be wrong.' I was flannelling, but I hoped my woolly answer would dig me out of the hole Mamma Harbinger had dug for me.

She stared searchingly at me before nodding. 'Good enough. There's someone I want you to meet.' She took me firmly by hand and led me towards the door. Despite being a big woman, her movements were graceful and distinguished.

Harkin got up, but she stopped him with a sharp, 'No!' Then, more gently, she said, 'This is sometin' for Drew alone, Harkin.'

She led me upstairs and along a corridor, the wooden floor creaking under our feet. Vases of exotic flowers released a powerful fragrance, overlaying the smell of wax polish. At the end of the corridor, she opened a door and ushered me in before her.

The shutters were closed, so it took a few seconds for my eyes to adjust to the gloom. It was a bedroom, furnished with solid oak furniture and a massive bed, with a cheerful patchwork counterpane. A tall figure lay on it and I stepped back in shock as I realised it was an ælf. He was still and in the dim light filtering through the shutters I could see there was a sheen of sweat on his face. Bandages covered his leg, shoulder and neck.

I looked at the Harbinger.

'I give you your wish, Drew,' she whispered. 'You may find out some trut' about ælves.' Closing the door behind her, she left me alone with the ælf.

His eyes flickered, then opened wide in alarm as he saw me.

'It's ok,' I said. 'I won't hurt you.' I stood awkwardly beside the bed, unsure what to do next. 'Do you understand me when I speak?' I asked.

The ælf nodded and cleared his throat painfully. 'I sspeak your tongue.' His eyes flickered nervously towards the door, probably hoping Mamma Harbinger would return and save him.

I sat on the edge of the bed, trying to look less threatening. I thought rapidly. Was this why Harkin had brought me here? Did he know there'd be ælves and maybe help could be had from that quarter? No, Harkin couldn't have known the injured ælf would be here. Mamma Harbinger was testing me.

'You were on the moor?' asked the ælf. 'You and the dog and the Bloodcap?'

I realised this was one of the ælves we'd tangled with earlier. 'Did I hurt you?'

He nodded. 'But it wass war. We wanted to hurt you, alsso.'

'Why did you attack us?' I asked. 'Did you know we'd be there?'

He shook his head weakly. 'We were patrolling and came acrosss you. Been told to look out for you. We missjudged your abilities.' He moved slightly and gasped. His eyes moved to a glass of water on the nightstand.

'Do you want a drink?' I asked.

He nodded, so I lifted his head carefully, put the glass to his lips and helped him sip, struggling to believe what I was doing.

'Thank you,' he said.

'Why were you looking for us?' I asked.

'Our queen wantss you. We hoped to capture you for

her, perhapss win her favour.' He looked away, then fixed me with his eyes. 'Our queen wantss something you have – but she musst not have it.'

I must have looked bemused because he went on.

'She iss old and no longer thinkss ass she should. Many of uss wish a better life, but she iss ssingle-minded and bitter. Thinkss of nothing but vengeance and ressurgence.'

'Surely if she regained the stone, the ælves could become great again. Don't you want that?'

He shook his head. 'Where would it finish? Never-ending war? No, I don't wish for that.' He paused. 'If I ever leave here.' He gasped.

I picked up a cloth from the night-stand and gently dabbed the sweat from his forehead. I hated that we had done this to him. At that moment, I hated myself. 'Tell me about your home,' I asked.

He told me haltingly about his life. The ælves were very different to us, with a social structure more like a bee-hive, and I saw how that gave the queen vast power.

'Our life wass peaceful and simple until the queen changed thingss. Our way is to help each other and work together to make the best for uss all and for the good of the earth.' He frowned at me. 'We don't harm our home like you do.'

'You make your people sound perfect. I know we have many weaknesses, but cruelty isn't often one of them.'

He looked sad. 'That iss not a thing I feel proud of. Some of uss hope for better, but our queen hass grown ambitiouss. She iss the worst of our people, when we would wish for her to be the finest. She twistss human minds to her purpose and seekss for ways to overcome the carved stones that limit uss.'

'My closest friend was tortured by your queen for no good reason,' I said. 'How can you pretend you're all sweetness and light with just a poor leader? Ælves use and abuse people and you don't give cruelty a second thought!'

His eyes flashed for a moment, then he seemed to diminish. 'Cruelty and manipulation have been our way, but we may change if we can rid ourselvess of her. There are other ways for you to see uss.'

'Such as?' I asked.

'We have poetry like your kind can only dream of. Our art and literature are far beyond yours. We co-operate and love one another in ways you could never understand. Only the queen can breed, so we are free of the need to compete and work against each other like you do. Pleasse, pleasse do not judge uss unfairly. People like you are our only hope.'

After a time, he drifted off to sleep. I sat on, watching his chest lift and fall with his shallow breaths.

Eventually I felt Mamma Harbinger's hand on my shoulder and looked up, tears welling in my eyes. She led me out of the room and outside, pulled me against her briefly, murmuring in my ear. 'You have a true heart.'

As we walked down the stairs, I realised I didn't know the ælf's name.

Mamma Harbinger smiled sadly when I asked her. 'Ælves don' have names. Don' ask how they know one from another between themselves, but somehow they do. I bin callin' him Stanley, jus' to make sense of it.'

She ushered me into the dining room, where we found Harkin seated at an enormous oval table, waiting for us. He leapt to his feet, but Mamma Harbinger waved him back down.

'You mus' both be starving, and what I take pleasure from is feeding hungry friends.' The daughter we'd met earlier turned out to be one of four, but none of them were actual daughters. Mamma explained that fostering the children of friends, raising them and teaching them, was a

Haitian tradition. 'I got none of my own and it wouldn' be right to live in this big house by myself.' All four had a self-confidence and warmth they'd presumably learned from Mamma.

The four girls started bringing in food, supervised enthusiastically by Mamma, who refused my offer of help with a laugh of, 'Not whilst you're a guest in my home.'

Harkin winked at me, as they fetched dish after dish, filling the room with incredible aromas of spicy, hearty food. As each platter or bowl arrived, Mamma explained what it was, helping us to sizeable portions until our plates were mounded high. 'Griyo fried pork wit' pikliz – that's vegetables in spicy vinegar sauce. Spice chicken an' beans – best on a bed of cornmeal, to soak up the gravy. Okra an' black mushrooms, an' this is fried plantain an' breadfruit. You'll like this – it's crab and lalo leaf stew, an' you mus' have some grilled conch.'

Hunks of casava bread and bowls of watercress dipping sauce appeared beside us. Finally, with a mischievous grin, she poured us each a large glass of klerin – spiced bootleg rum that took my breath away.

'Eat,' she ordered, beaming with pleasure. 'In my culture food is love, so eat an' enjoy, my friends.'

The food was delicious. It was no chore to do as we were told, and we both wolfed our way into our share. The four girls joined us once everything had been brought in from the kitchen, quickly filling the room with their cheerful chatter as they too tucked in. I recognised occasional words of heavily accented French and guessed they were speaking Creole. As we ate, Mamma Harbinger asked after Archer and Traggheim and sniffed with disapproval when I mentioned Archer's new alliance with the angelii.

'Nothin' good is likely to come of that.' She thought for a moment. 'But mos' likely nothin' bad, either.'

The big door opened and Garm walked stiffly in, the wound on his rump slathered in some sort of sticky poultice.

'Welcome, Garm, my frien',' said Mamma Harbinger, gesturing to two of her girls, who ran to fetch him a pile of blankets to lie on and a vast bowl of food to eat.

Mamma turned to me. 'I tink you don' truly know jus' who Garm is?'

'I know he's more than a dog, although he chooses to be one just now. And I know he's ancient. Experience has taught me he doesn't suffer fools! That's about it.'

'That is truth in itself. Garm is as old as the hills and as young as a spring flower. He has been reborn many a time in a new guise and he can choose to enhance himself whenever it suits him.'

'When we were fighting the ælves, he seemed to get bigger and more powerful.'

'If that was what he needed to be, he could choose to be that way. Never underestimate him. He chooses his current form, but it don' restrict him. Rely on him, Drew. I tink you may need his help if your path is the one that it seems to be. And Garm is one you can truly rely on – take my word on that.'

I promised to take her advice, which brought up something. 'Do you mind if I ask why you're called Harbinger?'

She smiled. 'What do you know about a harbinger?'

'I've heard the phrase "harbinger of doom", that's why I asked. It doesn't seem to me like doom is part of your lifestyle.'

She burst out laughing, slapping her thigh with pleasure and making the girls stop their chatter and stare. She wiped tears from her eyes. 'A harbinger is a foreshadow, a hint of what is coming. What am I a harbinger of? I be a harbinger of many t'ings to many people and you mus' decide for yourself what part of your future you take from me. But know this...' She leaned closer. 'It is not YOUR doom!' She burst out laughing and this time, the girls joined in.

Harkin grinned and judged it a suitable moment to raise the subject of Jamie. 'You know I think, why Drew and I came to you, Mamma?'

She frowned. 'I do, but that business and this pleasure. When our meal is done, we can talk 'bout that. Now, tell me more about the shade you faced in Edinburgh. I like a good ghost story!'

With our meal finished, Mamma Harbinger led us through to a sumptuous lounge, where we could 'discuss matters of business' and where I also hoped to do some serious digesting.

No sooner had we made ourselves comfortable on the brightly-patterned sofas than one of the girls brought in a tray of steaming cups. 'Chokola peyi,' she announced, placing a cup onto a coaster near each of us, before leaving the three of us alone. Garm remained on his palatial heap of blankets in the dining room, where the youngest girl had taken it upon herself to act as his personal servant, petting him and feeding him choice titbits. Ancient creature he may be, but Garm clearly had no objections to this treatment.

The unctuous chocolate drink had a heady scent of cinnamon, nutmeg and who knew what else. Harkin and I sipped, whilst Mamma watched approvingly.

'I love to see people enjoyin' my food an' drink,' she said. 'And whils' you enjoy that, I'll tell you what I tink about your cause.'

I sat up expectantly. This was my only hope of getting Jamie back.

'I tink you have two questions of me,' she said. 'First is, can I help you rescue your frien's soul and second is, will I do it. That seem right to you?'

We both nodded.

'Good. The second question is simple to answer, so I'll answer it firs'. Yes, I will help you. You know why I introduced you to our visitor upstairs?'

I nodded. 'I think so.'

Harkin looked at me curiously. I hadn't had an opportunity to talk to him about Stanley and I was in two minds about telling him at all, given his deep and personal hatred of the ælves. I certainly didn't want him skewering Jamie's chances by hurtling upstairs with his pea-shooter, to take vengeance for his incarceration at Yester.

'That told me what I needed to know,' Mamma was saying. 'You're Harkin's frien' and that counts for much wit' me, but now I know your heart is good. I will help you.'

I could feel my pulse racing. Was there a 'but' coming?

'*Can* I do it?' She paused. 'No, I cannot...' My heart sank. 'But you can,' she continued. 'And I will help you.'

'Me? I can't do something like that. I'm still learning basic galdr-lore.'

She leaned over, put her soft, warm hand on mine, and squeezed gently. 'You got more power than you know, Drew. You jus' need to know how to use it right. And there's a little somethin' I can add, to make sure you may complete the task.'

I looked across at Harkin. I was flattered, but certain she was misunderstanding what I could do. What had he told her about me?

Harkin grinned, reading my face. 'If Mamma Harbinger says you can do it, then I reckon – no, *I know* – she is right. Take a pride in yourself, learn from Mamma and you'll do it, lad.'

Mamma Harbinger and I worked late into the night, and the next morning Harkin and I left for Edinburgh. We left

Garm to make his own way back after recuperating and, no doubt, enjoying being the centre of attention amongst Mamma's girls.

Safely tucked in my rucksack was a package wrapped in green calico, entrusted to me by Mamma. Using it, I might break the Ælf-queen's hold on Jamie's soul.

As we left, Mamma hugged and kissed us both. She handed me a little bundle. 'Cashew ginger brittle for Archer. That daemon's a sucker for it! Now get away from me and go do what you mus' do.'

27. REVIVAL

I returned to Edinburgh with mixed feelings. Exchanging the fresh air of the hills and the inspiring company of Mamma Harbinger and Stent's team for a wet, grey city didn't seem a good bargain to me, even if it brought the hope of seeing Ashnil and Alyssum. Ashnil was enchanting and delightful, but her angelus heritage made her seem unattainable. I had grown fond of the feisty and practical Alyssum, but it was hard to tell if there was anything between us. These thoughts quickly brought a pang of guilt: my focus should be on Jamie, and I faced the ordeal of recovering his soul. Mamma Harbinger was confident I could do it. I was not.

I parked the Carpy and, after the ritual two attempts to make the door close properly, I parted company with Harkin. 'The elastic's a bit too taut for comfort,' he said. 'I need to visit Yester for a bit.'

I trudged along the cobbled High Street, splashing through puddles, with my coat collar pulled tight to keep the rain out, then turned reluctantly into the narrow wynd leading to Traggheim's shop. Could it really be just a few weeks since I first scurried through here on wobbly legs, trying desperately to keep up with Archer's long stride and fearing that the sceadhu might be close behind? Which reminded me that the sceadhu was another piece of unfinished business.

As I pushed open the flat door, there was a delighted squeal and Alyssum galloped across the room and flung her arms round me, before pushing me back and looking me up and down, critically.

'The country suits you, Drew. You look better than I've ever seen you. It's great to have you back.' She made me sit down whilst she moved happily around the kitchenette, making coffee.

'How's Jamie?' I asked.

Her face fell and she glanced towards the bedroom. 'I'm sorry, Drew, but he's no different. Did you...?' She tailed off awkwardly.

'I don't know, Alyssum. Maybe I have the answer, but it won't be easy. I'll tell you about it when the others are here. Where are they?'

'Traggheim's immersed in his workshop – he's trying to build a long-distance tocsin so we can communicate faster with Stent. He'll be delighted you're back, and not just because you're the only one who doesn't glaze over when he explains his machines.'

'And Archer?'

'Your guess is as good as mine. He's been banging about since you left. He's worried about you, not that he'd ever admit that, of course.' She handed me a mug and sat alongside. 'How's Stent doing?'

We talked about Stent's amazing team of hard-working drop-outs and her face grew grim when I told her about our fight with the ælves. She never liked it when any of us were in danger. I told her about Garm's injury, stressing that we'd left him well-tended and in the lap of luxury with Mamma Harbinger. When I tentatively told her about Stanley, she took my hand, her eyes bright.

'Be careful who you tell about that. Not everyone will understand.'

'I felt guilty keeping it from Harkin, but I didn't see any alternative,' I said.

'You did right.' She leaned over and kissed me on the cheek.

'What was that for?'

'For growing up,' she said simply, giving me a cheeky grin. I pushed her, and she shoved back, then turned serious. 'There's someone else you haven't asked about. Ashnil's been pestering us almost daily for news about you.'

'Oh?' I affected indifference, and she punched my arm, hard.

'What the hell was that for?'

Alyssum smiled sweetly at me. 'That was for your emotional maturity being so short-lived, you pillock. Anyway, she's tried Archer's patience – he's still struggling with the new concept of angelii on our side.'

Luckily, the uncomfortable direction of the conversation was cut off by the door opening and Traggheim peering round it, his spectacles slightly askew.

'Drew, my boy. You've returned.' He pumped my hand enthusiastically. 'It's good to see you back in one piece. You must tell us all about your adventures. Oh, but first I must share my news about the long-distance tocsin I'm working on. I'm going to use a very fine, rapidly modulated beam of light, refracted off a strategic location between here and Stent's camp.'

'Will it work?'

'It will, it will. I must show you, Drew.' I think he would have dragged me away there and then, to see his work, if he could.

'Perhaps a bit later? I really ought to see Jamie first and catch up with Archer, if I can find him.'

'Right here.' Archer strolled nonchalantly through the door. He stopped and stared at me, his eyes boring into mine. 'You've grown in galdr.' He reflected for a moment. 'That's good. We're going to need it.' He helped himself to coffee and arranged himself elegantly in a chair, with his heels balanced on the edge of the coffee-table.

I made my excuses and headed upstairs, feeling guilty for not sharing what I was about to do, but I knew they'd try to dissuade me. The door creaked as I pushed it open and edged into the bedroom. Jamie lay on the bed, as still and lifeless as when I last saw him. I shut the door firmly behind me.

I sat on the bed beside him. 'How're you doing, you big ginger goon?' Unsurprisingly, he made no response, and I sighed. Time to get on with it. I reached into my trouser pocket and pulled out my ancestor's stone, running my finger-tips briefly over the fine carvings on the polished stone. I placed it in Jamie's hand and closed his fingers over it.

Next I carefully unwrapped Mamma Harbinger's package, folding back the outer wrapping of oil-cloth to reveal a small figurine, wrapped in soft cotton: a thin, long-legged doll, painted white and with a thin gold circlet around its head. This I placed carefully into Jamie's other hand.

In the soft cotton of the package lay a small silver knife, and I picked it up and examined it carefully. It was not so much a knife as a miniature sword, wrought in solid silver.

Drawing a deep breath, I focussed within myself, using a technique Mamma Harbinger had schooled me in. I hunted through my mind until I found what I was looking for: the wyrm, curled up, sleeping. I gave him a metaphorical kick and rubbed at the wyrm-scar. It glowed, pulsing green and orange as I felt the galdr-heat build in it.

'Right, you scaly parasite. We made a deal,' I told it. 'You moved in here against my will, but the rent is a fat chunk of galdr when I need it. So keep your side of the bargain or get out.'

In my mind's eye I saw the wyrm uncurl itself slowly, yawning as it did so, to make a point. It gazed at me with its unblinking eyes. 'I have not been wanting, Duh-rew Mac-loud. When you need my galdr, you must seek it from me.'

'Well. I'm seeking it now, so get off your arse and gear up.' A momentary stab of pain showed his irritation.

I opened my eyes and clenched the werigend tightly in my hand, feeling it work. The motion moved and rotated in it, getting faster and faster. I felt the wyrm-scar burn as galdr welled up inside me, building into a crescendo that threatened to explode my head. When I could no longer contain it, I released it, directing it in two streams: one to the ancestor stone, the object of the Ælf-queen's desire and her reason for hunting me; the other stream I directed to the little mannequin. As I let it go, I could feel the werigend rattling furiously in my hand. I had to fight to stay on my feet, but Mamma Harbinger had hammered into me that I had to be ready for what would come next.

In my right hand, I clenched the miniature silver sword. It felt like I was standing in the centre of a hurricane, being thrown about like a wind-thrashed tree. Yet everything else in the room was unaffected. As I fought to keep my footing, suddenly something changed – the battering ceased – and in front of me stood the Ælf-queen in all her glory, her face a savage rictus of hatred.

'I ssee you, Drew Mac-loud,' she spat. 'I ssee you and I cursse you. I cursse you for all time. You and the devil Arch-urr.'

I recalled Mamma Harbinger's advice. 'She'll try to distract you and she will mos' surely behave like she is really there, but she isn't. She can only hurt you if you let her, Drew.'

The Ælf-queen moved closer. 'Oh yess, I cursss you with all the–'

'Shut the fuck up, ælf-bitch!' I wasn't going to let her get any further. All my rage and fury for the vileness she had inflicted on Jamie, on Harkin, on Stanley, and towards countless others, overwhelmed me and I'm not ashamed to say I saw red and lost control.

Without warning, I rammed the silver sword into her chest, making her scream and pull back from me. Although this was a manifestation of her and not the actual creature, the silver metal and the galdr washing out of me and through the sword, still hit her hard. I stabbed again and again so that she pulled back further, cursing and spitting at me, but unable to withdraw, held tight by the galdr I was pouring into her image. Then her eyes lit on the miniature ælf in Jamie's hand and as she looked, she clearly sensed the ancestor stone in his other hand and must have realised what was coming. Her eyes opened wide, and she opened her mouth to say something.

I didn't wait to hear what. I slid the silver sword into a carefully-made slot in the mannequin's chest. There was a noise like thunder, a blinding blue light – and then suddenly it was over. The room was quiet again.

I fell onto the bed, my legs lacking the strength to keep me upright. My mouth was dry, and a migraine burned through my head. My hands were shaking like leaves and I couldn't stop them. I leant back against the bedpost, my eyes closed against the pain, and heaved some big breaths, trying to drag oxygen into my body.

'You look like shit, Drew.'

I snapped open my eyes in astonishment, and in front of me, Jamie's big, daft, ginger-haired face looked back.

'What's going on?' he asked. 'Where are we? And most of all, what were we drinking last night? My head feels like it was beaten with a quarter-pound mash hammer – and you don't look any better.'

Perhaps it was the adrenaline, or maybe shock, but all I could do was laugh. I laughed and laughed until tears ran down my face.

Alyssum put her head round the door, obviously figuring that laughter meant the task was done. She introduced herself to Jamie, and I gently took the ancestor-stone back from him. As I slipped it into my pocket, there was a tinkling sound. To my horror, the werigend was bent and twisted, with small parts falling from it. But now was not the time to worry about that.

The next few hours must have been confusing for Jamie. My new friends, colleagues, or whatever the hell they were, were all strangers to him. The awful events at Yester were just his nightmare now – but sufficiently twisted and vivid to convince him there was truth in what I'd told him, after all.

He was still physically weak, but determined to learn all he could about the world he'd landed in. We talked for hours and, once Alyssum had forcefully convinced him he wasn't ready to leap out of bed yet, he sat back and listened carefully as I explained everything that had happened to me, asking occasional questions.

'All of this is going on around us all the time, but we know nothing about it. That's what gets me,' he said.

'But you can see how, can't you? You didn't want to believe me without seeing evidence, and why would you?'

'Sorry about that, by the way. But here's something else I don't understand–'

'There'll be lots of moments like this, believe me,' I put in. 'I think I've only scratched the surface so far.'

'Yeah, I bet. But, anyway, where is the Ælf-queen now? Is she still alive? Did you kill her, or banish her or what?'

'According to Mamma Harbinger, the Ælf-queen cannot be destroyed. What I did simply weakened her temporarily, so I could grab your soul from her. When the stones were first set up, they limited her power and kept her confined to a small area. If Stent's gang can get enough stones back into place, that should keep her in her contained for the time being.'

'Jesus, you'd think there was a silver bullet or something that could wipe her out once and for all.' Jamie shook his head.

'If there was, I'm sure Archer would have used it fifteen hundred years ago. I think it's also a kind of ecosystem thing – if you get rid of the ælves altogether, then it means a void that might leave the way clear for something even nastier.'

'Nastier than that vicious bitch? That's someone I don't want to meet.'

'About that... There's something else I need to tell you, Jamie.'

'What, you haven't told me enough weird stuff already?' he asked.

I tentatively explained about meeting Stanley and how he had made me realise the ælves were not just two-dimensional enemies. I observed him as I talked, worried about how he'd feel about me fraternising with the enemy.

'That makes sense,' he said finally. 'All normal sentient creatures have variable personalities. Why shouldn't ælves too? So is it possible there might be a mutiny?'

'That's what I'm wondering,' I mused. 'But will they do it themselves or do we need to kick-start it? And if so, how?'

'Sounds like your mate Stanley is the key to that – if he lives,' said Jamie. 'But look, if you only winged the queen, and your pal Stent's rocks aren't all in place yet, isn't there a risk she'll come after you? She must be really pissed off with you.'

That was a thought I was trying not to let fester in my mind. Giving her a bloody nose was satisfying, but a wounded and vengeful Ælf-queen was an unappealing prospect.

I left Jamie to sleep. Alyssum was stuffing him full of herbal concoctions she claimed would get him back on his feet. 'Besides,' she said, 'your happy little bromance will still be there tomorrow!' She ducked as she scurried past me into the bedroom.

I called in to see Traggheim. He was in his element, and his enthusiasm for the new tocsin was infectious. I suspected we might need it before long.

After I'd let him chunter on about it for a while, I confessed. 'I'm really sorry, Traggheim, but I've broken the werigend.' I handed him the battered gadget, which rattled, causing him to frown momentarily. He clapped his magnifiers down over his spectacles and examined it carefully, muttering under his breath as he did so.

Finally, he looked up. 'But, Drew, this is amazing!'

I raised my eyebrows.

'Don't you see what you've done? You've pulled such a huge measure of galdr through the werigend that it has literally disintegrated. Your galdr powers have grown far beyond what Archer and I hoped.'

'Yes, but it's not my galdr – it's the wyrm's.'

He shook his head. 'The werigend would only act on

your galdr, Drew. The wyrm's galdr, even drawn from within you and manipulated by your own hand, would bypass it. This was you. Perhaps your ancestor's stone has helped you to grow your strength.'

'Really? I wish I knew more about its history. What was the deal my ancestor struck with the Ælf-queen and did he keep to it? I don't enjoy feeling that the stone is stolen property.'

'Galdr has a habit of reacting to these things – a little like water, finding its own level. Galdr finds those who can justify holding it, in one way or another.' He clapped me on the shoulder. 'I'm proud of you, Drew.' Then he hesitated. 'But go carefully. The more powerful you are, the more attractive you are to potential enemies. And remember, success has as much to do with subtlety as with raw power.' He smiled. 'Still, I really am proud of what you've achieved, my boy.'

Later, I strolled across the moonlit grass in Princes Street Gardens, enjoying the smell of the wet grass as it was crushed under my shoes. It was chilly, but who cared? I looked up at the handful of stars visible through the glow of the street-lights, glad to see them, and intoxicated by the sense of having saved a friend and given the Ælf-queen a taste of her own medicine. Why didn't I walk around at night more often? The background sounds of the city added to the effect, and I felt truly alive, ready for whatever the parallel realm could throw at me.

Then I felt it. A susurrating hiss behind me, followed by the nausea.

'I wondered when you'd turn up,' I said, without turning round. The susurration swelled and deepened in a way that was all too familiar, and I clenched my teeth before whipping around to look at it. The writhing smoke and coal-red eyes of the sceadhu were growing rapidly and already it loomed over me, stretching tendrils of smoke towards me. I felt the sharp pain in my head as it attempted to gain a hold on me.

'Oh, I wouldn't go in there if I were you. You'll never believe what's taken up residence since you last had a poke about,' I said cheerfully.

The sceadhu recoiled momentarily, then pressed forward again. I decided to have a go at it myself before stirring up the wyrm. Apart from anything else, twice in one evening might be too much to ask for – I didn't want to be the boy who cried wolf. Or wyrm.

In my trouser pocket, I closed my fingers around the ancestor stone, feeling the warmth of its smooth surface against my fingers. Then came the knife-sharp pain as the sceadhu probed into my mind, but this time, I blocked it firmly.

Again, the sceadhu swirled back, its burning eyes glowering at me as it tried to understand. It would not give in easily and pushed forward, probing my mind again. I could feel it trying to hurt me and looking for a way to control me. It was time to treat this primitive aglaecan to a swift lesson, I thought. I pulled all the galdr I could from the stone and felt it swilling around inside me like a tidal wave, washing into every corner and subsuming all in its path until, when I felt I might drown in it, I let go. A brilliant white flash of light sucked the sceadhu from my mind and flattened it into a dark billow of smoke, the two red eyes still staring at me, unblinking. The susurration changed to a squeal so high in pitch it became barely audible – this was the sceadhu's turn to feel pain.

I'd had enough now. 'Take a hint, sceadhu. Your hunt is over. You lost. Now GO!' I pulled up another blast of galdr, plenty to see it on its way, and I rocked back on my heels as the last wisp of smoke dissipated in front of my feet and the squeal stopped, as though cut by a knife.

Across the grass a well-dressed couple walking a Shi Tzu sped up, the man hauling on the lead to make the dog catch up. I realised they had seen nothing except a weirdo shouting into the night and suddenly, it made me cold and vulnerable. Squashing the sceadhu was satisfying, but the adrenaline gone, I felt like a man focussed on setting mouse traps whilst a T. Rex loomed overhead. I shivered, shoved my hands deep into my coat pockets and hurried back to the flat.

28. GARDEN

The bell on Alyssum's shop-door jangled as I entered. So many pungent scents, all demanding attention at once, heralded an assault on my nose.

Alyssum bustled through from the workroom. 'Oh, it's you, is it?' She gave me a peck on the cheek. 'Are you going downstairs?'

'Actually, no. I was hoping for a coffee and a chat.'

'A chat you can have, but not the coffee. I'm miles behind, so you need to make yourself useful.' She thrust an armful of canvas bags in my direction and propelled me out of the shop, locking the door behind her.

'We're going shopping?'

'Gardening.'

'You have a garden?'

She stopped in her tracks and stared at me. 'For an intelligent man, you can be remarkably thick. Where do you think all the herbs come from? Mars?'

'I guess I thought they came from hedgerows or exotic suppliers, something like that.'

'There is a bit of that,' she acknowledged. 'But anything I use a lot of, I grow myself.'

'How come I never knew about this?' I wondered aloud.

'Because I normally go there first thing in the morning,

when you're still buried deep in your pit, snoring your head off like a wallowing hippo.'

The private gardens of Edinburgh's New Town are a collection of delightful hidden gems – or an outrageous scandal of outdated privilege. It depends where you sit on the political spectrum, but either way, the small urban parks are accessible only to those who own one of the Georgian apartments nearby. Alyssum led me along Queen Street to a point where the railing-imprisoned privet hedge met a line of neatly-trimmed lime trees. From her apron pocket, she took something the size of a matchbox and shook it.

To say a gate appeared in front of us would be to undersell it. It didn't appear – it was just there, in a way that made it clear it always had been.

'Traggheim?' I asked.

'Need you ask?' Alyssum pushed open the gate and ushered me through an archway. We clipped through the hedge and emerged into the garden beyond.

I'd expected a muddy, practical allotment, dedicated to growing herb crops, with perhaps a shed or a poly-tunnel. But laid out in front of me was about an acre of Edwardian formal garden. Each bed was geometrically related to its neighbours, with a miniature Box hedge around the edge of each. A vast array of plants grew within the beds and there was the continuous buzz of pollinating insects, flying from blossom to bloom.

I looked at Alyssum. 'You've been playing with the seasons in here, haven't you?'

She shrugged. 'Archer has his uses. Best way to get consistent quality.'

At the far end of the garden was an ornate glasshouse, built onto a south-facing brick wall. So much for the grotty poly-tunnel. At the garden's centre, a huge circular stone feature had water pulsing from the top and cascading over tiers of stone and into four rills, each of which led to a corner of the garden. Our feet crunched on gravel as we passed through a wooden pergola with yellow and cerise roses cascading from it.

'Do the roses, fountain and rills help with consistent quality too?' I teased.

She put her head on one side and poked out her tongue. 'I need water for the plants. Why shouldn't it be pretty? And I like roses. My garden, my rules.'

'Alyssum, this is idyllic. No wonder you keep it to yourself,' I said.

'I'd be lying if I pretended this isn't my happy place. But it's my work as well. And that's why I brought you here. Come on.'

She pottered about the garden, pulling up a weed here, clipping an unwanted shoot there. From time to time she'd select something she wanted, cut it with suspiciously sharp-looking secateurs and hand it to me to put in a bag.

We passed what was obviously a very large marijuana plant. I raised an eyebrow at her. She just shrugged and gave me a lopsided grin.

Gardening has never been my thing, but seeing Alyssum's obvious pleasure in what she was doing was infectious and she chattered on about the different plants as we went.

'This is greater burnet-saxifrage. It's useful for galdr-burns, but I mix it with fourteen other things to make a very strong painkiller with few side-effects.' She carefully trimmed some stems and handed them to me. 'Shaggy soldier – an awful name for a lovely plant. Useful for some dweorg ailments that resist anything else.' She passed a handful of leaves to me. 'Monk's rhubarb. Mixed with a special something, the flower anthers make you less noticeable.'

'So some of these plants have galdr uses, not just healing?'

'Well, not as such. You need to apply the galdr, but in

some situations, the right herbal mixture can help overcome a shortage of skill. Could be useful for you!' She gave me an impish grin and ducked. 'Aren't you going to ask me about love potions? Everyone does eventually.'

'You can create love potions?' I asked obediently.

'Actually, no. Though it is amazing what I can do with a straight face and a convincing placebo. Can be fun to watch.'

'You're a mischievous little minx, aren't you?' I jumped back as she aimed a sharp kick at my knee.

'Possibly. But I'll be who I want to be, as should we all. Anyhow, you don't need a love potion, Drew.'

'I don't?' I countered cautiously.

'God's teeth, why is it my ill-luck to be surrounded by awkward, useless males?' She looked at me closely and then, presumably seeing no light dawning, helped me out.

'Ashnil, you berk.'

'Ashnil?'

'Ye-e-e-s, Ash-nil,' she said slowly, as though to a confused toddler. 'The girl's infatuated with you. Can't you see it?'

At moments like this, I usually feel like a tongue-tied, spotty fourteen-year-old, trying to negotiate my way through the minefields of facial boils, awkwardness and rampant hormones.

'I'm not very good at reading women,' I confessed.

'You're really not. You like her, don't you?'

I admitted I did. 'But I thought you hated her? Anyway, she's an angelus.'

Alyssum whacked me over the head with a bunch of stems, then handed them to me. 'Put these in the other bag. I got to know her better whilst you were away. For heaven's sake, talk to her. She thinks you don't want her because she's an angelus.'

Light dawned, and a goofy grin betrayed me.

'Oh, good grief. When did I sign up to be Marjorie Proops?' she said. 'Let's have a drink in the greenhouse.'

Amongst the potting benches and seed trays were two period cafe chairs and a matching table.

'Do you entertain here often?' I enquired.

'Cheeky sod. I sometimes play agony aunt for Archer in here, but don't tell him you know. He can be sensitive about that sort of thing.'

I bet he could. I looked at the glass of pale-green liquid she handed me and sniffed it. 'What's this?'

'I'm not telling you, because you'll be a pain in the neck about it. It's good for you and it's nice.'

I sipped it. She was right on both fronts and a light apple flavour danced on my tongue as a sense of well-being rippled through me.

She leaned back, enjoying her drink, then drew a deep breath. 'What are we going to do with Jamie?' she asked.

This was a bolt from the blue. 'In what way?'

'He's caught up now. There's no way back for him unless we find a way of protecting him so he can revert to a normal life. Even so, he'll never forget what he's seen and what has happened to him.'

'Or the impact it's had on him?' I thought for a moment. 'He seems bomb-proof, but he's not. He's really fired up about the parallel realm – I don't think he'd willingly go back to whatever version of normal could be created for him. Anyway, surely it should be his decision.'

'You saw how hard it was to protect you when you became part of the realm,' Alyssum said. 'It would be harder with Jamie because he doesn't have latent galdr-powers.'

'But surely other galdr-folc get by with limited powers? And besides, I was being hunted. Nothing's after Jamie now. Well, so far as we know.'

'Minor galdr-folc keep themselves to themselves and don't come to the attention of ælves, sceadhu, shades and who knows what else. Now Jamie's known at that level, we don't know who or what might fancy using him to gain leverage on Archer or the angelii.' She paused. 'Or you.'

'Me?'

'You're daft if you don't think you've made waves in the parallel realm.'

I put that uncomfortable thought to one side. 'So, what should we do?'

'We need to set out the options for Jamie, preferably before Archer gets involved and bullies him into anything.'

29. TOCSIN

Entering the close leading to Traggheim's, a familiar sharp sound caught my attention. I looked around for its source and spotted a jackdaw, perched atop a lamp, its piercing blue eyes fixed on me and its head on one side as it 'tchak'-ed insistently. Since it was a jackdaw that presaged my first encounter with the sceadhu, I was immediately on my guard. Instinctively I felt in my pocket for the werigend, but found the smooth warmth of the ancestor stone, reminding me that things had changed.

'Tchak! Tchak-tchak!' scolded the bird.

'Ok, you've got my attention. What is it you want?'

The bird hopped from foot to foot, gave one more 'tchak' for luck, then flew to the top of a waste bin a few yards away and started tchak-ing again.

'Don't tell me, Lassie. Has Jimmy fallen down a well?'

The bird just glared at me. Sighing, I followed as it flew to a lamppost – and so we continued: me following as it flew from perch to perch, frequently tchak-ing and obviously leading me somewhere. But where? And who or what would be waiting? I followed warily, ignoring a group of Italian tourists, who seemed to think we were some sort of side-show.

Eventually, the bird led me into a small garden behind

a tenement. I entered cautiously and there found Rillan waiting for me.

'You!' I glanced around, but he seemed to be alone.

He held up his hands. 'I understand you have cause to dislike me, but hear what I have to say. You owe me that.'

'I owe you nothing. Why would I listen to you, Rillan? You betrayed us to the Ælf-queen and walked away when we needed you.'

'I disagree,' he said smugly. 'Who distracted the sceadhu so the daemon could rescue you? Who fought alongside you against the shade at Shrubhill? We may have our differences, Drew, but you at least owe me a hearing.'

'You have two minutes, and then I'm leaving.' Out of the corner of my eye, I could see another figure in the shadows and guessed it would be Eleleth, Rillan's sidekick and fellow traitor. I stepped back to keep a shrub between him and my back, glancing at the gateway to check it was still clear if I needed to exit in a hurry.

'You caused my chosen one to walk from me,' he said.

'One minute, fifty seconds.' I put my hand in my pocket to touch the ancestor stone. His eyes followed the movement, and for a moment, he hesitated.

'Drew, you do not need to fear us,' he said finally. 'We are here not to threaten or harm you. Much the opposite, in fact.'

I was getting curious but refused to give the smarmy toe-rag any latitude. 'One minute, fifteen seconds.'

'You are caught in an unfamiliar world – a dangerous world. It is impressive how quickly you have built up your powers and skills, but you are still at substantial risk. You *and* your friend. There are many out there who could – and would – harm you or destroy you and your only protection is the evil daemon who controls you.'

I gave an involuntary growl – Garm must have been rubbing off on me.

'Oh, I know you count him as a friend, but he is using you for his own ends. You must believe me in this.'

There was certainly a little truth in that, but I felt I had Archer's measure by now. Besides, if the alternative was Rillan, then any or all of the devils in Dante's nine circles of hell would make better friends than him.

'So what's the alternative? You, Rillan? Even the sceadhu could knock you for six, but he'll leave you alone now, because I despatched him yesterday.' I couldn't resist boasting.

His eyes widened. 'I congratulate you. And therefore, you must hear what I have to say. I am not speaking for myself. I am here to represent someone of great power, someone who would welcome you and guide you in the parallel realm. Someone whose fight against evil is a truly worthy thing. If you will meet with him, then I am sure you'll see that what I'm saying makes good sense.'

I resisted an urge to tell him to get lost. *Never throw away an opportunity.* 'I'll think about it.'

He smiled his most obsequious smile. 'You will not regret it.'

'I only said I'd think about it.'

'I'll send the jackdaw for your reply in two days. If you agree, he will lead you to the meeting. And your safety is guaranteed, I assure you.'

I left as quickly as I could, suspecting I knew who Rillan's mysterious fighter of evil was. I was wondering where Archer was when I felt a nudge at my leg and a 'wuff'. I looked down to see the whiskered face of Garm, sleek and well-fed, his wound healed.

'Garm! Welcome back, you little reprobate. Did Mamma and her girls run out of food, or did she get fed up and boot you out?'

He grinned at me, as only a terrier can.

'Well, I'm glad to see you looking better. I don't suppose you know where Archer is?'

He barked once and shot off down the High Street. I galloped after him, marvelling at the speed four stumpy legs can deliver.

Getting to the top of Calton Hill is a steep climb at the best of times. When you're trying your best to keep up with a hurtling terrier, it's even harder. I flopped against the wall at the top of the slope, gasping like a steam engine. When a disturbingly enthusiastic American tourist asked if I was ok, all I could do was hold up my hands to show I had no immediate plans to expire.

Garm was out of sight, but fortunately the top of Calton Hill was relatively flat and open, so I knew I was likely to find where he'd shot off to. Once I'd recovered my breath, I set off past the observatory towards the National Monument, suspecting that might be where I'd find Archer and Garm. I was right.

The usual smattering of tourists wandered about the giant pillars and stone steps of the monument. Our forebears got excited about winning the Napoleonic wars and set out to make the 'Athens of the North' epithet real by copying the Parthenon, but they ran out of money and so we have a partial Parthenon instead.

The tourists mostly occupied themselves trying to shoe-horn them and their loved ones into a selfie with the monument and the view in the background. I'm not sure if it was galdr or preoccupation that blinded them to the presence of a small dog and a tall daemon. Archer lay stretched out on the monument's pedestal, his head resting on a pillar and one knee drawn up. His long coat flapped gently in the breeze.

'All you need is a slim volume of poetry and a Fortnum and Mason hamper,' I said, sitting down next to them.

Archer considered this carefully. 'It really depends on what is in the hamper. I've never been enthusiastic about Gentleman's Relish and sherry seems such a waste of effort.' He offered me a polished pewter hip-flask. I took a cautious sip. Whatever was in it slid down my throat like superheated velvet.

'Besides,' he continued, 'poetry is too effeminate. Some excerpts from Sir Walter Scott's "Waverley" novels would be more appropriate. Or perhaps a decent translation of Virgil.'

'Are you a literary snob, Archer?' I was glad to find him in a relaxed and reflective mood.

'I suppose I probably am, by today's standards. 'I mean, "Fifty Shades of whatever nonsense", is hardly literature. That's the problem with an immortal life: it's difficult to settle on what you like, because people keep coming up with new things to compare it with. It gets annoying after a time.'

'Jamie would call that a First World problem.'

'And he'd be right. There are much bigger things to concern ourselves with. But it's good to exercise the soul a little, now and again. How is Jamie, by the way?'

'He's well, I think. Alyssum will release him into the wild soon, which is a whole other subject. But there's something more urgent we need to talk about.'

'I thought so. When Garm said you were seeking me, I suspected my peace was to be interrupted. At least he gave you a good work-out.'

I glared at the dog, who grinned back, before rolling onto his side to soak up the weak winter sun.

Archer swung his legs around and jumped neatly down. 'Come. Let's walk and talk.'

We strolled across the mown grass, taking in the city view, as I told him about my meeting with Rillan. 'We thought he was up to no good and now he's shown his hand. I'm tempted to tell him to get stuffed, but I reckon we should find out who he's acting for. What do you think?'

Archer sighed and looked at me. Suddenly, he seemed to show a little of his great age. 'I'm sure I already know.' He took out the flask, took a sip and offered it to me.

I waved it away. 'You think it's Obadiah?'

'I would be surprised if it were not. We suspect he's returned in some form and he would easily discover you are connected to me. This is exactly what he would do. Except there's something he's misunderstood.'

'Which is?'

'He hopes he can lure you away.' He stopped and, with his hands thrust into his pockets, he looked closely into my eyes. 'I believe he's wrong about that.'

The gaze was uncomfortable. After a moment, I looked away. 'You know he is. But what do we do about it?'

He jerked his head, as if to clear it, and then smiled thinly. 'For now, absolutely nothing, because I have faithfully promised Traggheim that I will attend the unveiling of his new tocsin. You should come too. Give me a little time to think about Obadiah and what steps I should take.' He clapped me on the back. 'Come, Drew.' He whistled and Garm shot past us, growling briefly to show his opinion of being whistled at.

'Yes, yes, as you say,' said Archer.

I followed them, wondering briefly why Archer had said "I" and not "we".

We gathered around the big table in Traggheim's workshop, on which sat a large brushed-aluminium box with riveted brass edges and corners. Various knobs and levers were on the front, and from the rear, a stiff metal trunk crossed the room to the fireplace, where it disappeared up the chimney.

Alyssum muttered something about 'Boy's toys,' and, although Archer had made the effort to be present, his face betrayed his cynicism. Garm, of course, was curled up beside the hearth, industriously licking his paw and taking little interest in proceedings.

I felt I ought to be encouraging and Traggheim's new creation certainly intrigued me, but the old dweorg's enthusiasm for his work would trundle blithely over the top of any amount of disinterest. His pride was overwhelming.

'As you know, we've had a tocsin for some time, using a narrow beam of galdr-enhanced light to communicate alarms between here and several locations.'

'We know, we were there,' muttered Archer, dodging a kick from Alyssum.

Traggheim lowered his glasses and looked censoriously over the top of them at Archer. 'You recall that it also provided very efficient two-way communication...'

'It did?' I asked, surprised.

'... if Archer had shown any willingness to learn the Morse Code,' continued Traggheim.

'Never going to happen, old friend. Move on,' Archer said, with a wink.

Traggheim doggedly continued. 'So we need a system to permit long-distance, two-way communication without Archer being required to develop any rudimentary skills. I took the Hólmganga design and developed an improved version of the Tocsin. The Hólmganga made use of the large reservoirs of background galdr present around the Ælf-queen's court, whereas for the enhanced Tocsin I have relied on intense light, with just a gentle nudge from galdr to assist it. As you know, Stent has no galdr. I won't bore you with technical details, but it works by bouncing a powerful beam of light off reflectors hidden in old Ordnance Survey trig points atop several hills. Although, as you know,

Stent's fierdwic has now moved to the Moorfoot hills. We may now speak with him.'

At this, Archer stopped playing around and took Traggheim seriously. 'Really? And it works?'

'We are about to find out. But I am confident. Stent has received the other machine, with detailed instructions on how to set it up.'

'Why was the fierdwic moved?' asked Alyssum.

'To let them work on the stones south east of Edinburgh,' I told her. 'They've done most of the ones around the Pentlands. But how did you get the reflectors up to the trig points?' I asked Traggheim. I couldn't visualise him with a rucksack and a packet of Kendal mint cake, setting off to install them.

'Actually, I arranged for them to be inserted for a different purpose when the trig points were built in the 1950s. Happily, they lent themselves to re-purposing.' He gave me a smug smile. 'And Stent should be ready to speak with us...' He glanced at a chronometer on the wall '...about now.'

'You theatrical old bugger. That was clever timing,' said Archer. 'Let's see then.' He leaned forward eagerly.

Traggheim extended a brass trumpet from the top of the machine, pushed in a bronze lever and applied a match to a small gas-jet under a wire-mesh flap. The hiss of the gas flame was followed by a clunk as Traggheim pulled out another lever. 'This inserts a fuel pellet into the flame, which ignites it to create an intense light. That is magnified, focussed, modulated and finally galdr-enhanced and cloaked from human view. Each pellet lasts around two minutes.'

He leant forward and adjusted a brass knob. 'Speak to Stent, Archer,' he said importantly.

Archer leaned in and spoke tentatively into the trumpet. 'Ah, hello, Stent?'

Traggheim coughed. 'That is actually the heat exhaust. You speak here.' He indicated a grille on the front of the machine.

Archer glared at him and tried again. 'Hello, Stent?'

There was a pregnant pause, during which nothing happened. All eyes moved accusingly towards Traggheim, but before anyone said anything, a sound finally came from the tocsin.

'Aye, err. Hello? Is that you, Archer?' It was recognisably Stent.

Traggheim raised his eyebrows. I whispered in the old dweorg's ear, 'You engineered that pause deliberately, didn't you?' A smile twitched in the corners of his mouth.

Archer leaned back into the machine. 'Stent, my friend, it's very good to hear your voice.'

'Aye, aye, it's great, man. This thing is pure brilliant, though it took a deal of setting up.'

'It will allow us to keep in better touch, Stent.' He mouthed, 'Thank you,' to Traggheim, causing Alyssum to nudge me.

'Stent, I trust all is well with you?' said Archer.

'No, Archer, I canna say it is. We're in a bit o' a mess here just now.'

Archer frowned. 'What do you mean? What's happened?'

'That bloody Ælf-queen's what's happened,' replied Stent. 'I reckon she's finally realised what we're up to and two o' my lads were laid into last night.'

'Shit,' muttered Archer.

Alyssum leaned forward. 'Stent, it's Alyssum. Are they ok?'

'They're alive, but badly burned. We got them to hospital and pretended it was a campfire accident, but I dinnae ken if normal treatment is effective, Alyssum.'

'Not if ælf-fire burned them.' She turned to Archer. 'I need to go there.'

'Stent,' I said. 'It's Drew. How is everyone else coping?'
'No' well, Drew. This isnae what they signed up for.'
'The pellet's running out,' Traggheim warned us.
Archer leaned back in. 'Hold tight, Stent. Help is coming.'
A moment later, the light in the machine faded.

30. OBADIAH

There are few things as frustrating as the feeling that you urgently need to be in several places at once. I was desperately worried about what was happening to Stent and his crew and wanted to get there and help as quick as I could. But my closest friend was recovering from an ordeal and I felt needed me. How could I abandon him again? We now knew that my prime enemy was the renegade daemon Obadiah and if I were not around to respond when Rillan's jackdaw came looking for me, I might miss our best opportunity to scope out the enemy. Meanwhile, there was a selfish, nagging voice in the back of my mind telling me not to lose my chance to be with Ashnil.

Still, whatever else was coming at me, I knew I owed Jamie some of my time first.

'Drew, mate. I thought you were never coming to see me, and Alyssum's like a Rottweiler if I try to leave before she's sure I've recovered.' Jamie had been standing at the living room window when I entered, with a listless air that changed the moment he saw me. His eyes lit up with enthusiasm. 'I've heard tonnes about the parallel realm and what you've been doing. It's incredible – just amazing.' Then his face fell. 'I'm sorry, Drew. I should've believed you when you told me, but you'd been so weird recently

I thought you weren't well. You must admit, it's all hard to take in.'

'Don't worry about it.' I grinned at him. 'Do you think I'd have believed you if you'd come to me with a lunatic story like this?'

'I doubt it. It really takes a situation where you're dragged into it unexpectedly, doesn't it? So you can see and feel the proof for yourself. That's what happened to us both.'

'Yes, but there's a difference, Jamie,' I said tentatively.

'I know, I know. You've done so much.'

'What've you heard?' I knew Alyssum had been cautious about what she had told him. The more he knew, the harder it would be to embed him safely into normal life again.

'Oh, Traggheim's a great old guy, isn't he? He's been coming up here and chatting about all sorts of stuff.' His pink face, fringed top and bottom with a shock of ginger hair and the stubble of beard, was flushed with enthusiasm. Like most gingers, his skin gives away his mood easily.

'Jamie, you don't have to remain in this realm,' I said and flinched when he looked like I'd slapped him. I soldiered on regardless. 'Look, you've been through a lot and your experience should've shown you how dangerous the parallel realm is. Yes, it's exciting and different, and I know you needed that as much as I did. But there's no way back for me. There still could be for you. It won't be easy, but Archer can set up protections that will keep you safely rooted in the normal world and, more importantly, protected.'

'Stop.' He held up both hands. 'Just stop, Drew, and listen to what I have to say. I get what you're saying and I'm grateful. I really am. But it's not what I want—'

'Jamie...'

'Let me get this out.' He took a deep breath. 'You're right, I know. There are parts of the parallel realm which are dangerous. I know I'm impetuous, but I've thought this through and I've talked it over with Traggheim.'

Devious old bugger, I thought.

'Yes, something more exciting is attractive,' Jamie was saying. 'You and I have both been sliding along, achieving nothing and hating ourselves for it. So, yes, some excitement is welcome. But I also want to stick with you, back you up. You're the only real friend I have and if you're up to your ears in something, I want to be there with you, getting your back. Oh, I know I'm never going to have your galdr ability and I'll probably be the parallel realm's equivalent of a gopher, but that's ok with me. It's what I want.'

There was something heart-warming about the way he stuck his chin out defiantly. 'Finished?' I asked.

'Yes,' he said, holding my gaze.

I knew I wouldn't get him to shift his stance. Jamie was like the castle rock once he'd made up his mind about something – immovable and impregnable. And dependable. He'd made his choice. I realised I was relieved.

'Besides,' he said. 'Alyssum's really nice, isn't she?' There was a sparkle in his blue eyes. Just when I thought Jamie had grown up, at last a little of the old Jamie bubbled to the surface. At that moment, I knew we'd be fine.

'Jamie, good luck with that one. She's a wonderful person and I love her like a sister, but...' I tailed off, struggling.

'Feisty?' he suggested.

'So you've already had your shin kicked a few times?'

'Oh aye, and got a few punched shoulders, but that's just her way.'

I got a couple of beers from the fridge and we settled down to catch up properly, and to prepare the fierdwic. I had an idea, and I thought Jamie could help.

Early the next morning, nursing a hangover, I hauled myself

off the sofa. Jamie was in the bedroom, snoring his head off, so I let him sleep longer. My patent cure of three Alka-seltzers, dissolved in a can of Monster helped, so I decided a run round Holyrood Park would either kill me or cure me, before I got ready to head to Stent's camp.

Running was an unexpected side-impact of becoming entangled in the parallel realm. Archer was insistent that exercise was essential to build sufficient physical strength to cope with the immense strain that use of galdr puts on the body. After a few experiences of his brutal approach to physical training, I decided the best defence was attack and had taken up running. With places like Holyrood Park and Princes Street Gardens within easy reach, it was no great hardship – provided I watched for the slippery cobbles in the High Street. As time passed, I had felt my body toughening up and galdr became easier to use.

I set off down the High Street towards Holyrood Palace, side-stepping a thoughtfully-placed dog turd. As I trotted along, swerving to avoid the occasional early tourist, I thought about what Alyssum had said about Ashnil's feelings for me and wondered whether I would find an opportunity to do anything about it. This brought my thoughts back to Stent. Problems were closing in around us and I felt helpless. I needed to get to Stent and help him deal with the ælves, but I needed to scope the Obadiah problem first. I was also worried that Archer didn't seem as engaged with these problems as I expected. Thank heavens for Harkin and Jamie, but neither had any real galdr-power to draw on. It was becoming increasingly clear that it was guile, rather than galdr, that would dig us out of this hole – if anything did.

I crossed into Holyrood Park and ran towards the crags. 'Where's the bloody jackdaw?' I muttered. The sooner it summoned me to meet Rillan's "someone of great power", the better. 'And please let it be Obadiah.' I wasn't looking forward to an encounter with him, but the thought of another powerful character on this stage frankly terrified me.

'Tchak!'

I skidded to a halt on the damp pavement, glaring at the bird, which was perched atop a lamp-post, looking down on me. 'You're just taking the piss now,' I told it.

It glared at me, then abruptly flew off without a backward glance.

'Odd,' I said out loud and jumped when someone behind me spoke softly.

'Not really. The bird has done his job and left.'

I birled round. There was nobody there a moment ago. Now, a figure sat on the metal park bench, looking squarely at me, and I knew instantly it must be Obadiah. He wasn't tall like Archer, he had more of a stocky build. He wore a tailored three-piece pin-stripe suit, with his shirt open at the collar, and a silver right-angled arrow was pinned to his lapel. His patent leather shoes gleamed in the sunlight, and he wore light-grey doeskin gloves. His hair was dark and slicked back and his narrow eyes were exceptionally pale, with a flash of violet. He gazed at me, then he got up, took off a glove and extended his hand.

'Mr Macleod, my name is Obadiah,' he said.

Offending a powerful daemon right out of the gate seemed a bad idea, so I shook his hand, albeit unwillingly. It felt soft and slightly damp, but his grip was strong. He never took his eyes off mine as we shook.

'It's a pleasure to make your acquaintance at last, Mr Macleod. I have heard a considerable amount about you and I feel sure you have been told things about me.'

I nodded. His voice was quiet, yet strangely commanding. He was smoothly well-spoken, but with a menacing undertone.

'I ask only that you set aside my reputation for a time and judge me as you find me.'

'That won't be easy,' I said.

He frowned. He was clearly unaccustomed to people speaking their minds, but then he smirked thinly. 'Archer and I parted ways a long time ago and a great deal has happened since then. Please.' He indicated the bench and, without waiting to see what I would do, he sat, crossing one ankle over the other.

I shrugged and sat at the other end of the bench, angling myself to look at him.

'Do you smoke, Mr Macleod?'

When I shook my head, he tilted his slightly.

'Perhaps you will not object if I do.' It was clearly not a question. He removed a silver case from his inside breast pocket and extracted a thin cigarillo, before clicking the case shut and returning it to his jacket. He regarded the cigarillo for a moment, as though deciding what to do with it. Then he flicked a forefinger slightly. Instantly, a wall of blue flame shot up from nowhere in front of us, making me shrink back instinctively.

He looked at me sideways, with the hint of a sneer, then extended the tip of the cigarillo into the flame and lit it. He casually waved towards the roaring flame-wall and it disappeared.

'Nice trick,' I said, with more bravado than I felt. How was this all going to end?

He ignored that. Instead, 'You dispatched my sceadhu with great ease,' he commented.

'What else did you expect me to do with the creature that was hunting me?' I asked.

He raised his eyebrows. 'I expected you to be hunted. I expected you to become the sceadhu's victim, not its nemesis. You intrigue me, Mr Macleod. That is why we are speaking and I am not seeking other ways to bring about your end. It is why I am ignoring the Ælf-queen's entreaties to help her retrieve her property. I think perhaps you are not meant to be ended. I think perhaps you need a new mentor.'

'You expect me to join up with you? To trample on all that Archer has done for me? To ignore what you have tried to do to me?' I replied, incredulous.

'Oh Mr Macleod, let us speak as befits my station and the station to which you aspire. Success in the parallel realm is not predicated on petty squabbles, on casual vendettas or hunts for vengeance. It is much purer than that. Good and bad have no relevance or reality, as I'm sure you have learned. The two simple questions you must ask yourself are: do you want to become all you can be? And can you possibly believe your current path will lead you there?' He pulled on the cigarillo and amused himself by weaving the smoke into a Pictish-style pattern.

'Nice touch.'

'I thought so.' He turned and fixed me with those penetrating pale eyes. 'You know as well as I do that Archer is a lost cause. His emotional attachments and refusal to see realities are slowly stacking up against him.' He held up his hand to stop me interrupting. 'Oh, your loyalty is admirable, in its own naïve way, but it will take you nowhere except to share in Archer's inevitable downfall.' He got up and turned to look at me.

'We will speak again, Mr Macleod. Consider, please, what I have said.' He strode away and after three steps, his body collapsed into the shape of a running fox and was rapidly gone from sight.

I sat back and breathed out slowly, leaning back on the bench. This was not just a recruitment attempt, it was a threat. The sceadhu had been nothing to Obadiah. He had much worse in mind if I didn't fall in line, I was sure of that.

*

Back at Traggheim's shop, things were in chaos. Harkin had returned, ready to accompany us to Stent's camp. Traggheim was bustling about, trying to be useful, largely by inflicting cups of tea on everyone, and Garm was lying beside the hearth with one eye half-open, waiting for the best moment for a foray out to trip someone up. Alyssum had several bags and cases of medicines neatly stacked and was being passively aggressive towards Jamie, who she clearly felt shouldn't be accompanying us. One person was conspicuous by his absence.

'Where's Archer?' I asked.

'Brooding, in his library,' said Alyssum. 'I don't know what's got into him. Sometimes he takes moody turns.'

'I'd better see him.'

She grabbed my arm and led me out into the hallway. 'It was Obadiah, wasn't it?'

I nodded.

'What did he want?'

'Exactly what you'd expect. He wants me to join him or else be part of Archer's downfall.' I shrugged. 'I'll be back shortly.'

'Be quick. We have to get going.' She sighed and raised her voice a few decibels, leaning back through the door. 'If this shower of imbeciles ever gets their act together!'

I slipped out and hurried across town to Scotland Street. Holding my breath, I endured the pain and nausea of a galdr-jump through the iron railings. Finding the right spot inside the tunnel, I tapped the correct bricks with my knuckles and they glowed briefly with the right-angled arrow before opening to allow me to climb the stairs to the library.

Archer was hunched on one of the leather chairs beside the fire, which was blazing. He barely acknowledged me as I approached, staring instead into the flames.

After a moment, he spoke in a low tone. 'Are you going to accept his offer?'

'How do you know he made me an offer?'

'It's what I would do in his circumstances.'

'Well, it wasn't so much an offer as a combination of threat and ultimatum.'

'So you've decided?'

'Yes, I have.' I pulled roughly at his elbow, so that he looked up at me. 'Do you really believe I would abandon you, after all that you've done to help me?'

'I think that you'd be a fool to refuse his offer. Surely you can see that my power is waning as his is growing?'

'And you could sit on your arse and bitch about it, brooding and staring into the fire, like a sad old man, or you could do something about it.'

He stiffened. 'I happen to be a sad old man, Drew. But you're right. I must take him on. That will be my challenge, whilst you and the others defend Stent's work. I will keep Obadiah occupied in Edinburgh for you.'

'Be careful, Archer.'

He smiled thinly. 'I am always careful. Please look after yourself, Drew.' He returned to staring into the fire.

As I left the library, I half-turned and saw he was still sitting there, looking as though he was already defeated.

31. ASHNIL

I hurried back to the shop to find Alyssum herding Jamie and Harkin towards the Carpy. Garm gave me a knowing look and Jamie winked at me as he passed. Then I saw why: Ashnil came through the shop door and smiled at me.

'I'm coming to help,' she said firmly.

I looked at her, smiling prettily, and inwardly melted a little. 'You'll get no arguments from me,' I said, grinning back. There was suddenly something unsaid, yet understood between us, though I wasn't entirely sure what.

Alyssum rapidly broke the spell, sticking her elbow in my side. 'Keys,' she said brusquely, holding out a hand. I protested, but she raised her eyebrows and I capitulated, meekly giving the Carpy's keys to her.

'That's how it's done,' she said to Ashnil, who sniggered and then looked at me, eyes wide and feigning innocence.

'Wait, what are you two up to?' I asked.

'No time now. Get in,' replied Alyssum. Whatever it was, it looked like it might benefit me, as well as entertain them, so I did as I was told and squeezed into the back seat, next to Jamie, who was crammed into the middle.

'Did she bully you, as well?' I asked.

'I've got more sense than to argue with Alyssum. If she says she's going to drive, then that's what's happening.'

He leaned forward. 'Even though it's MY CAR.'

'Suck it up, Ginge,' said Alyssum, happily. They had become good friends during the long hours whilst Alyssum nursed Jamie back to health and I suspected she was an excellent influence on him.

Traggheim appeared and thrust a small wooden crate onto my lap. 'No room in the back for this. Instructions are inside, Jamie.' he said. 'Good luck to you all.' To me he added, as he shut the door, 'And be careful.'

After dropping us off at the camp, Alyssum intended to drive to the local hospital for a sneaky visit to treat the two men injured by ælf-fire.

'How will you treat them without getting chucked out by the medical staff?' I asked, en route.

Before she could reply, Jamie answered, 'Would you argue with Alyssum?'

I said nothing, though I could see his point – I wouldn't like to be the one who tried to repel her.

'Exactly,' he said. 'Nobody argues with Alyssum.'

She stuck out her tongue. 'I know a few tricks to distract or displace them. A mixture of misdirection and a smidgeon of galdr will make sure they never notice what I'm doing.'

As the car left, we looked round. The atmosphere at the camp couldn't have changed more.

Whereas before everything had been bustling and enthusiasm, now there was a sense of defeat and fear.

'I dinnae ken how to turn them around,' said Stent. 'I've run out o' ideas.' He looked dispirited, and the dark lines under his eyes spoke of exhaustion. 'That ælf-fire knocked the spirit out o' them an' a couple have left already.' He sighed. 'I think we'll have to gie it up as a bad job.'

Ashnil touched my arm. 'I'll join you in a while,' she said, heading towards the tents.

Time to step up, I told myself. 'We have to get back to basics. We need to re-think how we're doing things and adapt to the new circumstances. Maybe if your team sees us taking action, they'll get behind us again?'

Stent was trying not to show it, but I could see doubt and defeat in his face. 'Won't hurt to try, I guess, but it'll need tae be one hell o' a plan. C'mon.' He nodded towards his campervan. 'Let's talk.'

As Harkin and I went to follow Stent, Jamie picked up the crate Traggheim had given him. 'Things to do. I'll catch you later.'

I nodded briefly and followed Stent and Harkin up the steps into the camper. Garm watched me, then turned decisively and trotted after Jamie.

'If I didn't know better, I'd think all the rats were deserting a sinking ship,' muttered Harkin. 'What're they up to?'

'A little idea we came up with,' I replied. 'I'll explain if and when it works. Right now, we need a plan to bring this project back on track.'

'It seems to me,' said Harkin slowly, 'that we have two problems we need to deal with and rapidly – before there's any hope of persuading these people to continue with their work.'

'And those are?' I asked.

'First, they must feel that some measure of defence exists that if the œlves attack again, they will be defended. These are not true galdr-folc and I suspect that having some of their number suddenly and viciously attacked with a thing as horrible as ælf-fire has had a powerful impact on their confidence. Am I correct, Stent?' Not for the first time, I thought Harkin was the ideal person to have by my side in a crisis: practical, down-to-earth, and reliable. He was in his element here.

Stent nodded. 'Aye, that's the matter, Harkin. The ælf-fire threw them all off-kilter. Me too, if I'm honest. It wasnae something any o' us had heard of before.'

'Sorry to be stupid,' I put in. 'But what exactly *is* ælf-fire? From what I'm hearing, this is more than any simple flame?'

Harkin nodded. 'You're right there, Drew. It's a fearful weapon they've used. Thankfully, it's hard for them to get the ingredients. They never used it at Yester or when we met them on the moor, and that shows their supply has limits.'

'But what is it?' I insisted.

They looked at each other and Stent spoke first. 'Like napalm,' he said.

'I don't know what napalm is,' said Harkin. 'But if it means a sticky, white-hot fire that attaches to whoever it touches and burns to naught, then that's about it. They concoct it from a mix of plant extracts, which they distil down in a process driven by ælf-galdr – massive amounts of it.' He considered for a moment. 'That may be why they could use it here – they're closer to their base and can draw on more ælf-galdr. Anyway, I daresay Alyssum can tell you more about it. It's vile stuff.'

'It sounds hideous,' I said, and they both nodded with vigour. I paused, thinking what a nightmare this could be, then pulled myself back to the here and now. 'So, what's our second problem, Harkin?'

'If these folks are so scared of ælf-fire, then defence alone won't bring back their confidence in the work. They need to believe that we have a plan so clever that they're unlikely to need defending. And you know what else, lads?'

We both looked at him expectantly.

'We'd bloody well better have such a plan or we're going to get some of the same.'

I tried not to notice as Stent slumped slightly in resignation. This was up to me. Not only was I, against all my expectations, the most powerful wielder of galdr here, but these two stalwarts were expecting leadership and I was going to have to deliver some.

'We need to meet this new threat in a way that the ælves don't expect,' I began. Both Harkin and Stent were listening intently. So far, so good, but this had better hit the mark. 'We can't protect everyone when they're out and about. We don't have enough people with the power to fight off ælf attacks. Basically, it's Ashnil, Harkin and I for the time being.'

'My power is small enough,' said Harkin. 'Though Alyssum has some skill too.' He sighed. 'But together it's little enough to defend these people.'

'Then we have to meet the threat head-on and neutralise it before it can get near them.'

'But how's that possible?' asked Stent. 'We dinnae ken where the ælves have their base. Nobody knows.'

'That's true,' said Harkin. 'The bastards have their fortress so well-hidden behind layers of ælf-galdr that nobody has ever found it.'

'So we need to bring them to us.' I was being as decisive as I could. 'What are ælves good at?'

'Being bastards?' suggested Stent, unhelpfully.

Harkin gazed at me for a long moment. 'Being arrogant and confident in themselves. Is that where you're leading us?'

'Exactly. I propose to use that arrogance to lead them into a trap. If we can draw the Ælf-queen into some trap which allows us to harm her, although we may not knock her out, we could give her a bloody nose.'

'And by that, give heart to Stent's stout folks,' finished Harkin for me.

'But these are ælves,' protested Stent. 'Some of the most powerful aglaecan there are.'

'But that's just it,' I said. 'They're not! Not any more. They're powerful, but thanks to the work you've been doing, their power is localised. There couldn't be a better time to do this.'

Harkin and I looked at Stent. His gaze passed back and forth between us. 'You're crazy – both of you.' He stared out of the window for a moment, and then a slow smile came over his face. 'But you might just be right.' He barked a laugh. 'This could actually work if we move swiftly, before any mair people leave. How do we set this trap, then?'

'Here's what I have in mind,' I said, and they both leaned forward to listen.

Some time later, we emerged from the van, feeling more positive. I immediately sensed a change in the camp. Wee Jeannie was emptying a bucket of water outside the catering tent and gave me a smile. Two others waved as they crossed the site. I turned to the others.

'Something's happened – the atmosphere's changed.'

Stent looked about him. 'Aye. What's going on?'

'I reckon *she's* what's happened,' said Harkin, nodding past me towards Ashnil, who was deep in conversation with the two Jackies in front of their workshop. I could see that, whatever she was saying, they were lapping it up.

'D'you know what we never reckoned on?' said Harkin. 'We never reckoned on the impact that there angelus would have on folk. She's got skills the likes of us can barely comprehend, skills that can cheer folk up.'

Of course! I realised she was using some of her glamorous influence on them, just as she had with me, back in the diner. That seemed a very long time ago… A thought struck me. 'Is it fair on them, to manipulate them like that?'

'All is fair in love and war, I reckon,' said Harkin. 'What do you think, Stent? They're your people.'

'Anything that turns back the tide o' despair looks good to me just now,' he replied. 'If they're happy, I'm happy.'

I walked across to Ashnil, who was finishing her conversation with the Jackies, both of whom were beaming. She gave me a radiant smile as she moved to join me.

'They seem happier,' I said, guardedly.

She looked at me pensively. 'You think I've manipulated their emotions, don't you?'

'Yes I do. You have history in that regard.'

'Touché.' She leaned forward and kissed me full on the mouth, lingering until the taste of her threatened to overwhelm me. Despite my worries, I didn't resist.

'What did you feel then?' she asked.

'That was... very nice.'

She giggled. 'You are deliciously repressed, Drew. I know what you felt, because I felt it too. And it didn't need any manipulation. You felt love because love was there to be felt. These people just need to be given reasons to feel good.'

I felt caught between this delicious moment and the reality of our situation. 'We're working on plans to defend them and distract the ælves,' I said.

'And I'm sure they're good plans, but you're being cold and logical. They needed someone warm and empathetic to tell them how much they matter and how much what they're doing matters. They needed hope, so I gave them some.'

'How did you do that?'

'The same way people have been doing it for thousands of years. I gave them a pretty face, telling them about their hero.'

I felt misgivings. 'Ashnil, who have you told them is their hero?'

'You, of course.' Before I could say anything more, she kissed me again, pulling my head down to her and holding the kiss whilst she gently probed my lips with her tongue. She was intoxicating. Eventually, she pulled back slightly and whispered in my ear. 'I told them about the hero who fought off an ælf attack and slayed a sceadhu. But they were most thrilled when I told them their hero is in love with the pretty girl and that we're going to live happily ever after together. Nobody can resist a romance.'

Over her shoulder, I could see Wee Jeannie pointing at us and smiling. 'Perhaps the romance should be real?' I whispered back.

She rested her head against my neck for a moment and sighed. 'I'd like that,' she said.

32. PASSING

The camp nestled in the bottom of a river valley overlooked by a small hill jutting out from the valley wall. In the iron age, our ancestors had turned it into a hill-fort, and the vestiges of circular defensive ditches were still visible amongst the sheep-nibbled turf. At the top I found Jamie, with his back resting on a hump in the ground, gazing down into the valley. Beside him Garm was sitting, his nose wiffling constantly at the scents being blown up the valley by the light breeze.

'You must be able to see miles from here,' I commented, flicking a few sheep droppings aside, then dropping onto the springy turf beside him.

'This'll do nicely, Drew,' he replied. 'We can see in both directions along the valley, and down that side valley opposite. Plus, there's a fair view across the hills behind us.'

'Does it work?' I asked.

'Seems to.' He indicated a brass and copper box sitting atop the small crate Traggheim had given him in the car. 'It's doing everything old Traggheim said it should.'

Every few seconds, the machine gave a loud click, as though to prove it was functioning. Traggheim had burned the midnight oil to make a machine that would sense heightened ælf-galdr and give us a warning if any ælves approached the camp. This was the first element of my plan to defeat the ælves: to prevent them from sneaking up on us. Jamie had volunteered to take charge of this. He also had a small compressed air foghorn which Traggheim had, in his own words, 'Knocked up.' It would allow him to raise the alarm in the camp below.

'How're things doing down there?' he asked.

'Better, but still fragile. Ashnil's busily creating the legend of Drew, Defender of the Just. They seem to be buying into it.'

He laughed out loud. 'Seriously? Your ego will be out of control, if you're not careful.' He considered for a moment. 'I suppose giving them something to believe in isn't a bad idea.'

'That's what Ashnil thinks. She's good at this. It seems to work.'

'On Stent too? I can't see him being a sucker for a pretty face, he seems a tough cookie.'

'Actually, yes, but this has knocked him off balance. Harkin's taken him in hand. By the time I get back down there, I think they'll both have had a few drams.'

'Lucky buggers.'

'Yeah. Have you got everything you need?' I looked at the sky. 'Looks like it might get chilly.'

He showed me his rucksack. 'I've got my bivvy bag and plenty of supplies. Fido here can keep me warm if need be.'

Garm's head slowly swivelled round to glare at him.

He held up his hands. 'Ok, ok.'

Garm continued to glare for a moment, then returned to sniffing the air. I gave Jamie a look. He shrugged.

'So, you and Ashnil, then?' he asked.

I smiled. 'Maybe. If we come through this unscathed. It's hard to look much beyond the next few days at the moment.'

'Only you could actually score yourself an angel, Drew.'

'She's an angelus. Trust me, there's a difference.'

'Yeah, whatever.'

We sat in silence for a while, looking along the valley. In the background, the click of Traggheim's latest creation punctuated the sound of a skylark singing.

'This isn't good,' said a strange voice.

'What!' I jumped, looking about, trying to work out where the voice had come from.

'I said nothing,' replied Jamie.

'Bugger – that's what I thought,' came the voice. 'Down here, you pillock.'

I dropped my gaze, to see Garm staring directly at me, nodding slowly. 'Garm?' His lips hadn't moved.

'For fuck's sake, catch up, two-legs,' said the voice in my head. 'You can hear me – get over it. WHY you can hear me is what matters. Something must've happened to Archer.'

'What's up with you two?' asked Jamie, frowning as I 'shushed' him.

'What do you mean "something"?' I asked.

The dog's eyes widened. 'He must be dead. Why else would his power to understand me have jumped?' He glared at me. 'You have big shoes to step into, sunshine.'

'What's going on?' persisted Jamie.

I groaned. Why did things just keep getting worse? 'I can hear Garm talking to me, which is something only Archer can do. Garm thinks that means something terrible has happened to Archer. He may even be dead.'

'Shit. What now?'

I stared at the horizon and thought for a moment, then decided. 'Whatever has happened in Edinburgh, we first need to finish what we've started here. And we need to do that now.' I turned to Traggheim's box, which was still clicking steadily. 'Now we can see if it's other function works.' On the lid were ten copper pads in two semi-circles. I placed my fingertips firmly on them, closed my eyes, and concentrated. *Time for some action, lizard,* I thought.

Deep in my mind, the wyrm stirred itself. My breathing grew faster and a terrible pain grew, but I held it in and kept pulling.

'More,' I told the wyrm and the flow of galdr increased. The agony grew until I could hold it no longer and released it. A massive magenta lightning bolt shot into the sky from the box. Reaching cloud-base it shattered into a profusion of glowing symbols, silhouetted against the clouds: geometric shapes, stylised animals and others, all meaningless to me, but with a clear meaning to their target. They slowly faded and I rubbed my forehead, grinning with relief.

'So, what's meant to happen?' asked Jamie. All he had seen was me touching the box and scowling.

'I just projected a massive "fuck you" across the sky. If it works, I've left the Ælf-queen with no choice but to respond. If she doesn't, she'll lose face with her people. And with any luck, she'll be so angry about it she might make a mistake I can exploit.'

'Err, I'm all for you waving your dick at that brutal bitch, but what exactly are you going to do when she comes galloping up that valley with a horde of ælves behind her, all hacked off and spoiling for a fight?' He looked distinctly frightened and I realised he was the only one of us to have suffered the worst she could do.

'Don't worry, Jamie. That will not happen.'

'How do you know? How can you possibly be so sure?'

'Because I challenged her to face me one-on-one,' I replied. 'The winner takes my ancestor's token.'

Jamie stared at me. After a moment, he said, 'You stupid idiot.'

I shrugged, then started, as Garm's voice appeared in my head again. 'Let's get it over with then,' he said.

I looked down to see the dog lying on his back with his legs in the air. 'If you're my new "master" (he actually pronounced the inverted commas around that) then the canine part of me must formally submit to you, however much it pains me to do this.'

I grinned.

He bared his teeth and growled. 'If you even consider rubbing my belly, there will be serious fucking consequences for you,' he said.

Leaving Jamie to keep watch, with the aid of Traggheim's gadget now clicking away merrily once more, I galloped down the steep slope, stumbling over tussocks and laughing with exhilaration. Strange to tell, I felt really alive. I knew I was soon to face possible, even likely, death at the hands of the Ælf-queen, but I could still make an impact and that felt good. Of course I mourned for Archer, but there was no time to dwell on the news. For now, my focus had to be on the Ælf-queen.

Garm bounded beside me effortlessly and kept glancing sideways at me. Eventually, he said just two words. 'You'll do.' Then he sped ahead.

Coming into the camp, Harkin and Ashnil met me, their faces grim. The news about Archer had already reached them from Traggheim via the tocsin.

'Tell me briefly,' I said. 'Then we need to focus on the ælves. They'll be marching to us by now.'

'That was you, Drew?' asked Ashnil. 'I thought it must be.' A smile flickered. 'Very impressive. If that insult doesn't bring her to us, then nothing will.'

Harkin cut in. 'I will make this as brief as is possible, Drew. Traggheim contacted Stent, using that contraption, and told him of what has taken place in Edinburgh.' He held out his hands. 'Archer must be dead.'

'Must be?' I asked. 'Or, is?'

'According to Traggheim, Archer went in search of Obadiah. Traggheim begged him not to, but without success. His machines showed massive galdr activity and then... nothing. The daemon has fallen.'

'That explains why Garm's allegiance has transferred to me.'

Ashnil gasped. 'Truly? Drew, that is incredible. That means your powers have grown to where, with no remaining daemons, you are the next most worthy.'

'What about Obadiah?' I asked. 'Does this mean Archer killed him before he died?'

'He's an aglaecan by choice, so he must be forfeit,' she said, squeezing my arm. 'But you're right. Now isn't the time to mourn Archer.'

Harkin nodded vigorously. 'Stent and his boys are right back in the doldrums from the news,' he said. 'I don't think we'll gain much help from that quarter.'

A loud honk, followed by shouts, floated down from the hill-fort. Looking up, I could make out Jamie, waving frantically across the valley.

'Here she comes,' I said, looking at them both.

We walked out of the camp to meet her and I was struck by how absurd I would have thought this just a few months ago. I was about to face mortal combat with the queen of the ælves, supported by a Bloodcap, an angelus, and a Jack Russell Terrier. But this was no fantasy and I could easily be dead in a few minutes. I laughed out loud.

'What's funny?' asked Ashnil.

'This. It's utterly mad. But if I've got to die a sudden and horrible death, what better way to do it?'

Harkin and Ashnil exchanged glances.

'I was right,' Garm growled in my head. 'You'll do.'

Arrayed in front of us were the Ælf-queen and her retainers. She sat astride a gleaming white horse. I idly wondered if she was riding the same horse as when I saw her meet my ancestor. Do ælves have immortal steeds? Who knows? A semi-circle of six retainers, similarly mounted, was behind her, each carrying an impossibly long spear, surely ceremonial. To my surprise, one of them was "Stanley". As I looked at him, he gave an almost imperceptible shake of his head and I moved my gaze away. Why was he here? And why had he risked acknowledging me?

'We meet once again, Drow Macleod, child of your forebearss.' The Ælf-queen smiled nastily, then spat onto the ground between us. 'Your little show doess nothing to impresss.'

'Yet here you are, you vile old termagant, worried enough to respond to my summons.' (I rather liked 'termagant,' an insult I'd pinched from Harkin.)

'You are–'

'Oh, shut up and let's get on with this, you sad old battle-axe.' I deliberately interrupted her, determined to raise her tempo, if I could. 'I've more important things to do than waste my time on you.'

Her eyes flashed and she leapt down from her horse, landing impossibly lightly, and clicked her fingers. Instantly, a glittering white sword appeared in her hand and she swung it twice, checking the balance.

Harkin stepped forward and offered me a blade. I do not know where he got it from, but I shook my head, knowing I hadn't the sword skills; it would only hamper me. 'I don't need a sword to deal with this worthless piece of shit.'

'Your dayss are ended,' she spat out, leaping forward, with the sword point extended, to run me through. As the tip struck my chest, I gasped and staggered back. I heard Jamie, who had come down the hill, moan behind me. The Ælf-queen's eyes flashed towards him and widened as she recognised him. Then, to her evident surprise, I caught my breath and took a step back, just winded – and mentally thanking the dweorg for the thin, galdr-infused chest-plate under my shirt. 'I'm not that easy to kill, you toxic bitch,' I told her calmly.

She scowled and, not for the first time, I wondered if I was out of my depth. Then I remembered Archer and, furious at his loss, I threw myself at her, grasping at her throat with my fingers. She let me do it, confident I couldn't overcome her overwhelming ælf-galdr, until her eyes opened wide as the wyrm's power worked. It allowed me to close my fingers round her wind-pipe and squeeze, at the same time as I poured galdr towards her sword, which shattered.

With a cough, the Ælf-queen used the lightest touch from her empty sword-hand to lift me off the ground, then hurl me back down, my grasp torn from her throat. She spat again and sneered, jumping forward, high into the air. Just in time, I saw her rapid descent towards my head and half-rolled away, throwing a blast of galdr to push her sideways. I jumped to my feet.

'Cease this nonsense and take action, Duh-rew Mac-Loud,' ordered the wyrm's voice in my head. 'You have power to squash this insect.'

It seemed a good enough insult, so I shouted, 'I'll squash you, you insect,' and, pulling as much galdr from the wyrm as I could, I threw myself at her and head-butted her face. She wasn't expecting that and as her nose shattered with a satisfying crunch, she screamed in pain. But now she was furious, and so were her followers. Two of them moved towards me and I thought I was in even bigger trouble, but to my delight Stanley lowered his spear in front of them and said something urgent in ælvish, presumably reminding them this was a one-on-one fight.

Suddenly, though, my head felt as though it would burst. I couldn't breathe or move, and I slowly collapsed onto my knees in blinding, incapacitating agony. The Ælf-queen stepped forwards, her fingers outstretched to point at me and I could do nothing to stop her. Agony overcame everything. I fell forward onto my own outstretched hands as she drew her glittering white knife from her waist to finish me. The pain doubled, my head feeling as though it were on fire. I thought it was over, when she inexplicably stopped in her tracks, and even stepped back, her eyes wider still. In an instant, my pain disappeared, but my arm felt white hot – and I realised the agony in my head had been the wyrm, repelling the Ælf-queen's advance.

I grabbed my opportunity and hauled myself to my feet. She had loosened her grip on the knife and, using a technique I'd never really perfected, I managed to pull it from her hand to mine using intense galdr, feeling the heat of it course through me until her knife landed in my hand. That was ice cold.

She was on the back foot now, but she leapt towards me, hissing, her nails grasping at my face. I ducked behind her and brought my leg around hers so her body was across my front, allowing me to press the knife to her throat. All of a sudden, everything went silent.

I slowly pushed her to the ground, my knee on her slim, ice-cold chest, keeping the knife pressed into her throat as blood dripped from her face.

'You would never dare,' she hissed.

'Stanley!' I called, not taking my eyes off her for a moment. 'What happens if I claim her galdr and let her live?'

'A new king or queen would be sselected.'

'Ashnil? What do you think?'

'Be careful, Drew. If you don't draw her galdr, she'll be back, but it would be dangerous stuff to have. Ælf-galdr is different and may be toxic.'

'Stanley,' I called again. 'Will you accept her galdr and swear fealty?'

'I will gladly accept her galdr, but I cannot swear,' the ælf replied. 'Instead, I will asssure peace with your folk.'

'Good enough,' I agreed.

I knew it was a risk, but I had a hunch that Stanley would play nicely. He stepped forward, took a silver rope from around his waist and tied a noose in it, slipping it around the Ælf-queen's neck. As he pulled it tight, she slumped and visibly diminished. The new ælf-king pulled her to her feet, nodded to me and said, 'That was well done. I give you peace.' With that, he turned and led his people and their former queen away.

'Bugger me! You lucky bastard.' Stent's praise was qualified, as ever, but it was welcome. So were Ashnil's hugs and Harkin giving me a mighty thump on the back. Disentangling myself, I looked after the departing ælves. Their new king stopped and looked back at me. He nodded his respect, and then he and his retinue disappeared.

'You should have forced them to give you fealty, Drew,' Harkin growled. 'Without it, we'll never be certain of peace.'

'Aye, I don't trust they ælf-bastards any mair than I can throw them. Could you not have done that?' asked Stent.

I shook my head, rubbing the throbbing wyrm-scar. 'History has shown us that subjugation causes deep-felt resentment that grows and comes back to bite you. If you finish your work here, Stent, we'll have them boxed in and, for the time being, they have a king with different priorities.'

Ashnil linked her arm through mine and pinched me hard. 'Don't get too full of yourself.'

'She's right,' said Jamie. 'What was it Roman Generals had when they marched in triumph? A slave muttering in their ear about being only mortal, or something of that sort?'

'A slave, you say?' Ashnil scowled at him.

'No, no. I didn't mean...' He trailed off, then saw her grinning and realised she was messing with him. 'Ha bloody ha. But it was good to see that vicious bitch with a bust face and a noose around her neck,' he said, with feeling.

'We'll never know what they do to a failed queen in private, but I'm sure it won't be pretty. And she deserves every bit,' I told him.

33. LEADER

With the Ælf-queen neutralised, we collected Alyssum and headed back to Edinburgh, leaving Stent and his gang to carry on the work to contain any future ælf activity. Jamie insisted on driving the Carpy and when I detected a unique aroma in the car, I realised Garm had joined us too.

The atmosphere in the car was strained, especially after we told Alyssum about Archer. She was distraught, and it was also obvious she had misgivings about Ashnil and me. In truth, I wasn't sure a relationship with an angelus was a good idea either, but Ashnil and I had had no time to discuss it and I had bigger priorities. I couldn't believe Archer was gone. That smarmy bastard Obadiah has taken out the person who had protected and trained me.

Jamie, who didn't really know Archer, was still riding the high from having seen the Ælf-queen humiliated, and at first he chattered on about the ælves and the camp. Gradually, he fell quiet. We drove the rest of the way in reflective silence.

Getting out of the Carpy, I rushed off to see Traggheim before anyone could try to join me. I wanted to have this conversation alone.

'Drew, my boy. You are very welcome indeed. I have been so worried about you,' the dweorg gushed. He chivvied me through to the back room and inflicted a pot of his smoked tea on me. 'You must tell me everything that happened.'

'All in good time, Traggheim. First I need you to tell me about Obadiah and Archer. What is the story with those two?'

His face fell. 'Ah, that is a sad and difficult tale, and not one I care to recall.' His bright, deep-set eyes regarded me, then he clearly reached a decision. 'But you are right, of course. These are things you need to know. In fact, I suppose you have *a right* to know.'

He drew his chair closer. 'These events I shall describe to you occurred a long time ago and I heartily wish they had stayed in the past. But the past has a habit of influencing the present and thus we must understand it.' Traggheim topped up his cup and continued. 'You have heard from Archer about Agnes Finnie, yes?'

I nodded.

'Well, I am certain he did not divulge the full story. I think he tried to pretend it didn't happen as it truly did.'

The window rattled. He got up and let Garm in. Garm jumped down and curled up next to the hearth, but his eyes were wide open, listening to the old dweorg's words.

'You see, the root cause of the brutal execution of Agnes was not a witch-hunting frenzy by the townspeople. Nor was it just their desire to avoid repaying their debts to her. It was much deeper than that.'

'It was Obadiah, wasn't it?'

He nodded. 'Obadiah was experimenting with ways to use galdr to his own advantage: attempting to gain vast power by using the misfortune of others as conduits. This was not only dangerous for Obadiah, it was destructive for those he used. Archer tried to discourage him and then to prevent him, but to no avail.' He looked towards the hearth. 'Garm was there and saw it all.'

Garm nodded slowly. In my head I heard him say, 'Bastard. Total fucking bastard.' But he seemed content to let Traggheim tell the story.

'Agnes was indeed a witch, as they would call it then. A healer, we would say today. Much like Alyssum, of course, Agnes' descendant.'

I gasped. 'Does that mean Alyssum and Archer are related?'

'No, no. Archer is not Alyssum's ancestor, but he has ensured Agnes' female descendants have kept to her path and he has protected them from harm. Alyssum is the latest in a long line. Obadiah manipulated Agnes to enhance her abilities and manipulated those around her to build resentment, jealousy, hatred, and anger. His goal was to create an emotional maelstrom and then use it to generate a large quantity of galdr, which he could snatch from her at the moment of her violent death. Archer didn't realise this was happening until it was too late and the die, as they say, was cast.'

'No wonder he's bitter,' I said.

'And more. He blamed himself. Not only did his fellow-daemon Obadiah first encounter Agnes through Archer, but Archer was so infatuated with her he failed to see the signs until it was too late.'

'Couldn't Archer do anything? He was a powerful daemon. I can't believe he didn't overcome Obadiah.'

'Oh, he tried. They fought. It was a battle royal on Arthur's Seat. They were well-matched, and the battle went on for days, each getting steadily weaker. Eventually, Obadiah slipped away. We hoped he was gone for good. It took decades for Archer to recover to full strength.'

'Well, that explains the irrational way Archer behaved when he realised Obadiah was back.'

'If I ever see Obadiah again, I'll rip his balls off,' Garm growled. 'And I'll enjoy it too.'

Traggheim, oblivious to what Garm was telepathing, continued. 'There's more. Whilst you've been away, I've been doing some research. The appearance of Major Weir's shade was troubling me. I think his inexplicable fall from grace and execution in 1670, twenty-six years after the death of Agnes Finnie, was also the work of Obadiah. That helps to explain the sudden appearance of his shade, in concert with the return of Obadiah.'

'But if Obadiah could do that so soon, does that mean their fight didn't weaken him as much as much as it seemed?'

'Just so,' said Traggheim. 'And worse. His powers are likely to be very substantial because of manipulating the diabolical behaviour and execution of the Major. And who knows what else he may have been up to in the intervening years to build his powers?'

'So, not only do we have a powerful renegade daemon, he's probably vastly more powerful than he would be naturally?'

'Worse,' Garm growled in my head. 'He killed Archer.'

I stared at Traggheim. 'Archer's powers?'

'I fear so.'

'Bloody hell.' I thought for a moment. 'Where did Archer go to fight with Obadiah?'

'We don't know, I'm afraid,' replied Traggheim.

'You?' I asked the dog.

'I was with you at the fierdwic, fuckwit.' Garm bared his teeth.

'Shouldn't you be more respectful to me now?' I asked him.

'Dream on.'

Traggheim looked at each of us and slowly shook his head.

I left Traggheim and went for a walk to clear my head. I needed some peace to work out what my next move should be. But it wasn't to be. As I stepped past Traggheim's shop sign, gently creaking in the breeze, I found Ashnil waiting for me. She gave me a winning smile and a hug, which I really wasn't in the mood for, and she sensed it and pulled back a little.

'What's the matter?' She frowned. 'Are we ok?'

This wasn't the right time, but my confused and worried mood brought out the worst in me, maybe exacerbated by the damp, chill evening. 'I don't know, Ashnil. I really don't know what to think.'

She touched my arm. 'Walk with me and tell me what's going through your mind.' She meant well, but sometimes I just can't help showing my worst side.

'I just don't think that we're suited to each other,' I blurted out. 'I can't see this working.'

She blinked away a tear, then a fighting look came across her face. 'Don't you dare just cast me off. It's clear how you feel about me. I can sense it, and I feel the same about you. I love you, Drew, and I'm certain that we belong together. I've been careful not to use my powers on you, so I know our feelings are real. So don't you dare pretend otherwise, Drew Macleod!' She drew herself up to her full height and glared at me defiantly. Despite myself, I thought how pretty she was, perhaps even more so when angry.

I took her arm and led her through the close and onto the High Street. 'Ashnil, I know that's all true and I can't possibly pull the wool over your eyes. If there's one thing angelii excel at, it's understanding human emotions.'

'Unlike you.' She put that in with a pout.

'I won't argue, but don't you see that's exactly why it can't work between us? How we feel about each other is only a starting point. We're different species, for heaven's sake! If we're together, you lose everything. Will you still be you? Will you change? I don't think either of us knows how it will affect you, and you might come to regret your decision. You could never go back, could you?'

'No, but–'

'Never mind "buts", Ashnil. We're not compatible. Being in love is wonderful, but it doesn't solve the problem of reality, which for us is that it can't possibly work. And what about Obadiah and the parallel realm, and where do I fit into that now? What room do I have in my life for love?'

Her eyes flashed with anger. 'Well, thank you for mansplaining that for me, Drew. The only thing that's truly clear here is that you fear committing to a good thing and you're scared to take a risk. You're right. It won't work between us, because only one of us can think clearly and behave like an adult.' She stepped back from me, glaring. Then she shook her head, turned and ran away into the mist, leaving behind only the vague sense that I had handled that badly and was probably being an idiot.

I briefly considered going after her, then thought better of it. Whatever else I did, I needed my head clear to focus on the bigger problem: Obadiah.

'I said you were a fuckwit.' Garm trotted out of the mist, giving me a withering look, and sat on the pavement beside me.

'What do you know about relationships?' I snarled at him. 'You live in a world of "meet, shag, move on".'

'Do you know you sound really jealous when you say that? Anyway, I choose how to live my life, but I can see what's bloody obvious. She's the best thing that is ever, *ever* going to happen to you.' He sniffed his leg reflectively before adding, 'So, you're a dickhead.'

I sighed. 'You're not helping, Muttley.'

He darted forward and nipped my ankle hard. 'Never think you can speak to me like that! Show me respect, two-legs.'

'Sorry Garm,' I said, rubbing my ankle. 'I'm distracted, and not just about Ashnil.'

'Fuck, you overthink things. You're standing there, all set to devise some clever plan to handle Obadiah. Aren't you?' he asked accusingly.

'Of course I am – I have to do something.'

He shook his head, slowly. 'I'll make this simple for you, stupid. Where's Obadiah?'

'I don't know.'

'How did he kill Archer?'

'I don't know.'

'How can you defeat him?'

'I don't know.'

'So, you're being a fuckwit! There's nothing you can do except wait for Obadiah to come to you, which he will definitely do. Then and only then can you answer these questions and make plans. Agreed?'

I nodded. 'I suppose so.'

'There's no bloody suppose about it. So stop being a fuckwit, go after that pretty girl, tell her you're a total twat and that you don't mean what you said.'

'But…'

He bared his teeth and growled menacingly.

'Ok, ok, I take your point.' It seemed easiest to surrender. Overwhelmed, I left him and walked off into the mist, wondering which way Ashnil had gone and debating whether I really should try to catch her up.

As I walked, my head was a swirling chaos of conflicted thoughts, almost too many to process. I stumbled over the wet cobbles with an image of Archer's death at the forefront of my mind. How could that vibrant, solid personality possibly be gone? How could I continue without his guidance? A pain in the arse he may have been, but I needed him. Didn't I? Of course I did. And what about Ashnil? Nobody like her had ever entered my life. I felt a fool for pushing her away, but how could it possibly work between us? And without Archer, who would protect people from the growing aglaecan menace? Could I harness the wyrm's powers and do it? He was fickle, and there's a world of difference between having power and having the deep understanding of how best to harness it. I was surely not much more than a novice. Then my thoughts came back to Archer. What had happened to him and where the hell was his body? Surely the least he deserved was a proper funeral?

As these thoughts circled round and round my mind, I unthinkingly left the High Street and descended The Mound into Princes Street Gardens. The trees dripped with moisture and the clammy weather was keeping people at home, but the quiet solitude suited my mood perfectly. I pulled my jacket collar up and shoved my hands into the pockets.

'Mr Macleod, it is far more pleasant within here, out of the weather.' The smooth, sneering voice was instantly recognisable. I spun round to see Obadiah, sitting in a shelter. I could have sworn he hadn't been there a moment before, but there he sat, relaxed and regarding me with a half-smile as he tapped the ash from a cigarillo. His pin striped suit jacket was unbuttoned, revealing a gold chain crossing his perfectly-tailored waistcoat. He could easily have been a bank manager, enjoying his lunch break.

I moved swiftly towards him, but he moved his little finger slightly and it felt as though I had walked into a plate-glass window.

'Oh really, Mr Macleod, please don't be so silly as to think I would permit you to harm me. You or your little doggy over there.' He waved his hand regally. Following his gesture, I saw Garm, sitting in the grass a hundred yards away, watching us both.

'Now, will you behave or must I cause you pain?' The smooth, oily voice made me more determined to destroy this toxic monster, but there was nothing I could, so with difficulty I mastered my emotions and nodded.

'Good. I wouldn't want you to go the same way as Archer, after all. So much potential wasted.' He tutted.

I clenched my teeth and choked back what I really wanted to say. Perhaps his arrogance might lead him to reveal something useful. 'What happened to Archer?' I asked levelly.

'Oh, something which had been brewing for centuries. Archer's gone, so you may as well forget him.' He smoothed his waistcoat and shot his cuffs, revealing the bright glint of gold cufflinks. He was clearly enjoying the situation. He stared piercingly at me and tilted his head. 'Oh, how charming. You want to find his body, don't you? You're actually grieving and hoping for a funeral to – now what's the modern phrase? – oh yes, you want to "find closure".' The smile disappeared and he snarled, 'There will be none. He is gone and you'll never find a body, Mr Macleod, so give up that naïve thought.'

'How could it possibly be a problem for you to tell me where Archer's body is? If you've killed him, there's no threat to you.'

'Oh, how positively delightful. You think you can persuade me to follow my better nature? Grow up, Mr Macleod. Better nature is not a feature of anyone who succeeds in the parallel realm, and that included Archer. You won't find his body, and that is all you need to know on the subject.'

Garm's voice cut into my mind. 'Don't! Don't even consider it, fuckwit.'

I breathed hard, my fists clenching and unclenching.

'I'm telling you,' Garm went on, 'Suck it up, buttercup. Milk the bastard for what you can find out and come away whilst you still can.'

A smile slowly spread across Obadiah's face. 'Your little doggy giving you advice, is he? How thoroughly amusing.'

'What is it you want, Obadiah?' I still kept my voice as level as I could.

'I want you. But I can see I have more work to do, to show you I am now your only option – unless you prefer to descend into the depths of chaos? You know, I assume, that there is no way to depart the parallel realm, now that you are entangled?'

I nodded.

'Then you need to consider the offer I made when we last met. Your options have narrowed considerably and my offer is strictly time-limited.' He stood up, buttoned his impeccable jacket and unfurled an umbrella. 'One more thing, Mr Macleod. I would advise you to think carefully about your girlfriend.'

'Meaning?' I demanded, hotly.

'Simply that her history is not as pure and pretty as you believe. She had another before you and I employ him.'

'Brother Rillan?'

'Just so, Mr Macleod. Who do you think assisted me in luring Archer into an ambush? Angelii are so delightfully gullible.' He shook out the umbrella and opened it. 'Good day, Mr Macleod. I guarantee we shall meet again soon.' He turned and strode away.

I looked at Garm, noticing as I did so, a fox's brush disappearing into the shrubs. Garm trotted across to me. 'Move it, two-legs. You're wanted at Archer's library.'

'By who?'

'You mean "by whom", and it doesn't matter. Shift your gawky, two-legged carcass or I'll bite your arse.'

We went in via Alyssum's shop. As we descended the spiral staircase, I could hear voices, but when the heavy door creaked open, the room fell silent. Suspicious, I thought, as Alyssum, Jamie and Traggheim, all looked at me expectantly. Garm nudged me forward.

'What is this?' I asked. 'Some sort of intervention?'

'That's exactly what it is,' said Alyssum. She gave me a brief hug, then pointed to the leather sofas facing the fire. 'Sit,' she commanded. 'And pin your ears back.'

I did as I was bid, Traggheim and Jamie sitting alongside. Inevitably, Garm settled by the fire and began toasting his backside, whilst Alyssum got down on the rug beside him, scratching his ear.

'Mate,' began Jamie. 'We're worried about you and we're worried about what will happen next. We need you to stop crashing about and get focused. I know I can't contribute much to this, but I'm inextricably involved...'

Alyssum looked away and stifled a cough. *Something going on there,* I thought.

Jamie continued. 'I'm involved in this, and I know you better than anyone. You're grieving for Archer, you've lashed out at Ashnil, and we're afraid you're going to do something stupid with Obadiah.' He looked at Traggheim.

'Jamie is right, Drew. This is no time for uncertainty and upset. Nor is it a time for emotional, cluttered thinking. We need to make plans and we need you in the centre, thinking rationally.'

Alyssum leaned over and patted my foot. 'What these two are trying to say, in their clumsy, roundabout way, is that you're the most powerful of galdr-folc remaining and the folc are threatened. You need to be the focal point of a collective action. A leader, even. So we need you back.'

She smiled warmly. 'Stop acting like you're on your own, Drew. You're not and you should know that.'

I leaned back into the creaking leather of the Chesterfield and looked up at the ceiling. A cobweb slowly waved in the rising air above the fire. I looked around at the tall shelves, packed with leather-bound books, and something occurred to me.

'Billions of words,' I said.

Alyssum and Jamie looked at each other.

'Drew?' queried Traggheim.

'These books.' I gestured around the library. 'Certainly millions, probably billions, of words of wisdom and knowledge about the parallel realm, about galdr-folc and aglaecan. The galdr-folc are threatened by a brutal person and they've lost the daemon who has protected them for many centuries. Somewhere in the library there must be an answer to how we stop Obadiah from rampaging through the galdr-folc of Edinburgh.'

'But you're now powerful,' said Jamie. 'Surely, with your own power and the with the power of the wyrm to draw on, you can defeat Obadiah? You took out the sceadhu and the Ælf-queen.'

I shook my head. 'It's not that simple. The sceadhu was stupid and her anger and arrogance blinded the Ælf-queen. I may have power, but Obadiah has more, and he's a daemon, with many centuries of knowledge and experience to draw on.'

'Drew is right, I'm afraid,' said Traggheim. 'This requires guile, tactics and capability, as much as it requires the application of raw galdr.'

'We need to search the library,' I said. 'We need to find the solution.'

'There are two other things we need,' said Alyssum. 'We need you to make up with Ashnil and stop being an idiot about her. She's good for you and you're the only one who can't see it.'

I raised my eyebrows and was about to object when Garm looked up and growled at me.

'Oh yes, you will,' said Alyssum. 'or I'll beat you to a pulp.' And I think she meant it.

'The other thing we shall require is to call a galdr-moot,' said Traggheim. 'I shall set the wheels in motion.'

34. GALDR-MOOT

'That thing is soooo ugly.'

I was sitting at the bottom stair in the main hall of the National Museum of Scotland, looking idly at the display of an old lighthouse lamp with its lenses. The complexity of it fascinated me: hundreds of fillets of glass, each with polished facets, carefully positioned. Alone, each was just a piece of glass, but together they took the light from the lamp and magnified and focused it until it was a powerful beam. Maybe we needed something which could do just that with galdr. I imagined a powerful blast of galdr knocking the smirk off Obadiah's face as it blew him into oblivion.

'Did you hear me?' said Jamie, sitting beside me. 'I said that Chinese thing is really ugly.' He pointed at an exquisite jade carving of a lion. At least I think it was a lion.

'So are you, but it's worth thousands, and you're definitely not,' I pointed out, and he elbowed me in the ribs.

The museum had closed hours ago, but we remained, using a simple cloaking technique I'd found in one of the many books I'd scanned in Archer's library. Fuelled largely by gallons of coffee and some rather suspicious "herbal brownies", Alyssum had made, we had scoured the library, looking for inspiration. What a waste of time.

'They should start arriving soon.' Jamie nodded at a large sixteenth-century clock. 'You know, that thing looks like Traggheim made it: all gears and moving parts, made of shiny brass.'

Of course, he was trying to take my mind off what was to come, or more precisely, our lack of the faintest idea of what was to come. The galdr-moot had been called, inviting all interested parties to come together at the appointed time.

'What if Obadiah comes?' Alyssum had asked, blowing the dust from a book and passing it down to me.

'I don't know. He's certain to have heard about it, but with luck, he won't try to attend. He knows nobody would engage with him and everyone would simply scatter.'

'Even he would never break the truce of the galdr-moot,' put in Traggheim. 'It's beyond sacred.'

To tell the truth, the likelihood that Ashnil would attend and how she would react to me was also a distraction.

'All clear,' said Traggheim from behind me. He held an anodised steel box with a meter on the front and a probe of some sort, which he had been wafting around the museum, to assess whether Obadiah might be present.

'Don't worry, Two-legs,' said Garm to me, emerging from behind the dweorg, his claws clicking on the marble floor. 'I've checked the museum properly, whilst he waved that thing about.'

'Thanks,' I said.

'What for?' asked Jamie.

'Oh, nothing.' Yet again I'd spoken out loud to the dog, instead of thinking about what I wanted to say to him.

'Pillock,' said Garm.

Gradually, people started arriving. Some I knew, many I did not. These were the low-level galdr-folc of Edinburgh, those who were entangled in the parallel realm, less from choice than because of ancestry or accident.

Stent had driven down from the camp and clapped me on the back. 'Go on, yersel', Drew. This'll sort the bastard!'

My heart fell as I looked across the hall. There must have been fifty or sixty people and more coming. Did they all think, like Stent, that I had a brilliant solution? Had destroying the shade of Thomas Weir and defeating the Ælf-queen created expectations I couldn't live up to?

Alyssum waved at me and pointed, pulling me out of my thoughts. To my surprise, Mamma Harbinger appeared, accompanied by Harkin. I hadn't realised she would come.

She hugged me and enveloped me in a miasma of perfume, then planted a wet kiss on my cheek. 'It's a trick,' she whispered. 'My house has a cupboard that opens downstairs here.'

Harkin bustled forward and pumped my hand with enthusiasm. 'This is excellent, Drew, excellent. You have brought together a cross-section of galdr-folc society. What an opportunity to meet and understand so many people.'

The bustle and chatter in the hall suddenly ceased. I looked to see why, fearing Obadiah might have come after all. A lemon yellow glow at the far side showed that the angelii were arriving in style, led by Jophiel. I craned forward to see if Ashnil was with them, but couldn't make her out.

Jophiel and his entourage processed slowly along the hall, the lesser folc parting like the Red Sea, to allow them forward unhindered.

'Now that's an entrance,' murmured Jamie, beside me.

Garm growled, his hackles rising, and with a sinking heart, I realised why. Jophiel's progress through the hall like a conquering hero, accompanied by his retinue, looked positively regal. He was gearing up to place the angelii front and centre of whatever came next.

'The bastard's making a bid for power, with Archer out of the way,' I whispered bitterly to Jamie. 'Why the hell didn't I see this coming?'

Then I spotted Ashnil. She was in the third row of Jophiel's followers, walking slightly apart. She looked stunning, with hair up and wearing the formal white robe of an angelus. Bathed in golden light, she was simply beautiful, but she didn't meet my gaze.

Jophiel reached us and stopped. He nodded gravely to me. 'I am so very sorry to hear of the loss of your friend. He was a loyal and dedicated protector of the deserving.' His voice was commanding, clearly intended to be audible to all. He stepped past me and climbed the stairs, faltering momentarily as he passed Garm, who bared his teeth.

He reached the balcony, where he could overlook everyone. Realising that we were being out-manoeuvred, I trotted up the stairs and stood beside him. He smiled at me and I realised my error – it appeared I was endorsing him. Well, it was too late now.

'My friends,' called Jophiel. 'The time has come for us to gather together for mutual protection. You no longer have a feral daemon to protect you, and a marauding danger threatens you all: another daemon, who has shown his true colours and terrorises all we hold dear.'

Out of the corner of my eye I could see Jamie, struggling to stop a furious Garm from hurtling up the stairs to rip a chunk out of Jophiel. I was tempted to signal him to let Garm go, but some of the crowd were smiling and applauding Jophiel's words, and that was when I realised – whilst we had been working to find the cause of Edinburgh's woes and to put the ælves back in their stone cage, these angelii-bastards had gone behind our backs, spread their lies amongst the small folc and built a following.

Jophiel held up his hands and the room fell silent. 'Fear

not, my friends. The angelii will not fail you. We have never left you and will always be here for you. And we have a plan to resist this new foe and to protect you all. Trust in the angelii and we will save you, I promise it.'

There was open cheering in the hall.

'We trusted Rillan, didn't we?' I spat at him, and Jophiel turned to me and smiled again.

'Rillan is no longer one of us. I forgive you for your anger, Drew.'

I couldn't believe it. These pathetic, self-satisfied people really thought they could step into Archer's shoes and defeat Obadiah! I wanted to shout out and tell the small folk how wrong they were to trust him, but below me I could see Alyssum and Mamma Harbinger, both shaking their heads at me.

Jophiel continued. 'We will call upon a solution nobody else would dare to use.' He glanced sideways at me, but with no idea what he meant, there was nothing I could say or do, and he knew it.

He strode to a glass case containing a massive Roman amphora and passed his hand over the lock, which unlatched with a loud click.

I looked quizzically at the others. Alyssum shrugged, and Harkin shook his head resignedly. They were as bemused as I was, all except Garm, who was now still and rigid. I heard his voice in my head. All he said was, 'Oh fuck.'

Jophiel reached into the case with both hands and withdrew the amphora. Dramatically, he raised it above his head and held it there.

'What is it Garm?' I asked, but no reply came.

Jophiel grunted with the effort as he hurled the amphora onto the floor below, where it shattered, causing a small cloud of dust to billow up.

Around the hall people asked each other what he was doing and what this meant, craning their heads forward expectantly, to see the broken remains of the amphora. But nothing happened and relief swept over me. Of course! It was just another angelus cock-up. Then two things did happen.

Garm's voice said, 'Fuck, fuck, fuck, fuck, FUCK!'

'What the hell is it, Garm?' I demanded. But before he could answer, there came an almighty roar from the other end of the balcony. It sounded like a massive beast had been released and people were moving away in alarm and trying to see past the displays on the floor of the hall to identify the source of the noise.

'Now he's really done it,' said Garm. 'Nobody's seen this for hundreds of years and for good reasons.'

'Seen WHAT?' I shouted at him.

'The bloody carnifex. That clown has unleashed the sodding carnifex.'

35. CARNIFEX

The roar came again, echoing round the hall, where everyone was now huddled into terrified groups. Jophiel looked at me and I could see in his eyes that despite his fine words he was out of his depth.

'Garm, what's happening?' I asked urgently.

'You'll see. He won't harm anyone yet.'

'Yet?' I repeated unhappily.

A massive figure appeared at the far end of the upper gallery and walked towards us with the gait of a heavyweight boxer, confident of his power and strength. When the figure was half-way along the gallery, it turned abruptly and faced the terrified gathering.

The carnifex was well over seven feet tall, with bulging muscles and rope-like sinews. His dark, shining skin was only partly hidden by the oiled leather harness and kilt of a Roman gladiator, but his face was shielded within a huge bronze myrmillo's helmet. All we could see was the glint of his eyes through the face-grille. He brandished a gladius – the short, broad-bladed sword of a Roman legionary – crusted with dried blood. He slowly scanned the hall, his rasping breath echoing loud in the now-silent hall.

'Garm,' I thought-said, urgently. 'What happens next?'

'Anything,' he replied. 'The carnifex is powerful and terrible and knows no rules. He makes them up.'

The carnifex's impossibly deep, gravelly voice boomed around the hall. 'EGO SUM CARNIFEX VENI.' He paused and his head jerked round to glare at Jophiel, before he continued. 'PARA TE AD IUDICIUM MEUM.'

'I am the carnifex. I have come,' translated Garm. 'Prepare yourself for my judgement.'

The carnifex raised his gladius and flakes of dried blood spiralled downwards as he swung it around the hall. The rasping breath and automaton-like movement were truly terrifying. Finally, the gladius stopped, pointing at Jophiel.

I stepped slowly to one side. I wanted no part of whatever was about to happen to Jophiel. The bronze helmet tilted, as though the carnifex was considering something. Then, to my horror, the gladius swung to point at me instead.

Jophiel stepped forward and grandiosely addressed the monster he had summoned. 'Great carnifex, we thank you for accepting our call and we welcome you. We seek your help with a great peril which faces the galdr-folc of Edinburgh…'

He stopped and gulped as the carnifex abruptly pointed his gladius back at Jophiel and rotated it, as though carving a hole. I heard the angelus gasp and choke. His hands reached to his throat and his eyes bulged as he gagged and croaked.

I tried to help him, but found I couldn't move. Something was stopping my limbs from functioning and I could only watch, appalled, as Jophiel turned blue. Finally, the carnifex released him and he fell to the floor, coughing and retching.

'I,' rasped the carnifex, 'will speak your barbarian language. I and only I will decide what will be done. You are a petty fool, angelus, and I will deal with you no further.' The eyes glinted again. 'Unless you irritate me.'

He looked back at me and the awful, blood-crusted sword followed. 'You, I shall deal with. I sense your galdr and I see your part in this.' He crashed the gladius against the cast-iron balustrade. 'ON YOU I SHALL GIVE JUDGEMENT.'

'Time to shine, two-legs,' said Garm, unhelpfully.

I opened my mouth to speak, but found the words would not come, the carnifex was holding me mute.

'I do not need to hear mortal words,' he grated slowly. 'You will learn of the time and place of my judgement.' With that, he finally lowered the gladius and strode slowly away into one of the side galleries.

Finally, I found I could speak again. 'Bloody hell!'

There was a hiss beside me and I saw Jophiel's face looking up, distorted with hatred. 'You,' he spat. 'Always you. What are you?' He coughed and continued. 'A mortal nothing. Why must it be you?'

The other angelii rushed up the stairs to help him to his feet, and he lunged towards me, Jamie and Harkin coming, hopelessly, to my aid. But like a flash, Garm was between us, suddenly bigger, with his hackles raised and his teeth bared. He slowly advanced, snarling and growling. Jophiel slumped in resignation and allowed the other angelii to help him away.

I looked back to the hall and saw that one white robe remained. Ashnil had not joined the other angelii and as I watched, Alyssum took her arm and gently led her away.

The scent of trampled grass and peaty soil on the summit of Arthur's Seat was enhanced by the night dew, and I shuffled slightly, trying to get more comfortable on the sharp-edged basalt outcrop. A slight haze hung over Edinburgh, causing the lights of the city to twinkle and fade. I thought back to being chased up here by a belligerent

Archer, forcing me to learn galdr skills and get fit at the same time. I sighed. He was hard work to deal with, but had taught me so much in such a short time and I missed him.

A pebble went skittering over the edge and I leapt to my feet, spinning around to find its cause. A large shape loomed out of the darkness.

'Peace, peace, Drew. It is only me. I t'ought I may find you up here.' The deep, velvety voice of Mamma Harbinger was interspersed with deep breaths, and her perfume drenched me with a tropical scent as she came closer.

'Can I sit down wit' you a while, boy?' she gasped, lowering herself onto the rock next to me, without waiting for an answer, and giving a deep sigh as she did so. 'Man, that's an awful steep climb, Drew. If I'd known how steep it was, I might never have started.' Her teeth flashed white in the darkness and she reached across and took my hand.

'How are you doin'? How are you feelin' after all that's happened to you?' Her face was in shadow, but I didn't need to see it to know that she was looking at me with her penetrating stare and would brook no prevarication.

'I don't really know,' I said. 'Most people seem to think I'll just step into Archer's shoes and somehow defeat Obadiah, but they're forgetting, or perhaps ignoring, that I'm not Archer. Just because I've inherited his ability to communicate with Garm doesn't mean I have his skills. I've had some lucky breaks and I can call on the wyrm's galdr, but he's a stroppy bugger and having power isn't the same as knowing how to use it. Then there's the carnifex. How the hell do I deal with him?'

Mamma's hand gripped mine like a vice. 'Stop, Drew,' she said. 'Jus' stop. You're tyin' yourself in knots, cause you're tryin' to answer stuff you can't answer.' She gave my hand another squeeze. 'Jus' take a breath, will you, an' listen to me a while.

She was right, of course. I took a deep breath and listened to the low rumble of traffic in the city below. A jet howled in the distance and I glimpsed its navigation lights over the Firth of Forth.

'What do you see?' she whispered. 'An' what do you hear?'

I thought for a moment. 'The city. Everyone going about their business. Probably mostly on their way home after a day at work.'

'Jus' so,' she agreed. 'Life goes on. People live their lives, an' they love, an' they work, an' they look after those who they care about. Jus' as they always have, an' jus' as they always will. The world continues. So does the parallel realm. You, without ever realisin' what you are doin', have taken up Archer's role of tryin' to protect all this. I'm proud of you an' so would Archer be.' She squeezed my hand even tighter, in emphasis. 'Don' you ever forget that.'

She pulled her hand away and became business-like. 'So, what do you know about that carnifex?' she asked.

'Not much. He's clearly powerful – when he turned up, even Garm freaked out. He looks like a gladiator and spoke Latin to begin with, so I guess his origins are probably Roman. And I know he's going to summon me for some sort of challenge.'

'So you see, you know a lot, Drew.' She folded her arms. 'All I can add is that he was the public executioner of Rome and he was galdr-touched, maybe cause of all that torturin' and ritual killin'. Who knows? Now he is called on for a sort of justice. But Rome was a twisted, vicious and unfair place, so his justice ain't what you or I might call justice. He might use torture on you. It was normal back then, an' he thinks nothin' of it. But jus' grit your teeth an' you will be fine.'

I stared at her. What in the hell had I got into now?

281

'Steel yourself, Drew,' she continued. 'This might be a rough ride for you, but you're gon' come through it. I have faith in you, boy.' She laughed suddenly, a deep and lengthy rumble that seemed incongruous.

'Now,' she went on. 'I'm gon' give you three pieces of advice and mind you heed them. Mamma Harbinger don't give out advice to jus' anyone and you're gettin' three bits.'

'Ok.' I gulped. 'Right now, I can use all the advice I can get.'

'My first, is this. Stop worryin' yourself stupid about experience or ability. You're young and you're clever and that lizard, he's givin' you a lot of galdr when you need it. And you've become pretty powerful in your own right too, so jus' you stop doin' yourself down.' She leaned forward and poked me in the chest. 'You jus' do what seems best, an' you won't go far wrong.'

I nodded, far from convinced.

'Second piece of advice is this. Be who you are. Be Drew. Don' try to be somethin' else. Don' try to be Archer. He was a daemon. You're a galdr-touched human. He was him an' you are you. Don' try to be somethin' different, or better, or cleverer, or anythin' else, cause it will jus' make you worse, not better. Look at Obadiah. He's what happens if you let aspirations and ideas get ahead of who are and what you stand for.'

'I understand,' I said. 'And the third piece of advice?'

'That's easy. When you meet the carnifex again and he tests you, just remember it ain't real. None of it's real. He doesn't do real. If you keep that at the front of your mind, you gon' be fine, Drew.'

She heaved herself to her feet. 'Well, it's good lookin' at this city wit' you, Drew, but it's gettin' chilly and I'm goin' back down. Goodnight to you.'

'Goodnight, Mamma, and thanks,' I replied.

She paused for a moment and half-turned. 'One more thing, Drew.'

'Yes?'

'If you don' get together with that fine young angelus and love her for all you're worth, I'm gon' beat you with a big stick, boy.' As she continued down the steep, rocky path, her laugh rolled back up the hill towards me.

I stayed a while, thinking, and finally followed her down the hill. Part way, I halted, the hairs on the back of my neck sticking up. I stared around into the darkness. Just for the briefest of moments, I thought I heard Archer's voice faintly on the wind, saying, 'Help me.' I whirled around, peering into the blackness of the night, but heard nothing more, and after a moment I realised I was hearing things that weren't there. I continued down the path, heading back to the rooms at Traggheim's, which I now shared with Jamie.

That night I woke suddenly and for a moment stared into the dark room, wondering what had disturbed me. Some sort of faint, metallic sound? From nowhere, a truly massive hand grabbed my shoulder and dragged me up off the bed, ripping the bedclothes as though they were tissue paper. An overpowering stench of stale sweat and leather told me who it was: the carnifex. He held me up, so that my face was close to his and his rasping breath was warm on my face. I flailed about, trying to get a purchase with my feet. I grabbed his harness with my left hand and, unable to see much, I dangled helplessly in his grasp, like a kitten in its mother's mouth.

He said just one word. 'NOW,' then released his grip, dropping me to the floor, before stamping out of the room, smashing the door wide open and breaking the lock as he did so.

And then he was gone. After a moment, I clambered to my feet, just as Jamie and Traggheim both arrived in the doorway.

Jamie fingered the smashed door lock.

'The carnifex paid me a friendly visit,' I told them.

'The summons?' asked Traggheim.

'You could call it that.' I pulled on my trousers. 'He doesn't waste words, but I'm clearly required.'

A short time later, they both accompanied me back to the museum, Garm appearing from somewhere as we climbed the steps and Traggheim activated the doorway.

In the main hall we found the carnifex standing on the gallery with his arms folded, glaring down at us. We stopped below him and waited. For some time, nothing happened and the hairs on the back of my neck prickled as that grim visage stared blankly down.

Suddenly he lifted that awful, blood-stained gladius, raising it high above his head before slashing it horizontally, muttering something as he did so. There was a flash of light and from nowhere, a body tumbled to the ground beside us. To my astonishment, it was Obadiah and for a wonderful moment I thought he was dead – until he groaned, stretched, and got to his feet. He brushed the dust from his jacket and straightened his tie, scowling at the carnifex. It only took him seconds to regain his composure, and he smiled smugly at us.

'Mr Macleod.' He inclined his head smoothly. 'And your little friends. How charming.' He looked up at the gallery. 'Great carnifex, was that strictly necessary? A polite request was all that was required if you wished me to attend you.' He gave a slight bow. Next to me, Jamie snorted.

The carnifex pointed his sword directly at Obadiah, who fell silent.

'You shall be tested,' growled the carnifex and spat on

the ground. As he did so, a shot glass of pale-yellow liquid appeared in my hand. I wasn't conscious of picking it up or even of gripping it, but it was there in my right hand and a glance showed me the same had happened to Obadiah.

'You shall both drink,' rasped the carnifex's awful voice.

'Don't resist,' whispered Traggheim.

I took a deep breath and then emptied the glass in one go. It tasted of fresh lemons and thyme. Alongside, Obadiah watched me. Then, as the gladius was raised to point towards him again, he gulped down the contents of his glass too.

Surprisingly, there didn't seem to be any kind of effect. I'd expected some dramatic and probably unpleasant sensation, possibly a truth drug or worse. Instead, I had the pleasant taste of a warm Mediterranean afternoon in my mouth. I turned to whisper to the others, but the words never came out.

Without warning, the floor beneath me disappeared, and I fell with gut-wrenching speed. I flailed as I fell, but there was nothing to grasp onto and darkness enveloped me. With equal abruptness, the sensation stopped without impact and I found myself in some sort of subterranean chamber. I almost lost my footing on the uneven flagstone floor as I got to my feet. Sconces with flaming brands threw flickering yellow light onto walls of rough, handmade brick. But what drew my eye was the centre-piece of the room: a massive, polished bronze bull, larger than life-sized. The dancing reflections of the flames seemed to bring it alive. Below it, a broad iron brazier crackled and burned, the flames licking at its belly.

I was alone in the cellar, but before I had time to work out what was happening, something propelled me towards the bull. Twisting round, I could see nobody was there, just a powerful force, moving me inexorably towards the bull.

I tried to resist, but it was pointless: I was heading for a nightmare and could do nothing to prevent it. As I slid closer, a large door on the bull's flank hinged open. I tried to fight the movement, but how do you fight something that isn't there? The unseen force lifted me off my feet and flung me inside the bull. The door slammed closed behind me and in the darkness I gasped as I felt the hot metal. I was truly terrified and should have been screaming blue murder, but a strange calm came over me. I have no explanation for it, but instead of blind panic, Mamma Harbinger's words came back to me. 'Jus' remember, it ain't real. None of it's real. If you keep thinkin' that, you gonna be fine.'

I took a deep breath and tried to think about Ashnil. 'This isn't real, but she is and she loves me,' I told myself. With something tangible to focus on, perhaps I could get through this.

The heat of the brazier was gradually increasing and I could hear the roar of the flames as they licked the bull's belly, transferring the heat to my arms and legs. I wriggled, trying to let each limb get a few seconds off the metal to cool a little, but it was pointless: the metal was getting hotter and hotter and my hands and legs were blistering. I breathed deeply and tried to overcome the searing, savage pain. 'This isn't real, but Ashnil is and she loves me. This isn't real, but Ashnil is and she loves me.'

The burning of my skin became unbearable. I bit into my lip and felt blood flow down my chin. It was now a fight between the intense pain and my determination not to surrender to this 2,000-year-old maniac. I kept telling myself the pain wasn't real, but the exquisite agony kept building. 'It's an illusion,' I told myself. 'This isn't real, but Ashnil is and she loves me.' I visualised her face, the deep blue eyes, the tiny freckles on her nose, her soft lips. But the agony drew me back. 'This isn't real, but Ashnil is and she loves me.'

The smell of burned cloth and charring flesh filled the black void as I writhed in pain. I choked on the smoke and my back and legs burned further. The pain was incredible, but somehow the thought of Ashnil and Mamma Harbinger's promise held me on the very edge of sanity. I shouted at the top of my voice, between coughs and gasps, my life-saving mantra, 'THIS ISN'T REAL, BUT ASHNIL IS AND SHE LOVES ME!' My body screamed back at me: millions of nerve-endings, burning away to nothing as my skin crackled and my flesh melted. The dim light cast by my burning clothing and the vile stench of burning somehow gave me a little more strength. I kicked and banged against the inside of the bull, screaming my mantra through a throat constricted by blistering skin and smoke. With a bright flash, my hair caught alight and then...

Nothing.

I felt cool marble beneath me and the heat was gone. The pain was gone.

I opened my eyes and saw Jamie and Traggheim kneeling beside me. Before I could say anything, Garm slapped his tongue across my face.

'Sorry,' he said. 'Bad habit.'

I lifted my hand and stared at it. It was fine. I was fine. The whole thing really had been an illusion. Jamie helped me to my feet. I looked up at the stark figure of the carnifex, still looming over us in the gallery.

'Not you,' was all he said to me. Then he pointed the gladius at Obadiah, who was lying on the floor close by. 'YOU!' he bellowed.

There was another flash of light, and Obadiah was gone.

'Sentence of one thousand years' incarceration,' rasped the carnifex. Then he simply turned away and was gone.

'What just happened?' I asked. 'Is it over?'

Traggheim reached up and put his hands on my shoulders. 'It's over, Drew. You impressed the carnifex with your strength and resilience.'

'Yeah, and Obadiah screamed like a little girl,' put in Jamie.

I frowned at Traggheim. 'Do you mean to tell me that the carnifex's judgement was based on who had the biggest balls, not on who was right or wrong?'

'Just so. Roman justice was brutal and often quite mad. Why do you think nobody except that fool Jophiel has summoned the carnifex for centuries?'

'Just wait 'til Ashnil hears how you resisted the pain.' Jamie laughed, poking me in the ribs.

'You bloody dare,' I said, thumping him back. 'You mention it and I'll tell Alyssum you said Obadiah cried "like a girl". She'll flay you alive.'

36. RETURN

We emerged across the sandstone steps of the museum, into a chilly evening, with dusk just setting.

'You must be knackered,' said Jamie. 'How about a pint or two?'

Nothing could've been more welcome, but then something occurred to me. 'Where's Garm?' I asked. 'He was remarkably quiet in there after I came back. He would never normally resist the opportunity of a sarcastic comment.' I looked around and right on cue, he came galloping up to me and head-butted my shin painfully, growling and snarling as he grabbed my trouser-leg in his teeth and started pulling.

'What the hell?' I asked him, but there was no reply, except for more snarling.

And that was when I realised.

'Archer's alive,' I told the others.

Not waiting for a response, I ran, Garm leading the way. How could I have been so stupid? I *had* heard something when I walked down from the summit of Arthur's Seat: that faint sound I recognised as Archer's voice, but dismissed as an over-active imagination. I upped my pace, running as fast as I could. Archer was alive somewhere on Arthur's Seat, but who could say what state he was in, after being bested in a battle with Obadiah and then missing for days?

Garm raced ahead, barking in frustration. I could no longer hear him because I had been Archer's stand-in and Archer was alive, so I was no longer needed. But if he'd been alive all the time, how come Garm hadn't sensed it and stayed in touch with him? A bat dived past my head and I knew Archer must be near.

We found him staggering down from Salisbury Crags. His clothes were torn and charred, his hair was matted, but his face was set with fury.

'Where the hell were you? And you, you useless little shit?' He aimed a boot at Garm, who danced out of the way. 'Ten days in a bloody hell-hole. Don't say you didn't hear me shouting to you: I know you did. I sensed you. But you left me there!'

We were saved from further abuse by the arrival of Traggheim, puffing heavily, followed closely by Alyssum. Traggheim put an arm around his old friend, to support him, and Alyssum took his face in her hands, staring into his eyes and trying to assess what state he was in, whilst Traggheim muttered reassuringly.

I stood back, shocked. Had I really failed Archer? He'd always been a grumpy bastard with me and had just been through an ordeal. Surely he'd settle down when we got him somewhere we could help him properly. Jamie arrived and he and Traggheim helped Archer down from the hill, but he kept directing venomous looks at Garm and me.

We took him to Alyssum's shop, where she could best treat him. She shoved us away, and we trooped down the spiral stairs to the library.

'What I don't understand,' I said to Traggheim as we pushed through the massive oak door, 'is how he's alive. When Garm started speaking to me, it could only be because Archer was dead. So how can he now be alive? Can daemons do that – return from death, I mean?'

'He wasn't dead, Drew. Death is death, even for a daemon,' replied the dweorg. 'But Arthur's Seat is volcanic rock, which is highly impervious to galdr. I can only surmise that Obadiah somehow stunned or froze him and deposited him somewhere deep in the rock – perhaps a bottle prison.'

'A what?' I asked.

'A bottle-shaped space in the ground, with a narrow neck leading to a small entrance, through which a prisoner can be cast in, with the intention that they will never leave. Obadiah must have carved one out of solid basalt. I suspect that's how Archer escaped: the carnifox exchanged them, thus ensuring the negation of Obadiah's works. Once he was in there, Archer would have had no means of contacting us, other than shouting.'

Alyssum came in later, wiping her hands on a cloth.

'How is he?' I asked.

'He's in a rough state, but he's bomb-proof,' she said. 'He'll recover with rest and the right treatment to help him rebuild his galdr and mend the hurts inflicted on him by Obadiah. But he's been badly affected by it.'

'In what manner is he affected?' asked Traggheim, concern wrinkling his brow.

'Mentally, of course. Think about what he endured. First, the pain and humiliation of defeat at the hands of Obadiah, quickly followed by Obadiah forcing him to suffer in some hole, with no expectation except the likelihood of being there for eternity. He's angry, frightened and humiliated and, being Archer, he's also vengeful and looking for someone to blame.'

'Obadiah's already had his comeuppance,' said Jamie. Then, seeing Alyssum's raised eyebrow, he groaned. 'But it wasn't Archer who delivered it, was it?'

She shook her head slowly.

'It's Garm and I who will get the blame,' I said. 'And I deserve it. I heard him! I faintly heard his voice calling me on Arthur's Seat and convinced myself I was hearing things.'

'That'll teach you to ignore instincts that matter,' flared Alyssum. She subsided and continued slowly, 'No, that isn't fair. You would've followed it up if you'd had reason to think it genuinely could be him, wouldn't you?' She looked at me oddly, before adding, 'His being back displaces you, doesn't it?'

'Oh hang on,' I said heatedly. 'If you think for one minute–'

Traggheim pushed forward and held up his hand. 'Both of you stop and think, I implore you. Of course Drew would never have left Archer to his fate if he thought he might be alive. You know that as well as I do, Alyssum.'

She sniffed. 'I suppose so.'

'I need to clear my head,' I told them and headed through the tunnel to take a walk along the old railway line.

I galdr-jumped through the tunnel grille, into the play-park beyond, and to my surprise, Ashnil was sitting on the edge of the roundabout, swinging it slowly from side to side. She smiled when she saw me.

'What're you doing here?' I asked.

'When things get stressful, you always go for a walk to unwind. It was a fair bet you'd come this way, so I waited.'

'How are things with the angelii?' I asked, as we slowly walked together.

'Pretty awful. Jophiel is unbearable. He did something amazingly stupid in summoning the carnifex and all the pain of that fell on you. He should feel guilty for that and he's lucky it didn't end worse. But he's swanning about and taking the credit for Obadiah's downfall and for Archer's release. So far as he's concerned, he's a hero and what happened to you was just collateral damage. It was horrible.'

'It was. But you know what got me through it, don't you?'

'I do, and I'm delighted, but...'

'Let's not dwell on that now,' I interrupted. 'What happened to Archer was far worse than what I got. Defeated and humiliated by an enemy he has opposed for centuries? For Archer, that's about as bad as it gets, but add a smug Jophiel and your mob making capital out of it...'

She scowled briefly. 'Not necessarily my mob. But remember, Archer is a daemon. He's hard-wired to cope with extreme situations. You are not.' She laid a hand on my arm. 'Take care of your own welfare and don't bottle things up. I worry about you.'

'And what about you?' I paused. 'And us?'

She smiled gently. 'I think we're good together, but I don't know where my world is going right now. Be honest – neither do you, do you?'

'Not the foggiest,' I admitted. 'Without meaning to, I lit the touchpaper and was dragged into an inescapable hidden world. I've got a vengeful daemon, who blames me for not rescuing him, a shed-load of galdr and little idea how to use it, an interfering wyrm resident in my head and a raft of galdr-folc I'm still coming to terms with.'

'Hmm. So, for now – friends?' she asked tentatively.

'Friends,' I said emphatically. 'Maybe with benefits?'

She thumped my arm and laughed.

I looked around us at the Edinburgh skyline. 'Look at this. The lights and sounds of a busy city, with thousands of people, all living their lives unaware of galdr-folc or the parallel realm. Just a few weeks ago, I was one of them.'

'You were never truly one of them,' she said. 'Your real life just hadn't started yet. Now it has.'

'Maybe it has,' I replied slowly. 'Maybe it has.'

ACKNOWLEDGEMENTS

Writing *Touchpaper* has been a joy, made better by the people who have helped me to make it better than it would otherwise have been. My wonderful wife Rona read several early versions and stopped me from permanently killing off Archer, amongst other useful suggestions. My brother, Ian also gave some very useful suggestions that helped me to re-focus. Dominic Newton and Alex Rougvie were great beta-readers and, as ever, stopped me from getting too full of myself.

My editor, Anne Hamilton did a sterling job of helping me turn my strange ramblings into something resembling a novel and she also proof-read the manuscript for me. The stunning cover was designed by Heather Macpherson of Raspberry Creative Type, who also typeset the book.

A SMALL REQUEST

As an indie author, reviews and publicity are hugely important. Please, take a moment to leave a review on Amazon, or wherever you bought this. A mention on the social media platform of your choice would be great too.

If you'd like to keep up to date with the parallel realm and hear when the next book in the series is published, why not sign up for my newsletter? I promise to play nicely and not dominate your in-box. As a thank you, I'll send you a free copy of an exclusive short story about Drew and Traggheim, "*The Artefact.*"

DavidDoddsAuthor.com

'A BLOODCAP, AN ANGELUS AND A JACK RUSSELL TERRIER.
THEY'RE ALL I HAD BY ME TO FACE MORTAL COMBAT WITH THE QUEEN OF THE ÆLVES.
I'D BE DEAD IN MINUTES...'

The historic streets of Edinburgh hide a parallel realm of shadowy killers, vicious ælves and deranged shades. All that stands between them and the unsuspecting populace are a daemon called Archer and the group of angelii he's feuding with.

Drew Macleod is caught in the middle. Someone, somewhere is hunting him. But why? Delving deeper into this parallel realm, Drew finds allies in a feisty herbalist, an ancient creature in disguise and an old clock-maker – but are any of them really who they seem to be?

Touchpaper takes us on an exciting journey in the footsteps of *Neverwhere* and *Rivers of London*

ISBN 978-1-068-56690-5

9 781068 566905

Cover design by Raspberry Creative Type